Hamelin
STOOP

Hamelin STOOP

The Lost Princess and the Jewel of Periluna

ROBERT B. SLOAN

HAMELIN STOOP: THE LOST PRINCESS AND THE JEWEL OF PERILUNA. Copyright © 2017 by Robert B. Sloan.

Printed in the United States of America. For more information, contact Twelve Gates Publishing at www.12gatespublishing.com.

www.12GatesPublishing.com

ISBN 978-1-4956-1990-8 (hardcover)
ISBN 978-1-4956-1991-5 (paperback)
ISBN 978-1-4956-1992-2 (e-book)

For purchase or information, contact www.HamelinStoop.com or visit www.12GatesPublishing.com.

February 2017

To Judy Ferguson
Treasured Colleague and Friend

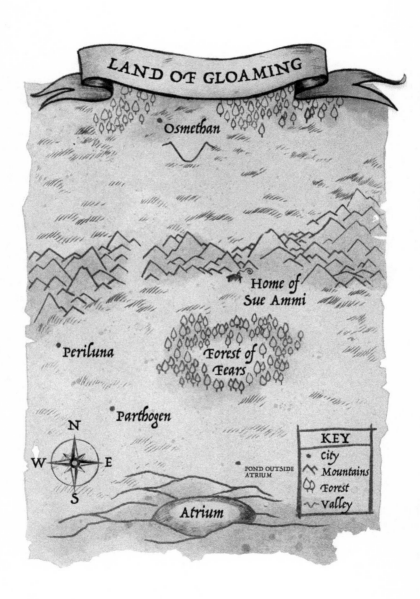

Chapter 1

The Other Side

H E MADE IT. HE WAS ON THE OTHER SIDE. BUT HE WAS more than disappointed. His main reason for coming—to find his parents and learn who he really was—now seemed like a distant goal.

The eagle started moving away from him toward the shaft the great bird called the Tunnel of Times. Hamelin had no time either to enjoy his success at passing the test or to keep his frustrations from simmering. He would have to follow the radiant bird unless he wanted to be left in this spot, with no light and no way back except across the footbridge and over the chasm.

He would follow, but it wasn't fair. He had just finished completing the hardest task of his life—coming back into this mysterious cave, following the eagle through dark spaces and along narrow ledges, and finally making his way across the footbridge over a massive chasm. He had failed to cross it three and a half years ago, but this time he had done it. And he had done it to find his parents.

The darkness below the footbridge had obviously tried to reject him. It was more than just darkness. It was a nothingness that was something. The burning smell of tar and the hot winds that blew at him as he tried to cross the bridge had nearly succeeded in knocking him off and into the abyss. But the gloves of strength that the eagle had given him had enabled him to hang on, even when one of the ropes of the bridge came undone.

The eagle had done nothing to help him, except of course for giving him the gloves years ago, when he was eight. Now, however, with agonizing effort, he had made it across, but the huge bird was pressing on, giving him no time to rest.

It's not fair! he thought. *I came over here to find my parents, and now the eagle tells me there are other things I've got to do, something about fighting in battles and recovering a kingdom. I just want my parents! I just want to know who my family is!*

Hamelin answered his own frustrations by remembering that the eagle hadn't said he couldn't look for his parents, only that there were other reasons as well to come over here and that the Ancient One would include Hamelin's reasons in his, whoever this Ancient One was.

Hamelin had been raised in an orphanage in West Texas in the early 1950s, and he knew what it was like to feel lonely. But even the loneliness of not having parents had hardly prepared him for the darkness of this cave. And now the eagle had told him that they were going through the Tunnel of Times and that the times would change, whatever that meant.

He had failed to cross when he was eight years old, but he'd been given another chance. He was now eleven and a half, and he had passed the test, according to the eagle. But what was this "Atrium of the Worlds" the eagle said they were heading toward? Would his parents be there? Probably not. The eagle made it sound like finding them was something a long way off, if it could be done at all.

Hamelin was tired, frustrated, and even angry. He kicked at some loose pebbles on the path in front of him, but he had no choice. The only light he had was moving forward. He had to follow.

They entered the shaft, and almost immediately the terrain began to change. Though they were still inside the caverns, the ground beneath Hamelin's feet felt a bit softer. There were still rocks in the path and low places overhead to watch out for, but the space was different, more confined. He remembered learning the word *claustrophobia* in Mr. Waverly's fifth-grade class, and now he began to feel it.

The light shining from the eagle gave the impression of rounded sides on both his left and right. Hamelin calculated that he could have stretched his arms out full length and there would have been only two to three feet remaining on either side. The ceiling now was eight to ten feet high in most spots, and it felt like the shaft was gradually but steadily descending. *This must be the Tunnel of Times.* He hoped that it would be only a short time before they emerged from the cave. But he was wrong.

The eagle ran on quickly in front of him, occasionally hopping and even taking short flights of thirty to forty feet. Hamelin found himself jogging at first, then running at nearly half speed to stay up with the great bird. He was in good shape, but he wasn't sure how long he could keep up the pace.

The air was stale, and now Hamelin felt no breezes whatsoever. He kept smelling a moldy odor and occasionally a faint rotten-egg stench, which he remembered being told at school was like burning sulphur. He had trouble getting a good breath of air. After fifteen minutes, the eagle slowed a bit, but Hamelin found that he still had to run to keep up. He knew from hikes and other activities around the children's home that he could jog for an hour or more if he had to. Still, these conditions were different. The ground was uneven, the air was not fresh, the path they were on always seemed to be moving downward, and the eagle's pace was much harder than a jog. The backs of his knees began to ache.

After what seemed like at least forty-five minutes, just when he thought he couldn't go much farther, the eagle slowed to a walk, and Hamelin caught up.

"We can't stop yet," said the great bird, "but we did make up a little bit of our time." Hamelin panted and nodded.

"Although," said the eagle, who looked at him for a second before continuing, "we lost three and a half years when you failed to cross the first time, we're close to being on schedule for our present assignment."

Hamelin looked down. While he had always had it in the back of his mind, there was something he knew he had to say. "I'm *sorry*," he blurted out. He was embarrassed that it sounded so childlike.

The eagle looked at him carefully and then responded, "I am only a guide. There are others you must tell—"

"I . . . I just couldn't do the footbridge before—"

"I know," said the eagle. "You were younger then. Perhaps—"

"So why didn't you just carry me?" said Hamelin with a sudden note of frustration in his voice. "The first time, when I failed, you carried me back to the opening. Why didn't you just fly me over the bridge?"

The eagle stared at Hamelin. He blinked slowly and finally said softly, "Because you begged to go home."

"Well . . . why didn't you help me this last time when the footbridge was coming undone? You just stood there."

The eagle's eyes narrowed. "My strength wasn't in question. Yours was. It was a test. Both times. But you've passed. And now you know—and so does the Ancient One—that you can go forward."

Hamelin looked down. "It's just . . . I was afraid of—"

"No need to explain," said the great bird. "You've already apologized. That's a good beginning. The consequences are still with us, but even your failure, in the hands of the Ancient One, may give us other opportunities. But that's not ours to know ahead of time. There will certainly be other tests. So you must stay alert and never again turn back."

Hamelin still wasn't sure who this "Ancient One" was, but he was glad that the great bird seemed to accept his apology.

"May I ask again . . . if you don't mind . . . where are we going?" he said softly.

"You may, but I'm not sure I can tell you, as there are many points along the way. You'll have to learn as you go along. That's part of the plan that will allow you to succeed . . . if you can."

Hamelin was stung by the eagle's *if*. "So what am I supposed to do along the way?"

"Others will tell you more," said the Great Eagle, "but I can tell you that you're going into a very dangerous realm. On your way, you'll meet others who also have their assignments. You must join them. In helping them, you will also discover your mission. The Hospitable Woman will give you more details as to where you'll go after you meet her and what you're to do."

"What's her name?"

The eagle fluffed his wings slightly and shook his head but said nothing. Hamelin figured he had said something dumb and now was afraid that the great bird would quit talking.

"She sounds like a nice person," he said, trying to keep the conversation going.

The eagle had a rasping sound in his throat, the scraping wood sound. Hamelin thought maybe it was the way eagles groaned.

"Nice?" the great bird finally said. "I wouldn't call her nice, but she is kind."

Suddenly the eagle stopped and turned toward him. He lifted his head and looked at Hamelin for a long moment and then spoke. "I know you want to find your parents, but what you have been summoned here to do is not a task designed to make you feel happy. That may happen, if you succeed, but first of all you must do what is good and true, and perhaps we may join in the Ancient One's defeat of the rebels."

The great bird continued to stare at him, and Hamelin dared not look away. He suddenly had many questions, but now was not a good time to interrupt, since the eagle was talking, and he normally didn't talk much.

"You are entering a war," the eagle continued. "And as you go forward, you must remember that the fight is not *fair*."

"Not fair?" said Hamelin. "Why not?"

"Didn't I say it was a fight?"

Hamelin's eyes widened. He was used to short fights, ones that some adult came along and stopped before anything bad happened.

"And of course *you* are limited by the truth and good of others."

Hamelin had been taught to tell the truth and to be nice to others, but from what the Great Eagle said, the task ahead sounded a lot bigger and harder than just staying out of trouble or being nice and not telling lies.

The eagle quickly turned again and said, "Come, we must be off. Time grows short." The pace immediately returned to a steady run for Hamelin, and there was no more time, or breath, for questions. The eagle was apparently making up for the minutes they had spent talking.

As they went on, it struck Hamelin that the insides of the hills were bigger and more expansive than they appeared from the outside. In fact, he had long since lost all orientation with respect to the width and depth of the hill, much less the direction of the opening where he had entered.

As for time, Hamelin likewise had lost his sense of how long he had been gone from the children's home. He knew it had been several hours, perhaps as much as five or six, he guessed, but he really didn't know.

The eagle's pace picked up, and Hamelin had to take his eyes off everything but the radiant bird. The eagle now seemed to be in a low glide, and Hamelin found himself running at top speed. He knew he couldn't keep it up for long, and just when he thought he'd have to break stride, the Great Eagle's feet touched ground and everything slowed down. For a brief moment, he had the strange sensation of running in slow motion.

Just then the shaft leveled off and took a sharp swing to their left. The eagle noticeably slowed his pace. The tunnel continued for another hundred yards or so, then suddenly opened into an expansive cavern.

The Great Eagle paused for a moment at the entrance, looked around as if remembering something, and then strode into the cavern. As he entered, the light that shone from him leaped up to the walls. If the great bird had the ability to increase the light emanating from him, then at this moment he must have done so, for Hamelin found himself looking in awe at what could have been the inside of a natural cathedral.

The area was massive. With walls and ceilings of enormous height, the cavern must have been one hundred twenty-five feet long and at least sixty feet high and maybe forty feet wide. Magnificent stalactites hung from the expanse of the ceiling, and there were natural nooks and arches on the lower walls and what appeared to be small benches and tables here and there on the floor. The features apparently were not hand crafted, but they were somehow—Hamelin couldn't figure out how—molded right there within the cavern itself.

The great bird led Hamelin across this hall of splendor and out the other side. After walking about twenty paces through a smaller, adjoining cavern, almost like a hallway, the eagle stopped, sniffed the air, and shook his great shoulders and beautifully shaped head. He looked at Hamelin, who thought the radiant bird seemed almost sad. Had something happened here?

They then rounded a corner, came to what looked like another, much larger area, and stopped. The eagle's light was present, but not as extensive here. Hamelin knew that there was much he couldn't see. This cavern was huge. It appeared to be a perfect square, about one hundred fifty feet in length and width. The spacing between the walls was, for the first thirty feet up each wall, the same size as the square floor, but as the walls continued upward, the corners rounded, and the sides of the cavern arched and grew closer together. It was like the inside of a great rounded tower that grew smaller as it went higher. So high was the dome-like ceiling inside this last but very beautiful cavern that Hamelin couldn't even see it.

The walls glistened. Were they moist? Four great boulders were visible at equal distances from one another around the sides of this cavern. The boulders, which almost looked as if they had been hand carved of granite, were smooth and resembled chairs without legs. If they were chairs, the people, or creatures, who sat on them would have to be huge, Hamelin thought.

"How high is the ceiling of this cavern?"

"I don't know," answered the eagle, "unless you could measure the sky itself."

"You mean, it has no ceiling?"

"No rock ceiling," said the bird.

"But I can't see the sky," said Hamelin.

"That's because it's nighttime. If it were daytime, you would see an opening at the top."

"Nighttime?" asked Hamelin. "But I haven't been gone from the home that long. Surely it can't be night."

"You started your journey nearly twelve hours ago. In any case, as I said before, once we crossed the footbridge and came through the Tunnel of Times, time didn't change, but the times have."

"I still don't know what that means," Hamelin said.

"I mean that now you are at a different place in time."

Hamelin's eyes narrowed. "So where am I?"

"This place intersects with many kingdoms, but the people you meet here will look the way they would have looked to you hundreds of years ago. Time moves at the same pace for them as it does for you, but the times are different."

The talk of time reminded Hamelin of something. With a slight hesitation in his voice, he said, "Earlier . . . you said we had lost three and a half years."

"Yes, it has been almost forty-two months of great evil. It would trouble you greatly if you knew how much loss and suffering have occurred since then."

Hamelin looked down and shook his head. He realized then that the tension and exhaustion of fighting his way across the bridge and the hard pace through the tunnel had made him forget the girl he had failed, the one who had waited on him in vain. He wanted to ask more questions about her, but the eagle had already explained that she had joined Chimera's side. There was apparently to be no more talk of her. The eagle was pressing on to other topics.

"The times of evil are still with us, but remember—your own failure is in the past," said the eagle. "And with that failure, and perhaps even because of it, we have, finally, another opportunity."

"Another opportunity?"

"Yes. Often that never happens. One failure just closes a door. But the Ancient One does unusual things. Though we can't go back to the former time, what happened then can be used for something new."

Hamelin didn't want to hear any more about the past, so he said quickly, "Well, I'm ready to go on."

"Not yet. First, we must pass from the Atrium of the Worlds into the other kingdoms. But to pass into those realms, we must wait for the sun to rise. We need its light. For now, we need rest. Lie down over there." The eagle indicated a spot slightly behind Hamelin.

Hamelin understood nothing of what the great bird meant by the sun's light and how it would help them enter "other kingdoms," but he was more than happy to rest for a little. He moved to the area pointed to by the eagle, found a spot that felt smooth and dry, and made himself as comfortable as he could. The eagle walked away, and suddenly the room was pitch dark. Hamelin took off his jacket and used it for a pillow. But though he was exhausted, he couldn't fall asleep. His legs and back were sore, and the rock floor was hard. And the darkness was the darkest he had ever known. He kept the gloves on. His mind was cluttered with questions. What was he doing here? Why couldn't he find his parents now that he had passed the test? Was this where he should have been forty-two months earlier?

On top of all that, he suddenly realized how hungry he was. He reached into his right blue jean pocket and pulled out the apple, biscuit, and cookie he had stuffed there when he left the children's home so many hours ago. The apple was bruised and the biscuit and cookie were in pieces, but thanks to the long pocket Mrs. Kaley had sewn into his jeans, they were still there. He wolfed down everything and wished he had some water. He sat there in the darkness and then heard something.

Was that the sound of running water?

He was thirsty, but the apple had helped. Besides, it was too dark without the eagle's light to go stumbling around. *Where is he?* Finally, Hamelin fell asleep.

Chapter 2

The Thrones,
the Pool, and
the Light

W HEN HAMELIN AWOKE, THERE WAS NO SIGN OF THE eagle. He wasn't sure how long he had been asleep, but it felt like several hours, though he had no idea what time it was, except that it was still dark. As he sat up and looked around, there was no direct light in the cavern, but it did appear that there was more light now than when he had fallen asleep.

As his eyes traced the area around him, he noticed that the overhead opening referred to by the eagle was now a very dark blue. But he also detected high up on the wall opposite him another opening. At a height of at least forty feet, it appeared to be small, roughly circular, and perhaps only some six feet in diameter. Through this opening, Hamelin could see a patch of sky that looked like a mixture of streaky gray and dark blue—the kinds of colors you see in the farthest reaches of the east before the sun comes up.

He stood and, at that moment, realized how stiff and sore he was, a result of the previous day's hard march—plus the fact that he had slept on a rock floor. He stretched out his arms as he put his jacket on over his sweater, and he could feel the soreness running from his neck and shoulders all the way down his back and into his legs. *A hot shower back at the children's home would feel good*, he thought. *And where's the eagle?*

The eagle was still nowhere in sight. Hamelin's thoughts concerning the whereabouts of the huge bird reminded him of the deep disappointment that he felt—mixed with irritation at the Great Eagle. He had passed the test of the footbridge over the chasm. *So where is he? Has he just left me in the night?*

His questions were interrupted by a sound that just now registered on his conscious mind again—and reminded him of last night. It was the sound of running water. He was very thirsty, and there was just enough light for him to risk moving. As he made his way toward the sound, his eyes grew more accustomed to the darkness, and he could make out a pond.

There was insufficient light for Hamelin to see a reflection of any sort in the water but enough for him to know that he stood at the water's edge. He kneeled down, took off the gloves and put them snugly in the left pocket of his jacket, and placed his right hand in the water. He was surprised at what he felt. Instead of the coolness he expected, the water was warm. More than warm, it felt light and bubbly. He put both hands in the pond and splashed water on his face. *Oh, that feels good! Even on my neck and shoulders*, he thought. He took a deep drink and immediately felt better.

Hamelin stood and made more efforts to survey his surroundings. By now, some light was gathering in the cavern, and it was obvious that the sun had started to come up, though no direct shafts of light yet appeared through the opening in the eastern wall.

He again glanced at the pond at his feet and could now see that he was looking at a narrow pool some twelve feet wide from his left to his right and some twenty feet long from his feet to the east wall, where the pond touched the wall. He could also now identify the reason for the sound of running water. He watched as thin sheets of liquid flowed in tiny ripples down the east wall and then streamed lightly into the pool.

The pond itself, though fed by that steady flow of water, was mostly still, particularly where he stood. Hamelin felt a great attraction to the pond, especially since his face still felt amazingly refreshed from the water he had splashed on it.

As the sun continued to rise, light was rapidly filling the cavern, and he could see his surroundings even more clearly. *The eagle called this place the "Atrium of the Worlds." Maybe I should look around*, he thought.

He could see that he was in a spacious area that, as he had dimly made out the previous night, was a perfect square. He walked toward the middle of that end of the cavern and, in the growing light, realized that at his feet and all around him were the rich and beautiful colors of a massive indoor garden. Far from being a barren cavern, this was what in some places would be called a park.

Now that he could see, he realized that the great bird had led him into the Atrium through a large, curved doorway. The doorway led to a polished stone patio, which broadened out from the opening into the Atrium. Where he had slept was merely the entry area of what he could now see was a larger and truly magnificent space.

As he stood in the Atrium, Hamelin realized that the pond was straight across the room from the spot where he had slept. Then from the pond, there was a broad path, clearly a trail of some sort, that meandered northward through the length of the cavern. As the path approached the north wall, it made a soft turn to the west and eventually wandered back south.

He decided to walk from the pond northward along the footpath and continue counterclockwise through the chamber. As he walked, he could see that there was always about thirty feet—roughly ten adult steps—from his right side to the cavern walls. He also realized that, at the end of the trail, he would find himself back at the entrance where he had slept.

What Hamelin saw along the way no doubt gave this magnificent cavern its name, the Atrium of the Worlds. Between the path and each wall to his right, there were beautiful examples of a rich plant life—in beds with shrubs, flowers, and vines of every variety and color.

These magnificent flowerbeds were interrupted only by the large thronelike boulders that he had vaguely made out the night before. One stood in the middle of each of the four walls—to the east, north, west, and south.

The gardens were so stunning that they seemed almost out of place in this cavern, but Hamelin figured the humidity and the sunlight coming through the openings high above provided the perfect conditions for such a variety of vegetation. He was used to the sparse plant life in southwest Texas, so he found the colors almost overwhelming in their vividness. Vibrating with radiance, they seemed to shake and mingle. *These flowerbeds look like creeks of colors flowing out of the boulders*, he thought.

Though he didn't know all their names, he saw tulips, irises, peonies, hydrangeas, yellow daffodils, purple bachelor's buttons, and gerbera daisies of orange and yellow and red. There were shrubs of oleander with pink flowers, burning bush in its radiant red orange, Indian hawthorn, gray sage, rose of Sharon, and zinnias of red and white, yellow and purple.

These fragrant shrubs and flowers were so arranged that they almost blended into one, but still, if Hamelin looked closely, he could see each one in its distinctiveness. He thought he could see some deeper pattern, especially in the flow of the flowerbeds around and next to each boulder, but if it was there, he couldn't quite grasp it.

The smells from the flowers combined into a soft, wispy scent that reminded him of cactus blooms and sweet bread. And climbing along the stalagmites and boulders were vines of jasmine, clematis, antique roses, and honeysuckle. To his left, which was the inner, middle area of the cavern, the space was open, and the floor was a black, rocky surface, not as smooth as the entry area where he had slept but covered with small, gritty pebbles that looked like they had been burned repeatedly.

When Hamelin had finally circled the room, pausing in front of each throne and its own river of shimmering color, he returned to the smooth surface of the entry area.

Then he noticed that the room was filling up with light. There was as yet no bright shaft of light streaming through the side opening high up on the eastern wall, but the air sparkled, and the room was fairly shining. Hamelin's eyes were drawn upward to the opening at the very top of the Atrium's dome. It revealed the deep blue of the morning sky, so he knew the sun must have cracked the horizon in the east and was giving off the light now filling the room.

He also knew the temperature in the room was rising. But the increasing warmth was not uncomfortable, as the air in the Atrium seemed rich, full, and fresh. He breathed deeply, and the soreness in his body began to slip away.

Hamelin, however, gave little thought to his sore limbs, because his eyes were now fixed upon the upper walls of this magnificent chamber. Whether it was real or only apparent, the four walls, with their eventually rounded corners, seemed almost to converge directly above him as they stretched toward the patch of blue sky visible in the opening high overhead. He looked straight up, bending his back and neck to stare at the upper spaces, and for a second, he lost his balance. But he took a step backward and quickly regained it.

He then stepped on something odd and instinctively glanced at his feet. *What's this? Looks like a hammer of some kind.* He bent down and picked it up and realized that he had never seen one just like it. It wasn't at all like the one Mr. Moore used. The handle was short—too short to put his entire hand around—and made of wood. And the head was very different. It was forged metal, and instead of having two distinctive sides, one for driving nails and a clawlike side for pulling them out, it had two identical sides, both squared and evidently made for pounding. In such a strange, isolated spot—in this place not made by human hands—it was odd to see something so practical and so artificial. But it was obviously lost there on the floor, so he slipped it into the extralong right-hand pocket in his blue jeans. The handle and head were small enough that the hammer easily fit.

Hamelin's attention quickly returned to the room. There was still no sign of the eagle, but he could now see, because of the radiant light flooding the chamber and being magnified in the Atrium, that the massive converging spaces above the thrones were glistening. At first he thought he saw moisture on the upper walls, but then he realized that they were made of a glass that sparkled like an ocean of crystal. The glass wasn't clear; it was far too thick for that. It was, however, clear enough to reflect its surroundings and to magnify the light and heat of this fertile, glowing cavern.

The room continued to get warmer and was now somewhat uncomfortable. The heat wasn't unbearable, but it was steadily increasing from the light reflected off the upper walls, which was in turn bouncing around the room at multiple angles and filling every corner and space. *I've got to quit looking up. All these reflections are like mirrors, and it's making me dizzy.* He stood still for a moment to regain his balance, but his momentary dizziness reminded him of his frustration with the bird. *Where is he? I should never have followed him!*

He took a deep breath and let it out in an angry sigh. He looked around at his feet and then noticed that the flowers were becoming even more dazzling and spellbinding. *Like a flowing rainbow on the ground*, he thought. And the throne-like boulders now revealed brilliant sparkles of light around their outer edges and sides. Hamelin wondered for a second if they reflected natural diamonds embedded within the surface of the rock.

Contributing to the climbing heat and now glaring, almost overpowering light of this natural hothouse was the elevated ocean of crystal itself. Above the flowers and thrones, it gathered up every ounce of light within the room, magnified it, and then cast it forcibly outward, to be multiplied over and again.

With every passing second, Hamelin felt more intensely the heat and humidity in the chamber. He was beginning to perspire heavily, and his shirt, sweater, pants, and jacket, though mostly made of cotton, were sticking to his skin like thick, wet wool. *The pond. The water felt so good before, and I could sure use another drink.*

He moved quickly toward the pond, almost stumbling in his haste to gain relief, and then fell on his hands and knees, panting at the water's edge. Just before he plunged his hands into the water, he also saw from the effects of the light in the room that the pond was much deeper than he had first thought. Though he could see its subsurface rock sides around the edges, he could detect no evidence of a bottom, even though the water itself seemed beautifully clear. The pond was almost still, and when a faint image of himself flickered back into his eyes, he was surprised to see how tired and weak he looked.

He scooped large handfuls of water onto his face. Again and again he splashed it around his cheeks, ears, and neck, not caring where it splashed or how wet his clothes got. It felt so good, so invigorating upon his skin, that Hamelin placed both hands at the edge of the pond, ducked his whole head beneath the surface, and drank. He pulled it back up, slinging his hair backward and enjoying the full pleasure of the water, which, though still warm, left his face and skin feeling cool and full of life.

"You must be careful there."

Though the rasping voice at first startled him, he knew a half second later that it came from the great bird. Hamelin, still on his knees, looked to his left and saw the resplendent creature standing near him, more radiant than ever as the light from the room danced off his majestic plumes.

"Oh," Hamelin said, puzzled that he should have to be careful about getting a drink. "But I'm thirsty, and the water feels so good—and even tastes good."

"Yes, it should. Those are powerful waters, able to do far more than you can imagine."

"My face feels like new," said Hamelin.

"Yes," said the great bird. "Imagine what those waters could do for your whole body if it were plunged in."

"Can I?"

"No, not yet," replied the eagle quickly. "Those waters *are* refreshing. It is said they are life giving, but they must not be entered or even drunk lightly. In fact, they can be entered rightly only once."

"Rightly?" asked Hamelin, a little puzzled.

"Yes. They may be entered wrongly many times, but rightly only once. And whether rightly or wrongly, they bring danger to all who enter—but health to those who choose to enter and pass through rightly."

"Oh, I know not to dive in a shallow pool," said Hamelin, remembering the one back at the children's home. "So how do I get in?" After saying that, he looked back at the water.

"Not now," said the Great Eagle with a note of warning in his voice, "and not *that* way!"

But by the time the great bird had spoken, Hamelin had already lowered his face slightly closer to the surface of the pond and was gazing—even staring—into it. The light that had entered the room was full. It was intensified and multiplied by the beauty of the Atrium and the deep ocean of crystal that filled the converging walls above the thrones. The pond now reflected back at him with a surprising clearness.

He could see his own mirror image, and he looked suddenly better. The great bird opened his wings and stepped toward Hamelin. It was an eagle's screech, but in it the word *"No!"* came through clearly.

Hamelin, however, was paying more attention to the image in the pond than the eagle's voice. The water he had freely splashed over his face must have cleaned all the sleep and bleariness from his eyes. He had never seen himself look so strong, so alive, and so handsome.

The shrill sounds of warning shouted by the eagle were hardly audible to him. His eyes and mind were held by the mirrored image of beauty that stared back at him from the depths of those powerful waters. Hamelin ached to have what he saw in the pond. It made hearing the eagle almost impossible. Besides, why listen to a guide who so far had only misled him?

Chapter 3

Reflecting
the Image

AS HE STARED AT THE SURFACE OF THE POND, HAMELIN felt himself being drawn, almost absorbed, into his image in the water. The eagle saw that Hamelin couldn't hear his warnings, so he knew he would have to change the boy's focus, if he couldn't immediately change his mind. The eagle spread his broad, powerful wings and, with a few quick strokes, took flight toward the overhead opening where all the walls converged. Higher and higher he flew until it seemed that he would disappear through the opening.

But just as quickly as the great bird ascended, so then with massive strokes he reversed his course and began a downward flight. Instead, however, of plummeting straight toward Hamelin, he flew in circles clockwise around the Atrium, as if flying down a spiral staircase as wide as the walls of the chamber. The added distance of his circular descent enabled him to gain greater speed as he propelled himself ever downward. So great were the bird's strokes and so increasingly rapid his clockwise descent that he created a tornado-like wind within the Atrium.

Hamelin stood. He wanted to see as much of his body as he could in the water's reflection. He leaned forward, still gazing at the pond, and was slowly increasing the tilt of his upper body, about to fall in. But he momentarily stopped his forward movement. He hesitated because at that very moment something—maybe—caught his eye. Or was it a picture in his mind? Yes, a faint recollection of standing at the edge of the new pool at the children's home on his ninth birthday, ready to jump. He lifted his eyes for just a second and glanced around. But there was no one else at the side of the pool with him—not the other children, not the Kaleys, and certainly not Bryan and Layla. He looked down again, and once more he looked closely at his image. There was a handsomeness, even a beauty, in his reflected face and body that—in spite of the aloneness of the moment—started drawing him down once again.

The Great Eagle's spiraling descent was now at top speed. The bird was on a path that, in his final lap around the walls, would drive him squarely into Hamelin, but Hamelin did not—could not—lift his eyes from the pond. At the last possible instant, the eagle tilted his massive wings and swerved slightly. His flight path altered and took him directly over the pond and just in front of Hamelin's face before he banked around him and landed. Many things then happened at once.

The force of the wind created by the Great Eagle's descent, combined with his changed flight path at the moment of his greatest speed, flooded the cavern and Hamelin's senses with distracting sights and sounds. The near brushing of the eagle's wings against his face, the stirring of the wind, and the repeated flashing of the bird's radiant image as it reflected off the glistening crystal above and around Hamelin competed with his spellbinding image in the pond. Most of all, the force of the Great Eagle's tornadic flight created a rippling in the pond that momentarily broke the seducing effect of his reflection.

"Hamelin."

Did someone call my name? Layla? Still in a daze, he slowly lifted his eyes from the pond and then, seeing the eagle perched on the eastern throne and facing him, mumbled, "Help me."

"Turn away from the pond and look at the light in the crystal—above the western throne!" the great bird shouted in a raspy screech.

Hamelin tried to obey, but he lost his balance for a moment and rocked back on his heels. Slowly, however, he finally turned his body. With his back to the pond, he looked at the flashing glory that shone high on the western wall and then gazed deeply into the ocean of crystal that projected upward above the throne. At that very moment, the direct rays of the morning sun burst through the hole now behind him in the eastern wall of the cavern, and the whole room flashed with a magnified radiance that was beyond white light. The explosion of sunlight carried with it a spectacular splash of colors drawn from the Atrium's flowers that rushed into and reemerged from the ocean of crystal above the thrones.

Hamelin blinked and shook his head.

"Hamelin."

There it is again. Was it the eagle? No. It sounded like a man's voice. Bryan? He opened his eyes and looked again at the western wall and saw in the white crystal expanse the back of a human figure. The glowing glare of the multiplied light made the figure appear to be standing in a cloudy mist, but Hamelin assumed it was himself—at least a reflection of a reflection of himself. Though he could see it only dimly in the semiopaque crystal, the back of the human image was apparently being reflected from the pond back into the crystal walls. The sunlight through the eastern wall was bouncing off the western wall at just the right angle to simultaneously reflect from the crystal—who knew how many times or from how many angles—down into the pond and from the pond somehow back to the crystal. It reminded Hamelin of the times he had stood between multiple mirrors. From the back, and ever so faintly, he could see his true image receding into the crystal, the reverse of the mirror image of the pond.

At exactly that moment, the Great Eagle flew around him, hovered with outstretched wings, and called to him from the direction of the western boulder. "*Now* you can!" he said.

"Can what?" replied Hamelin weakly.

"Enter the waters!" screeched the great bird. "Are you willing to pass through the waters of death and life?"

"Yes," said Hamelin. His voice was low but decisive.

No sooner had he submitted to the great bird's question than the eagle flew directly toward him from the west. With wings still outstretched but talons now projected in front of him, he shot toward Hamelin and buried his mighty claws into the boy's upper chest and shoulders, one on each side. So powerful was the force of the eagle's two-legged strike upon him that Hamelin had no time to catch himself or break his fall. He hit the water first with his upper back, with his arms stretched out and his feet off the ground. Then, the two—the great bird still holding and pushing Hamelin with his talons—plunged into the waters.

Pain shot through Hamelin's shoulders as he immediately realized that this time, unlike three and a half years ago, the eagle's talons were not sheathed. The searing, knifelike pain in his chest and shoulders was coupled with the surprising jolt his body felt as he and the eagle plunged into the waters. Then to his surprise, Hamelin realized that, instead of hitting the bottom of the pond as he had expected, the two of them were diving deeper and deeper into the waters as the great bird's legs continued to drive him downward, back first.

Though he wanted to trust the eagle, Hamelin also feared him. In what he thought might be his last conscious moments, he asked himself, *Is the eagle pushing me to my death?*

Chapter 4

Through the Waters of Death and Life

H AMELIN AND THE GREAT EAGLE PLUNGED DEEPER AND deeper into the waters of death and life. The pain in the boy's chest and shoulders was sharp as the eagle's talons pierced his skin like burning needles. But around the burning was a cooling surge of water. Each movement of the eagle to push and guide Hamelin through the water painfully jabbed, jammed, and reset his talons into previously untorn areas of muscle and flesh but was quickly followed by the healing waters that rushed past and over his wounds.

The water was also amazingly clear. In spite of the pain and the churning of the water caused by the force of the eagle's powerful downward plunge, Hamelin was aware of objects swirling past him on either side. However, since he was looking backward with his face near the eagle's chest, he couldn't immediately make out their form or shape.

Then, just when he began to worry about the length of time he would have to hold his breath, the eagle's downward thrust leveled out, and Hamelin felt the powerful and painful grip on his chest and shoulders begin to loosen as the eagle relaxed his claws—followed by the sharp extraction of the talons from each point of entry. The great bird's body then turned slightly upward in the water, and he began to make powerful strokes with his wings. Hamelin, though fearing the bird's power, also knew that the eagle's plan, whatever it was, was his only hope. He had to hang on.

Just as the eagle's taloned grip broke, Hamelin, with his right hand, reached across his body and grabbed the great bird's right foot as the eagle also made another powerful thrust upward. All of this happened so quickly that Hamelin found himself spun around. He was now facing in the same direction as the great bird and being pulled, not pushed, upward through the water. The eagle stretched his left foot downward, and Hamelin reached up with his left hand, but the backflow from the bird's strokes pushed him back.

Hamelin was furious with himself for not having the gloves on. The grip on his right hand was weakening. Unexpectedly, however, the eagle made one quick reverse stroke, which slowed his ascent slightly. At that point, Hamelin's momentum moved him forward, and he was able to grab the great bird's left foot. He regripped his right hand and held on with both hands as the eagle powerfully pulled them upward.

Even with the hard streams of water rushing at his sides from the eagle's thrusts, Hamelin could now see the other objects in the water more clearly, though his first instinct was to close his eyes and duck his head. Afraid to see, but also afraid not to, he watched bizarre scenes all around him as the eagle's wings propelled them through the water. Large-headed creatures with humanlike faces but fish bodies swam directly at him. Some were contorted with pain and grief; others had jaws and jagged teeth that snapped and snarled. There were other deformed heads, scarred and pitted, with bugged eyes and hooked noses. There were twisted smiles, pointed chins, hollow cheeks, and gnarly skin stretched across bony disfigurements. They reminded Hamelin of the exaggerated monster masks that he and the other children had worn on Halloween.

Some of the creatures had arms and hands connected to their fish bodies. These grotesque heads rushed at Hamelin from every side. In each instance, just as he thought he would be bitten or slashed by their mouthy attacks, the creatures would vanish a split second before reaching him, only to be followed by others more deformed and frightening than the last.

But these were not the only faces in the water. There were also dragonlike animals with slashing teeth and snakelike heads. Some had clawing legs that snatched and swiped at Hamelin as they swarmed around him. Others groped and swirled at him with deadly tentacles that sprayed an oily stream as they tried to wrap themselves around him.

Just when he thought the swarming was over, another school of creatures—this one resembling rats with fins— rushed him. They flew toward him in the water, their mouths wide open, dripping blood. And there were others, human-like with something like bodies, appearing to be fully robed with crowns on their heads, that didn't attack but stood nearby. One of these figures stood out among them, having a sly smile, with young, weary servants moving about him on hands and knees. One of the servants, a beautiful young woman with golden hair, quickly, almost secretly, glanced up at Hamelin with a look of sadness and longing. And the figures with crowns waved their arms at him as if drawing him toward them in a friendly way. He wouldn't consider for a second letting go of the eagle, but he felt sorry for the woman and wanted to wave.

Finally, he saw one last creature, larger and looking more vicious than all the rest. It flew at him in a rush, simultaneously pawing, clawing, slashing, whipping, and threatening. It was one creature, but it appeared to come at him in parts, parts that were each fierce and hideous. It was such a mixture of beasts that it was hard for Hamelin to compare it to anything. It had the head of a lion, with fire flashing from its open, roaring mouth; the body of a goat; and the long, slithering tail of a snake. Around this creature, Hamelin saw a ball of light, but it was smoky and spread out—more like a bright fog than a clear, radiant light.

Finally, like waking up suddenly from a nightmare, when he thought he could hold his breath no longer, one last powerful stroke of the Great Eagle propelled them both out of the water and up, up above the waterline. As his face hit the air, Hamelin almost all at once gasped, coughed, and spat, his lungs alternately wanting to explode for lack of oxygen and then violently panting in quick breaths for the life-giving air that rushed to fill them.

He could no longer hang on to the bird and was unceremoniously dumped on the ground, his arms and legs sprawling. As he lay there drenched, he glanced up at the Great Eagle. The bird, also dripping, never looked more majestic. In fact, Hamelin almost thought he detected a brief look of pleasure on the eagle's face.

Minutes passed while Hamelin's breathing regained a steady pace. Finally, he glanced around and realized that they were no longer in the cavern. They were outside—with a sunny, blue sky above them—on the banks of another pond that was evidently connected underground to the one in the Atrium. His shoulders and chest no longer bore any claw marks or cuts; Hamelin now felt wonderfully alive—and strangely strong and peaceful. His body didn't hurt, his breath was deeper and fuller than before, and his skin was clean.

And everything seemed different. The frustration and even anger he had felt toward the eagle had lifted. Clearly, in spite of his strange words and actions, the eagle was good. Hamelin remembered that, even though the eagle had led him several times toward danger, he had more than once saved his life. And even when he seemed to do nothing, like back at the bridge, he was still doing something for Hamelin's good.

Hamelin looked at the bird and knew he should trust him, in spite of the pain he caused. Which reminded him of the eagle's talons.

"That really hurt," he said, rubbing his chest. "And then I thought my chest was going to explode. But now—what happened? I mean . . . why do I feel so different now, like I'm rested and strong?"

"A lot happened," said the great bird.

Hamelin shook his head and pressed his lips together. "But I don't get it . . . how come you didn't want me to go near the water, but then you pushed me into it? And what was my reflection in the pond doing to me? And what was in that shiny wall? And—"

"All that would require a lot of explaining," said the eagle. "For now, it is enough for you to know that the reflection in the pond was *not you*. What you saw was killing you."

"But I looked so good—"

"A distorted beauty. Those are the waters of death and life. If you enter those waters while looking at your reflection, under the spell of your own false appearance, the waters will bring nothing but death."

"You mean I could've died?"

The eagle nodded. "When you look at yourself in pride, you are deceived. And when you enter those waters in such a mind, the deception grows until you lose your very self, your true self."

"I don't get it. So why did you push me in?"

"Because those are also the waters of life. Once the spell was broken, you were no longer looking at yourself."

"When was the spell broken?"

"When you willingly looked away from your reflection, your false self, and at the western wall."

Hamelin thought for a minute about the wall and its images. "What did I see in that wall?"

The eagle hesitated and then answered. "You saw the crystal."

"But I saw something *in* the crystal."

"Yes." The eagle nodded slightly and blinked slowly, as if conceding a point he didn't want to admit. "The wall reflected the sunlight between itself and the pond and reversed the mirroring effect of the pond. You saw a true image."

"Of *me*?"

The Great Eagle sighed as his chest filled and then returned to normal. Finally, he spoke, though still reluctant. "It wasn't just you, but it was more you than you have ever been."

"So it was *me* in there?" Hamelin asked.

"Yes." The eagle paused, then said, "But there's more to your question than you understand . . . and . . . more to the answer than I know. I am only a guide."

"Tell me what you do know," insisted Hamelin.

The great bird narrowed his eyes and looked at the boy. Finally, he answered, "This I know: by looking away from yourself, you became more yourself, and when you gave me permission, I was able to guide you through the waters of death and life."

"Guide me? It felt like you were pushing."

The eagle was still and silent.

"So what were all those faces and horrible monsters in the water?" asked Hamelin.

"They are the appearances of death."

"But were they real?"

"Of course they're real, but they have no strength in themselves."

"But they sure looked dangerous."

"They are dangerous," said the eagle, "but they live off borrowed power."

"Borrowed? Who lends it to them?"

"Enough of this!" said the eagle. "I don't think you'd understand if I explained it, and I've already stated my limits. You have come safely through the waters, and that's enough for now."

"But every time the monsters came at me, I thought I was done for. But each time, just before they got me, they disappeared. Why?"

"Because," said the eagle after another big sigh, "you entered the waters rightly, and their powers were broken. If you had gone into the water looking at yourself, you would have become like your reflection, and then you would have been theirs."

"But in the pond, I looked so strong and healthy," said Hamelin.

"Yes, you looked that way, but you were tricked into thinking you were something you're not, which weakened you."

"But how?"

"You were enjoying what you saw, and pride was growing in you so rapidly that you were losing your mind."

"Losing my mind?"

"Don't you remember? I was shouting to you, but you could hardly hear anything. Despite the light and the swirling winds, you couldn't stop looking at your reflection."

"Then why did I stop?"

"It helped when I stirred the waters, but that's only part of it. For the rest, you'll have to figure it out yourself, if you can. I do not understand it myself."

The eagle's admission that he didn't know surprised Hamelin. What else did the eagle not know? The great bird was obviously frustrated at his questions, but Hamelin couldn't help himself.

"But what if I hadn't stopped?"

"Then the creatures would have . . . no! Enough! You ask too many questions about yourself! Your story is only part of a bigger story." The eagle looked away in silence, but just when Hamelin thought the conversation was over, the great bird added in a softer voice, "There is one who did enter the pool deceived by her own reflection. Perhaps one day you can ask her. She resisted for a while, but eventually she gave in and is again a captive of her vanity."

Hamelin wanted to ask more, but the eagle had scolded him about his questions. He remembered the bird's anger on an earlier occasion. He paused.

The Great Eagle stepped back and looked around, extending his legs and pushing his chest out. Hamelin was suddenly afraid he was about to leave.

"Where are we?" he asked quickly.

"We're now in the Land of Gloaming, which, like all lands, belongs to my master, the Ancient One. But it is under attack."

"Who's attacking it?"

"Chimera—I have mentioned him before. He is the powerful pretender who seeks to rule these lands. You are going to Osmethan, which Chimera has captured and given to his son Tumultor."

Hamelin noticed the eagle said "you."

"So," he said, in a voice that was a little higher in pitch than usual, "which way do we go from here?"

"*We* don't go anywhere. You must travel without me."

"Alone? But, Mr. Eagle, sir," Hamelin stammered, the words tumbling out, "how can I go alone?"

"I didn't say you'd be alone. I only said that for now you'd be without *me*. There will be others who will join you on this trip. But, young man—and to this you must pay close attention—you cannot accomplish your mission alone. Only as you help the others you meet can your work be done."

Hamelin wanted to ask about finding his parents, but he feared raising that topic again. So he settled for something vague. "What am I supposed to do?"

"You will discover that in the doing of it. For now, you must travel northward along this path. You will meet the others along the way. Together you will come to the house of the Hospitable Woman, Sue Ammi. All of you will receive other instructions there."

"Who are they? And how will I know them?"

"One seeks a sister held captive by Tumultor. The other companion seeks light. Help him too."

Hamelin was now fully confused by all the people mentioned by the eagle and what he was supposed to help them do. But it was more and more evident that the eagle was about to leave. Trying to stall him, Hamelin fumbled for a question.

"But—the one looking for light—what kind of light is it?"

"Enough!" And this time Hamelin knew he meant it. "For now, that is all you need to know. I must go. Your present task is before you. You are strong, Hamelin. Now be brave."

With that, the great bird suddenly took flight. Hamelin quickly rose to his feet and stared into the sky. The eagle shot straight up and then flew off to the west. Hamelin watched him until he was completely out of sight. Suddenly, he felt very alone.

He didn't understand a lot of what the eagle had said, and he would have to think about what had helped him pull his eyes away from the pond. But he felt some relief knowing that there were others he would meet.

For now, though, the path. There was a path right there at the water's edge leading northward. At least he was pretty sure that way was north, based on the sun's location. There was another path, but it seemed to head mostly west. So Hamelin started walking. He still felt refreshed from the waters, but now all he could think of—and try to remember—were the strange words of the eagle. He would have to be alert. Crossing the footbridge yesterday was obviously just the start of a lot of things. If he ever wanted to find his parents and learn who he was, he couldn't turn back now. He patted his pockets and felt the gloves in his jacket and the hammer in his jeans as he kept walking.

Chapter 5

The Forest of Fears

THE MORNING WAS BRISK, AND HAMELIN CONTINUED TO feel unusually strong from the waters of death and life. The air was cool, so he kept his jacket on, which reminded him to put on the gloves. He followed the road as it wound its way north. The countryside where the path led was pleasant, with grasslands as far left and in front of him as he could see and a mountain range in the distant horizon beyond that. To his right, Hamelin could see a thin line of trees that appeared to run generally north, but he wasn't certain how far.

In the early afternoon, just as he started to get thirsty, he came upon a small cluster of trees, in the middle of which stood a large boulder. He looked back to his right and realized that the thin line of trees that had been some distance away had slowly meandered in front of him and now ran to his left. The trees nearest the path shaded the boulder, and at the bottom of the large rock was a soft, damp area. On closer inspection, he realized he was looking at an underground spring bubbling up from the base of the rock.

Hamelin had seen such natural springs in Texas, and so he didn't hesitate to get down on his hands and knees for a drink. By bending his elbows, he could lower his head enough that his lips could drink in the cold water constantly flowing up from somewhere underground.

It was a good place to rest with the large boulder to sit against and the trees to provide shade. The air was fresh, and he was soon breathing deeply. Within a few minutes, he was close to a sound sleep. But as he dozed, he remembered the words of the eagle—that his earlier failure had cost three and a half years and that they had to hurry. Whether he was on schedule now or not, he didn't know. But he did know he had work to do, so he stood up, stretched, and took another drink. He was hungry, but the water was refreshing. He started off again. He crossed the line of trees, and the path picked up on the other side.

The air remained brisk, and Hamelin wondered whether it was winter in this land, just as it was back in Texas. The sun was high, but things didn't seem as bright as they were at the children's home. The colors were distinctive enough, but somehow the level of light seemed lower than normal, almost as if it were just after sundown, like the light at dusk. Then he remembered the eagle had called it the "Land of Gloaming."

He walked steadily on through the grassland that still spread all around him, but as the afternoon stretched on, he could see that he was approaching some woods. The closer he got, the more he could see that the trees were large, thick, and nothing like the sparsely wooded area back home. This was more like forests he had seen pictures of.

A sudden breeze then chilled him, and he could tell that, with the sun now sinking in the west, the temperature was also dropping fast. These conditions reminded him of Texas, where the days in the winter could be very mild but the nights were cold. He could also now tell that the days were not any longer here than they were at the children's home, so he decided that it must be winter here too.

These deductions left Hamelin with a dilemma. By now, judging from the sun, it must be almost five o'clock, and he could see that the forest was only a few hundred yards in front of him. On the one hand, he didn't want to be alone in those dark woods—which obviously went on for a great distance—at night. On the other hand, he didn't want to be out in the open grassland during the night either, with no protection from the cold air.

He decided to make the best of both options, so he walked on into the edge of the forest, going only far enough to find some protection under the trees but not so far that he couldn't get back out of the woods if he needed to.

He sat down against a large tree, settling in for the night. But he began to realize that he didn't like his circumstances at all. He was out in the country with no signs of civilization and no light whatsoever—not even from the moon. The darkness rapidly enveloped him, and he had only his jacket and the protection of a tree trunk to warm him from the cold night air.

But the worst of it was that Hamelin was by himself in the dark. He hated to admit it, but though he had always been somewhat afraid of the dark, like most children, being alone was even worse. And while he had mostly overcome his fear of the dark as he got older, he still hated being alone.

And now his fears made his mind fly in every direction. He tried to focus on his best memories of people he cared about. Of Mrs. Regehr and Mrs. Frendle, the Kaleys, Bryan and Layla, Marceya—but then he remembered the time she cried for her parents and then ran away. Which made him think of his parents. If they were over here, where over here? Thinking of the parents he had never met made him once again feel alone, which then brought him back to his dark, lonely present moment. And as the darkness around him deepened, he started to feel it—the isolating, suffocating weight of blackness that fell on him like a huge blanket, wrapping itself around his head and face and arms, with no way to crawl out from under it.

He wanted to scream—but who or what would hear him? Just as he thought he couldn't take it any longer, he heard a whooshing sound and felt a slight ripple in the air—it almost sounded like a flag whipping in the breeze. Hamelin couldn't see anything in the total darkness, but he could have sworn that someone or something had just run past him. He listened. It was quiet.

Then a short distance away, he heard a bump and a thud, and then maybe something like a big cat or raccoon thrashing on the ground, followed by a voice.

"Ow! Ow!" someone cried out. "That hurts! Ow!"

Hamelin jumped up, not sure whether he should run or be ready to protect himself. Once again he heard a cry of pain, "Ow!"

"What is it?" he asked. "Who's there?"

"What? Who's there?" asked the voice in return.

"I asked you first," said Hamelin.

He got up and made his way in the darkness, using the sounds to guide him. As he got closer, he could see the figure of a boy close to his own size sitting on the ground. He wore baggy clothes and a hood. From the looks of him, he was a good five years older and a couple of inches taller than Hamelin. His voice sounded friendly enough, under the circumstances, and he certainly didn't seem to pose any threat as he sat rubbing his shin and knee.

"Are you okay?" asked Hamelin.

"Yeah, I think so. I tripped over that tree root there and fell on my knee. Then I bumped my shin on that rock. But it'll be okay," added the boy quickly, apparently embarrassed that he had yelled so much.

"My name is Hamelin. What's yours?"

"I'm Lars," said the boy slowly as he sat on the ground with his right knee pulled up to his chest and rubbed his shin.

Glad to have someone to talk to, Hamelin sat down next to Lars and said, "Why were you running through these woods at night?"

"Because it's dark, and I'm anxious to get through it."

"But it's pretty hard to see in the dark."

"Well, not *that* hard," Lars answered. He noticed the quizzical look on Hamelin's face and so added, "I come from Periluna, the underground land west of here, where the light is growing dim, so I guess I can see in the dark better than you. And I'm running, if you have to know, not just because it's dark but because I'm in a hurry. I've got some important things to do. Besides, I didn't want to get stuck in the Forest of Fears all night."

"The Forest of Fears? Where's that?"

"Right *here*! That's where you are! And that's its name."

"Why?"

Lars's eyes widened, and his eyebrows squeezed together, but after a big huffing sigh, he realized Hamelin was serious and answered, "Because it's scary! It . . . it makes your worst fears *worse*! So I . . . I just started running."

Hamelin could understand that. He had wanted to run too, though he felt a little better, now that he had met someone else.

"So where are you headed?" asked Hamelin.

"Well, through this Forest, and then I'm going over those mountains just north of us to Osmethan, the city of Tumultor."

"Really?" said Hamelin, surprised to hear the names Osmethan and Tumultor. "That's the direction I'm going."

"Oh," said Lars, equally surprised. "Did Tumultor steal something from your family too?"

"No," responded Hamelin. "At least I don't think so. I'm really not sure who my family is, but I just know that I'm supposed to help someone whose sister was captured by Tumultor. Why are you going there?"

"I'm going to recover the stolen jewel that belongs to my father's kingdom. Without it, we die."

"Die?" said Hamelin with amazement. "Why?" he asked. "What does the jewel do?"

"It provides light to our kingdom! We need it to live." Lars paused but then continued. "And it's not just our kingdom at stake. If we fall to Tumultor, then other kingdoms will follow, and soon the Land of Gloaming will belong to Chimera."

Hamelin was quiet. There was the name Chimera again and the Land of Gloaming. All this was so strange.

"You're not from around here, are you?" Lars said.

"No," said Hamelin. "But I'm supposed to help some people—"

"There's only one thing I need," said Lars abruptly, "and that's the jewel. My father's kingdom is dying, falling into darkness." He looked to the north and whispered, "The jewel is the only thing that will restore the light and save us. I *have* to find it."

Hamelin was surprised that the eagle's words about meeting others were coming true so quickly, but it was obvious—Lars was the one in search of light. And Hamelin knew he had no choice but to help him.

Chapter 6

Another Traveler to Osmethan

A
S THE TWO BOYS RESTED AGAINST A LARGE TREE, HAMElin gave Lars a very quick version of his story, telling him about his journey, about the Great Eagle pushing him through the waters of death and life, and about how he was to meet two others on his path and help them—including someone searching for light.

Lars listened carefully and seemed to believe him.

"Then," he said, "it's no accident I tripped right here. So if we're in this together, let's go."

"I'm ready," said Hamelin. "And I'll be glad to get out of these woods."

The two got up, and Hamelin confirmed that Lars was indeed a little taller, but not a lot given their differences in age. Since Lars could see better in the dark than Hamelin, he led the way. As they walked, they told each other more about themselves, their journeys, and the worlds in which they lived.

Lars was a prince, the son of Elwood, a great king who ruled over the land of Periluna. Their land, as Lars described it, was a beautiful underground kingdom that had for centuries derived its light, warmth, and other life-giving properties from a great jewel. The jewel was fixed at the top of the underground sky—really a cavernous ceiling—that covered the entire land. It connected Periluna and the upper regions. The size of a man's fist, the massive jewel had special, powerful qualities that enabled it to draw light from the sun, since the top of its surface was open to the upper world, and then transfer its warmth and life-giving light to every inch and corner of Periluna below.

"If your source of underground light and power is gone," asked Hamelin, "why don't all of you just move and build new cities and towns up here?"

"We've tried," answered Lars, "but after so many centuries of living below ground, we're just not fit for direct sunlight."

That explained Lars's unusual clothes. His shirt had a hood that, during the day, could be pulled over his forehead and was evidently long enough, like a monk's cowl, to provide shade for his entire face. Every other inch of his body was also covered with clothing: his hands were gloved; he wore high-top shoes, which his long, baggy pants were tucked into; and his shirt came down well beyond his waist, its sleeves ending just below his wrists. The baggy pants made a whooshing sound when he walked, which explained what Hamelin had heard in the dark. He thought that Lars almost looked like a circus clown with his baggy clothing.

"My father told me not to try it, not to leave Periluna, but I had to," said Lars.

"So you've never been out here before?"

"We can make short trips, but we have to stay covered like this. We know about these upper lands from maps and drawings we studied in school."

After Lars told his full story, they talked at greater length about their lives and experiences. Hamelin described again the cave, the eagle, and the pond he was brought through. But then he came again to the eagle's instructions about finding two companions and then remembered another point.

"The eagle also told me that we are supposed to go to the home of the Hospitable Woman. Do you know—?"

"What?" Lars said with a strange note in his voice. "What name did you say?"

"The Hospitable Woman. Sue something. Do you know her?"

"Know her? Of course not. I mean, no one I know does. But everyone's heard of her." Lars realized he'd have to explain. "My grandmother told me stories about her. She supposedly lives in the mountains, and you can't see her unless she wants you to. She's supposed to be the wisest woman in the world. But there are also stories of her being fierce against those who are inhospitable to others."

"Well, the eagle told me that we are supposed to go to her home and receive instructions from her."

Lars slowed down and considered Hamelin's words— meet the Hospitable Woman? Then he shook his head and picked up his pace.

He remained quiet until Hamelin cleared his throat and said, "There's also, as I mentioned, someone else I'm supposed to help, someone trying to find a sister who's held captive by Tumultor. Do you know anything about that?"

"No, I don't. But I guess we'll find out."

The two boys continued north through the woods for a long way. Hamelin was getting tired, but he knew that Lars was in a hurry to get to Osmethan and wanted to walk through the night. He wasn't sure he could do that, but since Lars could see better in the dark, Hamelin certainly wasn't going to get separated from him and didn't want to look weak by asking to stop. They fell silent.

As they continued to walk, Hamelin thought he saw a light flickering in the distance. Lars had already noticed it, though he hadn't said anything.

"What's that over there?" asked Hamelin.

"It's a campfire, I think. See how it flickers?"

The two boys walked on, and the path led them steadily closer to the light. As they approached, they began to hear a sound. About thirty paces from the light, they realized it was the soft crying of a girl.

Before they reached the fire, though, the crying suddenly stopped, and they heard a sharp, stern voice. "Who's there?" demanded the voice.

The boys continued to walk, and as they got closer to the fire, they could see the girl, of medium height and about fifteen or sixteen years of age, rise to her feet. "I said, 'Who's there?'" she demanded angrily. By this time, the boys had emerged into the light of the fire. They stood there together still several steps away, the fire between them and the girl. The three young people stared at one another for several moments. The light from the fire flickered onto the girl's head and shoulders, revealing brown hair and soft skin. She stood there, obviously ready to fight, but even with her pursed lips and clenched fists, the light in her eyes and on her face reflected her beauty. Finally, she broke the silence again: "What do you want?"

"I'm Lars."

The girl didn't budge.

"I'm Hamelin."

Her eyes moved from Lars to Hamelin and back to Lars.

"Nice names," she said with a hint of sarcasm, "but I didn't ask for them. I said, 'What do you *want*?'"

"Nothing," replied Lars, "except . . . could we sit by your fire?"

She quickly wiped the tears from her eyes with the back of one hand while indicating with a wave of the other that they could sit down at a spot on the other side of the fire, still several feet away from her.

After more silence, Hamelin spoke again. "What are you doing here?"

"I'm sitting by a fire," she snapped. "What does it *look* like?"

He decided to try again. "Well, I hope we're not bothering you, but we saw your fire and thought it would be a good place to stop and rest. I'm very tired."

The girl looked at Hamelin and noticed that he was younger than she and the other boy. Her face softened just a little.

"What are *you two* doing here?" she asked.

The boys started slowly, but the more they told of their stories, the more she seemed to soften. Lars repeated what he had already told Hamelin, but Hamelin was so tired, he told only briefly of coming from another place, being led by a talking eagle through a cave and a mysterious pond, and now being sent to help Lars and someone else. The boys then looked at the girl and waited for her to speak.

"My name is Eraina," she finally said. She paused and stared briefly at Hamelin and Lars, who glanced at each other, but neither of them dared to say anything about her odd name.

"I come from Parthogen," she continued, "the capital city of the kingdom of Parthogen, ruled by my noble father, King Carr. Our troubles began some four years ago when our mother, the queen, suddenly died. My father, as were all of us, was grief stricken. While he mourned, our beautiful kingdom was overrun by a monster named Landon who is half man and half beast. The part that is a man scarcely deserves to be called a man, and the part that is a beast is a ferocious wolf. He alternates in personality—and some say also in appearance—between the two. He overran the city of Parthogen that winter with an army of wolves and wild dogs who seemed to sense his every thought and obey his every wish.

"Until he appeared, the beauty of our kingdom was unsurpassed, but now the city is ruined by Landon's canine packs. We now know he is a son of Chimera. On Chimera's orders, he enslaved many of our people, though some of us escaped, including my father, my two sisters, and me. We are in hiding, but many from the outlying areas of my father's kingdom are now rallying to us. We are looking for ways to defeat the monster and restore my father to his throne."

"How do you expect to drive him out?" asked Lars. "Do you have any armies to fight for you?"

Signs of doubt, detectable even in the firelight, appeared on Eraina's face. Though hesitating, she nevertheless answered. "Yes, we still have many people and soldiers who are loyal to us, but my father cannot lead them, at least not now."

"Why not?" asked Hamelin.

"Well . . . in the sacred scroll of our kingdom, there is a prophecy. It foretells the coming of beasts who will take the land. That has now happened. But it goes on to say that later all the heirs of the king shall return, and when the four thrones are filled—obviously by our father and his three daughters—the beasts will be scattered and our land restored."

Hamelin's eyes widened as he frowned. "That's . . . scary."

He wanted to ask what the four thrones were, but Lars broke in: "Hamelin, you've heard already about Chimera, but one important thing you may not know, since you are a stranger to these lands, is that Chimera is the master of Nefas. At one time, Nefas, the Abyss, was only the dark realm here in the Land of Gloaming. But now this hidden kingdom has come into the open. Chimera, through his three sons, is the lord of almost all the kingdoms on this side. Landon is one of his sons, and Tumultor is another. Landon, I'm sorry to say, seems to have Parthogen, or at least its greatest city. As I told you before, Tumultor—who controls Osmethan—stole our great jewel, the powerful gem that spreads light and life to Periluna. Once we are weakened by the loss of the light and its warmth, Chimera's plan is to take our kingdom too, and then his rule will be almost complete."

"What about the third son?"

Lars and Eraina looked at each other, as if reluctant to say anything, before Lars finally lowered his voice a notch and spoke. "His name is Ren'dal, and it is said that he is the worst of all, a deceiver who has long since ruled Ventradees."

"Ren'dal?" Hamelin said. "Say that again."

"Ren'dal?" Lars said.

"No. Where he rules."

"Ventradees," said Eraina.

"That's it," Hamelin said. But before he could say more, Eraina went on. He realized the word *Ventradees* matched the unfinished letters in his mother's note. He wanted to ask more, but then he remembered the eagle's warning and tried to focus on Eraina's words.

"And according to rumor," Eraina said, "Tumultor now also has one of our sisters, Charissa, who was apparently sent to him by his brother Landon. They are no doubt holding her, maybe using her in some way to prevent the fulfillment of the prophecy. She has been missing for nearly four years. That's why we haven't yet fought back to reclaim our city. If we rise up too quickly, we fear he will kill Charissa. So I'm going secretly to Osmethan, the capital city of the kingdom of Tumultor. My father thinks I'm going only to gather information, but I'm determined to rescue my sister and take her home to Parthogen."

Hamelin tried to interrupt when he heard of this sister held captive by Tumultor, but Eraina pressed on. "Then, when we three sisters and my father are reunited, we will be the four rulers who lead the uprising against Landon and his canine beasts, as the prophecy says. And then maybe we can even push Chimera out of all our kingdoms and back to his dark lands."

Hamelin looked at Lars, eyebrows raised, and then to Eraina.

"Then you're the *other* one!" he said.

"I'm what?"

"The other one Hamelin is supposed to help," explained Lars.

"I was told that I would meet someone who seeks to save a sister held captive by Tumultor. That's you!"

Eraina frowned. "I don't want your help. My mission is secret. You two would just get in the way."

Hamelin opened his mouth to respond, but Lars shook his head and shrugged, so Hamelin decided to stay quiet. The three stared into the fire. It had gotten late, and now all Hamelin wanted to do was lie down and rest. He was also hungry, but he hadn't seen—and she hadn't offered—any food. So while Lars and Eraina continued to share tales of the evil Chimera and his sons, he lay on his back and closed his eyes. But as his thoughts drifted into sleep, a sound rustled him awake. He sat up.

"What was *that*?" asked Lars.

Eraina kept staring into the fire. The sound grew closer, and now it seemed that it was a staccato sound, with more than one voice at its origin.

"Yeah," said Hamelin. "What *is* that?"

The sound grew louder, and it became obvious that it was a combination of howling and barking, sounds that dogs or wolves make in the night.

Eraina, who seemed not to care what it was, finally looked up from the fire, stared at the two boys, and with an expressionless face said, "It's the wolves of Landon."

"What?" asked Lars, rising to his feet quickly. Hamelin jumped up too.

"They've been chasing me ever since they discovered I slipped away from Parthogen. Landon is determined to make sure that the three sisters are not reunited with our father to start a revolt against him. That's why I have this fire," said Eraina.

"Why didn't you tell us *sooner*?" said Lars, his voice rising. "We could have kept going!"

"Because it wouldn't have mattered," she replied. "I know they will eventually catch me, no matter how fast I go. I've been waiting to make a stand here with this fire and fight them off. They are creatures of the night, and though they are attracted by this fire, they won't come right up to it, especially as long as I have the breath to fight," she said with clenched teeth. "You should run now. It's me they want."

"But, listen," said Lars, "there's no reason to stay here and fight when we can run. I can lead the way. I can see almost as well as those wolves in the dark."

"Maybe," said Eraina, looking at him up and down, "but they'll still eventually catch us. They're faster than we are."

"But they're not smarter or stronger," added Hamelin. "I say we make a run for it. Lars, lead the way. I've got an idea or two."

They both looked at Eraina.

"I'm not running anywhere!" she said.

"Please, Eraina," said Hamelin. "I don't have time to explain. But I've got a plan. Come on! *Run* with us!"

She hesitated.

"We're losing time!" said Lars.

She looked at Lars and, with what sounded like a sigh of disgust, said, "All right. Just *run* then!"

Lars led the way, and the three took off as fast as they could along the northbound path. The wolves' howls continued to get louder, which meant they were closing the gap.

It wouldn't be long before the creatures would overtake them, and Hamelin knew it was all up to him and his plan—and the gloves he had so far not mentioned.

Chapter 7

Hanging by a Limb

LARS, ERAINA, AND HAMELIN CONTINUED TO RACE AS fast as they could along the path. Since Eraina had built her fire somewhere in the middle of the woods, they knew they had no chance to run all the way through the Forest, and even if they could, that wouldn't stop the wolves from pursuing them.

Though the howling grew closer and closer, it paused for a short while. When it resumed, it sounded somewhat farther away. Evidently, the wolves had finally made it to the campfire and had rushed all around it, looking and sniffing for Eraina—and now her two additional companions—before tearing off in hot pursuit up the path to the north.

By this time, the three young people were still several hundred yards ahead of the wolves, but they could tell from the growing volume of sound that their pursuers would make up the difference in a matter of minutes.

As the barking pack approached, Eraina shouted, "Well, Mr. Hamelin, I hope you've got your great ideas ready, because we sure need one now!"

Hamelin yelled out, "Lars, look for the biggest tree you can find that has plenty of room between the ground and the first limb."

"What good will *that* do us?" Lars yelled back. "If the wolves can't get up it, we can't either! I hope that's not the best idea you've got!"

"Just do it!" shouted Hamelin.

"Oh great!" said Eraina. "I *knew* I should have stayed by the fire!" But within a few seconds, Lars could see the kind of tree that Hamelin wanted. It was huge. From top to bottom, it measured a hundred feet. From the ground to the first sturdy limb was at least fifteen feet.

"Well," yelled Lars, breathing heavily with his hands on his knees, "there it is, but I don't know what good it will do."

"Just stand there!" yelled Hamelin. He pulled at the heels of his gloves to make sure they were on tight. It was still dark, but some light was pushing through in the east. It was enough for Hamelin and Eraina to see the dark outline of the big branch Lars pointed to. With that, Hamelin grabbed Lars first, placing his right hand in the small of his back and his left hand just below his left knee.

"What are you doing?" Lars hollered indignantly.

"Look, just lean back. I'm going to throw you up to that first limb. You gotta catch it on the first try!"

"What?" yelled Lars, but it was too late for Hamelin to explain.

He pulled Lars backward a little from the waist and then yelled, "Okay, get ready! On the count of three, I'm throwing you, and you better grab it."

Before Lars knew what had happened, Hamelin had done just that. From the strength in his gloved hands, Lars was suddenly flying vertically through the air. Wide-eyed but just as Hamelin had instructed, he grabbed the first horizontal limb growing out from the trunk of the tree. Holding it with both arms, he swung his left leg up first, and then, using his left leg and his arms, swung himself over the limb and gained his balance while straddling it. It was a big limb, so large that he was able to keep his balance on it easily.

"Okay!" Hamelin yelled up to him. "We've got to hurry now, but here's the hard part. I'm going to throw Eraina up, and you've got to catch her."

"Well," said Eraina, both surprised and insulted, "I don't know how you did that, but obviously you've got some interesting powers. But let me tell you two things."

"Fine," yelled Hamelin, "but *hurry*!" The barking of the wolves was getting louder.

"First, I am a *princess*, and you better be very careful where you put your hands!" Hamelin looked puzzled, and Lars rolled his eyes. "Second, I'm perfectly capable of catching that limb myself, without any help from . . . what's his name? Lars?"

"Whatever!" shouted Hamelin. But without waiting for any more advice or scolding, he grabbed her in exactly the same way he did Lars and tossed her up with both hands. She flew just as Lars had done, grabbed the same limb, and then, allowing only a little help from Lars, swung herself around the branch, swatting away Lars's efforts to help more. Eraina and Lars were amazed—in fact, stunned—at what Hamelin had done. But what about Hamelin? They both leaned over and looked down.

The wolves were getting close. Less than a hundred yards away, they were thundering upon him, having caught the scent and now able to see their prey. Their barking became faster and its pitch higher.

Hamelin jumped. Of course, the gloves were on his hands, not on his feet, but he was beginning to learn more of what his powerful hands could do. When he jumped, his body bumped up against the tree trunk, while his arms, especially his hands, gripped it in a powerful hug. His gloved hands dug into the bark of the tree on each side, just as three and a half years earlier—which crossed his mind in a flash—his fingers had dug into the rocky ground of the cave after he had thrown himself backward off the footbridge.

Climbing the tree was slower than being tossed, but Hamelin managed it steadily. His knees hugged the tree as he pulled his way up, hand over hand. Using the strength in his fingers to press down into the flesh of the trunk, almost as if it were molding clay, he kept moving up.

But before he made it to the limb, the wolves reached the tree. They jumped at his feet, using the tree trunk and their forelegs to pull themselves even higher than they normally leaped. Hamelin's shoes were about eight feet off the ground. Just as the pack leader, a giant white wolf, made one final, snapping leap, he pinched his hands deep into the bark and lifted his feet as high as he could. Then, still clutching the sides of the tree, he swung his legs up quickly sideways, almost shoulder height, just in time to avoid the pack leader's bite. He then reversed the swinging arc of his legs, brought his two heels together, and slammed them into the wolf's head. The white wolf flipped and fell body first into the pack of barking, snarling wolves below.

Hamelin then quickly continued his climb and reached the limb. The three young people, with Hamelin panting from his exertions, sat there staring at one another, fatigued and amazed.

While Hamelin was still breathing hard, Lars and Eraina broke out laughing. He looked at them and, with a sheepish smile, joined in their laughter. For the moment, they were safe. The wolves and other wild dogs of Landon were still barking and howling below, but the new friends were safely out of their reach. Among the three of them, they hoped that by morning they could figure out what to do next.

Chapter 8

leaving the forest of fears

THEY HAD BEEN UP ALL NIGHT, AND HAMELIN WAS SO tired that once or twice, as he leaned against the tree trunk, he caught himself dozing off. But then the growls below snapped him awake.

Lars and Eraina obviously wanted to know more about how he had accomplished the feats of strength that had rescued them, so he explained that the eagle had given him the gloves and that the gloves gave him incredible strength whenever he wore them.

The barking and growling and jumping against the tree continued for a while, but the three really didn't have to devise a plan to escape. The rising sun worked to weaken and scatter the wolves, who were worn out from their efforts and preferred darkness to daylight. One by one, realizing that their prey was not going to come down, they skulked off. By sunrise, one or two wolves seemed determined to lurk about the area, but Hamelin decided to motivate them to take off with the others.

First, he stood up on the limb where they all sat. Next, with his left hand on the tree for balance, he raised his gloved right hand to the next large branch above him and broke it off with one tug. Then, gripping this five-foot limb and taking careful aim, he fired it like a javelin toward the wolf at the base of the tree. The limb found its mark. The wolf howled in pain, and with bruised ribs and a noticeable limp, he scampered off into the woods, still yelping. The other wolf quickly joined his injured partner. Grinning with satisfaction, the three young people listened as the wolfish whimpering faded into the distance. Eraina seemed especially pleased.

Safe for now, they started climbing down, but it was harder than they expected. Hamelin first shimmied his way down, his hands gripping the sides of the tree as he reversed the process he had used on the way up. Once down, he stood underneath Lars, who suspended himself by his hands from the limb, the bottoms of his high-top shoes still some nine feet above the ground.

"Okay," said Hamelin. "Let go." Lars did as he instructed, and though Hamelin's gloves helped him catch Lars and break the fall, Hamelin lost his balance and the two boys went down in a heap, laughing but none the worse in spite of the somewhat muffed catch.

Now it was Eraina's turn. The look on her face showed she was not altogether pleased at the prospect of suspending herself, with her ankle-length dress, from the limb. After some hesitation, she realized there was no other way.

She hung from the limb as though it were a chinning bar and then dropped down to Lars and Hamelin, who had promised to catch her. She fell with her back to the boys, who faced each other, with just enough space in between to catch her in an almost perfect sitting position. They made a smooth catch and, with hands interlocked, found themselves holding Eraina between them, forming a human swing for her. She gave them a faint nod of approval, placed her hands around their necks, and said, "Very good, boys. A little more practice, and I shall let you be at the front of my litter when my sisters and I return to rule Parthogen with our father!"

"Great," said Lars dryly. He then winked at Hamelin, wanting the two of them to pull their hands away quickly to drop her unceremoniously on her backside, but Hamelin wasn't sure what the wink meant. And his grip was too strong for Lars to pull away. So Eraina hopped off their arms, smiled, and said, "Thank you." Lars rolled his eyes.

The three new friends started out again on the path, and by now Eraina was convinced they were all supposed to travel together. They were tired, but Hamelin especially was dragging. Lars and Eraina, however, were evidently determined to make it through the woods as quickly as possible, so they kept going.

The sun was only a fourth of the way across the sky when they emerged from the woods and discovered before them a long stretch of barren, rocky ground, which extended from the woods to an east-west mountain range quite some distance in front of them. It appeared that the northward path they were on would lead straight ahead to the base of the highest mountain in the range.

By the time they had covered the distance from the edge of the woods to nearly the base of the mountain, it was easily midday, and Hamelin thought he could go no farther. It was cold, he was exhausted from staying up all night, and he ached with hunger. Being the youngest, he hesitated to say anything to the other two, but he did notice that they were beginning to slow down too. Several times he started to ask them to stop, but there was no place to get any relief from the cold, so he never did. Besides, they were by now not far from the base of the mountain, so he made up his mind he would definitely ask to stop there and try to find some shelter, whether they wanted to or not.

He and Lars had told Eraina what the eagle said about meeting the Hospitable Woman. Like Lars, she had heard stories about the mysterious woman but knew nothing about how or where to find her. Hamelin wished the eagle had given clearer instructions.

As they approached the mountain, a huge, gray cloud covered the sun, and the winter air suddenly got even colder. As they instinctively looked up to see the cloud, there was a flash of light, right up next to the mountain, like a mirror catching the sun. Then, all at once, the three of them saw something they hadn't detected until then. It was a sturdy looking cabin with features and colors that caused it to blend almost completely into the mountainside.

Smoke was rising from the chimney, and the signs of life at the cabin looked as inviting as anything Hamelin had ever seen. The house faced west, but its porch wrapped around it from the west to its south side. They looked at one another and nodded, silently agreeing that they would approach it. Hamelin hoped whoever was in that cabin could tell them where to find the Hospitable Woman.

Chapter 9

Sue Ammi

AMELIN, LARS, AND ERAINA HAD TAKEN ONLY A FEW steps in the direction of the house when the tall, stately figure of a woman emerged from the front door and came to the southern side of the porch. As they approached, they could see that she was facing in their direction, shading her eyes with both hands, and looking directly at them.

As they neared the cabin, her features came clearly into focus. She had the hair and eyes of someone very well along in years but the upright posture and smooth skin of someone much younger. Her hands were now clasped in front of her, about waist-high, with her right palm facing down over her left, as if she had just dried her hands from work and was now waiting for her family to come in for lunch and a rest. Her hair was a whitish silver, and it must have been extremely long, but how long was difficult to say since its strands were wrapped in a bun on top of her head.

Her mouth bore a smile that seemed on the verge of breaking into a laugh, and her eyes were wide with anticipation.

Her dress was simple, its color a light gray with faint hints of blue. The sleeves came down halfway between her elbows and her wrists, and the dress itself was full below her waist and extended to her shoe tops. She wore an apron that looped around her neck and covered the front of her dress.

She looked so welcoming that, for a moment, each of the three friends wondered if perhaps her eyes had failed her and she thought they were some other people, maybe guests she was expecting.

"Welcome!" she said as they approached. "I've been waiting for you. I worried last night that you wouldn't make it through the Forest, but now you're here!"

How had she known about last night? The three stole glances at one another, with eyes widening.

"Well done, Hamelin Stoop," she said. "You were wise and strong, and those qualities saved all of you from those wolves, despite your exhaustion."

"Eraina, daughter of Carr, I must say that your tongue was a bit tart with these boys, but I suppose we women know how and why that sometimes needs to happen. You were brave enough to stand and fight but wise enough to run when you did." She smiled at Eraina and then looked at Lars.

"And you, son of Elwood, were courageous to lead the group in the dark, and you were wise to trust in Hamelin when you did—the three of you would not have escaped had you not."

The woman was at least six feet in height, not counting the soft, silver-stranded bun that circled her head. Hamelin and Lars smiled but didn't say anything. Eraina stepped forward.

She bowed and then said softly, "We're on our way to Osmethan, the city of Tumultor. If you would be so kind, we would like to pause here for rest."

"Well, of course," the woman said with a twinkle in her slate-blue eyes, as if amused at the question but pleased with Eraina's politeness. "You need rest, and I have a late brunch all prepared for you. Come in! Come in!"

She motioned to them to follow and walked into her house. The young people entered cautiously. Inside, they found themselves not in a small, dark space—which the outside of the cabin prepared them to expect—but in a huge well-lit room that served as a combination kitchen, dining room, and living area. Farther back and a little to their right was the kitchen area, with baking pans lying around and a fine layer of flour on the cabinet. Delicious aromas wafted from the kitchen and filled the entire cabin.

In the middle of the room stood a simple wooden table with six chairs around it, though it was large enough to seat ten. Back to their left and farther in, the three friends saw a warm, comfortable living area, and on the far wall, the one tucked closest into the mountain, they noticed a fireplace with a sword mounted above. In front of the fireplace stretched a rug of some luxuriant, fluffy material, and around the room were large, soft chairs and a small sofa.

To the left of the fireplace, the friends noticed a wide opening where a stairway led to the second floor. The cabin was clearly larger on the inside than it appeared from the outside. It reminded Hamelin of the cave. They were staring all around in wonder and curiosity when the woman's sweet voice caught their attention again.

"Come, come, sit down and eat. I know you are famished." The beautiful woman—who looked old and strong at the same time—then took a seat at the end of the table nearest the kitchen and, with her hands, showed her three visitors where to sit. Bowls and platters of delicious foods had already been placed on the table—breakfast and lunch items, just right for a late brunch. The meal included scrambled eggs, sausage, roasted potatoes, pancakes, biscuits, fruits, and cereals—plus baked chicken and hot onion soup for those who preferred lunch. There were glasses of cold orange juice and milk and steaming cups of hot tea with cream, if anyone wanted it.

Hamelin started to reach for the closest platter, but the woman's voice, which earlier had filled the room in soft conversation, fell quiet. The children looked at her, expecting her to begin passing the dishes of food, but her hands were in her lap. She smiled at them and then looked up. At first Hamelin thought she was looking at something on the ceiling, but then she began to hum. It was a middle soprano note, soft and smooth.

Hamelin felt his whole body relax, and he remembered how tired he was. He closed his eyes for just a second. He saw in his mind the Atrium, and he could hear the water trickling down the wall and filling the pond. He saw the four smoothly shaped boulders, and the eagle was there, and two other creatures were talking with the eagle. He saw blue sky in the opening above the crystal, and then the four thrones floated up toward the opening and blended into one great, jewel-studded throne.

Streams of water flowed down from it, and the sweet pitch of the woman's voice blended into the gentle sounds of the rippling water. Clouds swirled around the one great throne, and Hamelin thought he could see a hazy figure moving toward it. He felt himself leaning forward as if to see more clearly through the clouds, but then the sounds—the waters and the woman's voice—stopped. Hamelin opened his eyes. He was embarrassed that maybe he had been asleep at the table, but no one teased him. He looked at the woman, and she caught his eyes with hers.

She glanced at Lars and Eraina and then back at Hamelin. She was thoughtful and almost looked sad before she smiled and said, "Please, eat. I made it just for you."

For Hamelin, it was the kind of breakfast that only Mrs. Parker could come close to matching. The three of them took many helpings and were more intent on eating than talking.

At the end of the meal, Lars was the first to express his appreciation. "Thank you very much, ma'am. I mean, Mrs. . . . I'm sorry, but I don't know your name."

She smiled warmly. "My name is Sue Ammi."

"You're the Hospitable Woman?" Hamelin asked.

She chuckled at that. "I must say, I'm always amused when they refer to me as the 'Hospitable Woman.' That name is a little stiff, don't you think? Of course, it's true I'm not a girl anymore. And I do love having company." She winked and then turned to Lars. "Thank you for your gratitude. You are all very welcome. Please, call me SueSue or Ammi, whichever suits you."

They were all silent, not knowing what to say. "Oh, I know you've been taught to address adults by their last name, but SueSue is the name my father gave me, and since I've given you permission, you're not rude in calling me that. Ammi is a name I received much later, after many troubles and much pain. But those stories are not for now. For now, you are sleepy. So I want all of you to go upstairs immediately, and I'll show you rooms where you may wash and rest."

So Sue Ammi, the Hospitable Woman, led them all up the stairs and assigned each of them a bedroom. Within a few minutes, they had undressed and bathed and were soon deep in sleep on feather beds softer than anything they had ever felt and between luxuriantly soft linen sheets.

They slept for hours, each dreaming of adventures, great banquets, holidays and parties, kings and queens, parents and children, and laughter all around. They rested well.

Downstairs, Sue Ammi worked to organize the special provisions her young guests would need to face what lay before them.

Chapter 10

Commissions and Gifts

FROM MIDDAY THROUGH LATE AFTERNOON, THE THREE travelers slept. By early evening, Hamelin started to stir. He thought he heard voices, so, feeling rested and figuring that the others were getting up, he got out of bed and quickly dressed.

To his surprise, his clothes had been washed, dried, ironed, and laid on a chest at the foot of his bed. As he put them on, he could smell the cleanness that clung to the fabrics.

As Hamelin walked toward the stairs that led to the large room below, he glanced back down the hall onto which the three bedrooms opened. At the other end of it, there was a large door that he assumed was the entry to a master bedroom where Sue Ammi slept. Just to the side of that door was a smaller one. As he stood there looking at it, the small door opened. Peeping around the doorframe was a beautiful child, a girl Hamelin judged to be about six or seven years old. Her hair, which was a blondish brown, flowed in well-brushed wavy strands down to the middle of her back. Her clothing was a light, rose-colored gown of a simple style, and she wore big, furry slippers. She stared at Hamelin before quickly closing the door.

He went on downstairs, and when he walked into the room, he realized, a bit sheepishly, that he was the last one to get up. Lars and Eraina were sitting in chairs at either side of the fireplace, and Sue Ammi, whose beauty was even more striking to Hamelin in the light of the fire, was between them on a small sofa.

"Ah, there you are," said SueSue. Her quick smile took away his awkward feelings. "I hope you rested well, Hamelin."

"Yes, ma'am, I did."

Her smile vanished. "We've been having some good conversations about important things. I want to talk to you later as well, but for now, let's go outside and enjoy the sunset. And I also want to point out a few things to you."

After stepping outside, the three of them were immediately taken by a beautiful evening sun, fully visible yet close to touching the western horizon. The clouds around it gave off hues of purple, red, orange, yellow, and gold, which mixed magnificently with the blue sky higher in the horizon. The evening air was still, but crisply cold. SueSue gave them blankets to wrap up in as they enjoyed the sunset, seated on comfortable chairs around the western side of her porch. They silently watched the sun as it dropped into its distant hiding place.

For a moment, they thought SueSue was sleeping, but then they could hear her humming softly, as if putting a baby to sleep. She then stood. "Look, children," she said as she pointed to the mountains that stood on their right and extended westward toward the horizon. She pointed to a break in the distant peaks.

"There," she said, "between those mountains, you'll find a passageway north. The path you'll now follow will first take you westward before it turns back to the north. Through that pass between the mountains, you'll come to a canyon that will stand between you and Osmethan, the city of Tumultor. You must stay on the path. It will lead you west around the canyon, where you'll find your way into the city.

"Eraina, you and I have spoken, and your quest is to rescue your sister Charissa. Lars, you and I have also spoken, and your mission is to recover the great jewel that Tumultor has stolen and return it to its place in your father's kingdom before it's too late. And, Hamelin," and here she paused, "you and I must talk."

By now the sun had fully set, and a damp coldness had moved along the base of the mountain.

"Let's go inside," she said.

As much as the three had eaten before, they were all amazed to realize that they were hungry again. The food that SueSue set before them was not sparse. There were vegetables, meats, and fruits, some of which Hamelin recognized, but some he didn't. He was too shy to ask what the strange foods were, but he tried some of everything, and not a single thing disappointed him. Their flavors were fresh, and with every bite, he felt content. For dessert, SueSue brought out a bread pudding that was light, creamy, and sweet, like Christmas in his mouth. Without feeling too full, Hamelin still felt satisfied.

"And now," she said, still at the table, "before you go upstairs again to rest—because you must start off very early in the morning—I have some things to give you." Her voice was grave and low. The easy smile on her face was gone.

SueSue reached somewhere behind her and retrieved two items. The first was a long linen cloth of various shades of blue, purple, and red, blending the colors of a sunset like the one they had just witnessed. It was generally rectangular in shape, though not perfectly. The edges were stitched, and across the middle of its width was a seam, as if the cloth had been mended or perhaps originally made of two pieces sewn together. She looked at Eraina.

"My dear, I give you this scarf. It will enable you to see both far and deep. It will work whether it is over your head or around your shoulders or neck, but you will see best when you intentionally spread its width over your head and hold its ends in your hands. Guard it, and use it with great care."

Eraina took the scarf with both hands and rubbed the fabric between her thumbs and fingers. "It's beautiful, and so soft. Is it fragile?"

"Oh no. Linen is very strong. Though, as you can see, it was torn once, but even then it took a great burst of power."

Eraina then raised the scarf over her head and draped it over her shoulders.

"That's right," said SueSue. "Wear it just like that. It covers, then it reveals. You can pull it over your head and face, or just let it cover your shoulders and neck. But the more you cover, the more it will enable you to see."

"How was it torn?" asked Eraina as she held the ends of the scarf in front of her in both hands.

"Oh, that's a long story for another day. The scarf and the larger cloth it came from have quite a history."

SueSue shook her head softly, lost for a moment in memory, and then focused again on Eraina.

"Be careful with it, my dear," she said quietly. "We do not know what would happen if it were torn again. We know some of what tearing it before accomplished. Great mysteries were revealed, but at a great cost.

"And one more thing: while it is yours for now, you may not give it to another. I advise you always to wear it on this quest."

"So will it—?"

"You'll learn what it does as you use it," the woman said quickly. Eraina seemed disappointed to be cut off, but then SueSue added softly, "I shouldn't say more. Sometimes too much explanation will keep you from learning." Eraina nodded.

The second item SueSue had brought out was a pair of ordinary-looking shoes. She turned to Lars. "And to you I give these shoes of speed and balance because time is short for your father's kingdom. Already you are inclined to run, but these will give you a speed far beyond what you already have, plus a balance that will amaze all who see you. You've shown yourself capable of making decisions, even when you don't understand all that is involved. Therefore, I give you this footwear because you have learned to combine haste with humility. When you wear them, you will receive even greater balance, speed, and agility. For this journey, I advise you never to take them off." Lars nodded as he took the shoes.

The woman then turned to Hamelin. He wondered what she could possibly have for him, since nothing else was near her.

"The gloves from the eagle give you great strength, Hamelin. And to wield what I am about to give you will require it." She stood and walked across the room to the fireplace, and from above its mantle, she removed the sword. It had a simple two-edged blade, uniform and sharp on both sides. The handle likewise was symmetrical and could be gripped with either hand or both, having only a plain hand guard across the top of its leather grip. From the bottom of the grip to the point of the blade, it was three feet long. From the way Sue-Sue lifted the sword, Hamelin could tell it was heavy.

Before handing it to him, she said, "You'd better put on your gloves."

Hamelin did as she advised and took the sword in both hands. Immediately it flashed, and he felt a surge of energy that went from the sword into his hands and body. Sue-Sue then quickly returned to the fireplace, pulled a stone from the left side of it near the floor, took something out, and walked back to Hamelin with a belt and sheath held in both hands. She strapped the belt around him and stepped back. The sword fit his hands perfectly, and the belt rested comfortably around his waist.

SueSue took a deep breath as her eyes widened and moved quickly from sword to sheath and then to Hamelin. In a voice soft and deliberate, she said, "Good. Now . . . put the sword in its scabbard."

Hamelin, holding the sword in his right hand and keeping the belt steady with his left, sheathed the sword; when he did so, he felt its energy subside just as he removed his right hand from the handle. The sword and its belt and scabbard immediately became invisible, though he could still feel them.

"Now," she said, "unlike Eraina's scarf and Lars's shoes, this sword, according to tradition, may be used only once by the same person. You need not always wear it, but I advise you never to have it far from you. And when you think you may need it, place the belt around your waist. But be warned:

the sword and the sheath now once again are together. Never take the sword out of its sheath unless you intend to use it, because once drawn, it must not be resheathed until its unusual power is spent. When it is drawn, it will become visible, and at that point, you must not delay in using it. You must strike and immediately let it go, for it will bring death to those it wounds, but also to you if you cling to it while the power is present."

All of them were silent. The words she spoke to Hamelin seemed to hang in the air.

"I am confident you will all be successful in your quests, for each of you has already shown the ability to overcome your worst fear. Hamelin, you fear more than anything being alone. Yet you went alone into the Forest last night before Lars came along. And Lars, you took the long way around from Periluna, needing the Forest for cover but trying to avoid as much of it as you could. You ran around the edge of it and entered from the south. And though you see better than most in the dark, nonetheless you hate the darkness. The darkness that is falling at Periluna has increased your fear, which is similar to Hamelin's fear of being alone. You were running from the dark last night, but you didn't turn back.

"And, Eraina, you, for good reason, fear those wolves. You once had a sister attacked by a dog when she was but a small child. Ever since you heard that family story, you have feared it would happen to you. You have dreamed about it. And now your father's kingdom is overrun by the wolf-man Landon, who rules by using his packs of dogs and wolves. Last night you built that fire to make your own last stand against those creatures. You knew they were coming long before Lars and Hamelin heard them, didn't you?"

"Yes," she said as she lowered her eyes.

"That is why it is called the Forest of Fears, because it uncovers and magnifies each person's deepest fear. But now you have all shown courage. I have great hopes for you. But remember, you must work together. Your quests are different, but they are all connected to a larger plan, so you must work together for the interests of each other. When you return from Osmethan, come back here. You'll need rest but also more instructions.

"And now, Hamelin. We must talk."

Lars and Eraina knew that it was Hamelin's time to hear about his mission, so they quietly climbed the stairs and went to their rooms.

Hamelin and SueSue each took a place near the fire, and he waited for her to speak, but she said nothing.

Finally, he couldn't wait anymore, and he blurted out, "So what am *I* supposed to do? I wanted the eagle to tell me more, but what he told me was mostly for Eraina and Lars."

SueSue looked at him and then gazed deeply into the fire. "Hamelin," she said, "you must tell *me* what your quest is. What is it that you most deeply want?"

Hamelin was quiet. The question surprised him because the eagle had warned him not to let his own reason for crossing the footbridge—his desire to find his parents—get in the way. That the Ancient One had bigger reasons. Now Hamelin wasn't sure what to say, so he tried a question.

"Are you asking me what I want to do?"

"No," she said. "I didn't ask what you want to *do*; I asked what it is you most deeply *want*."

Hamelin didn't speak quickly. He thought about Lars and Eraina and knew they had kingdoms to restore, a jewel to find, and a sister who was a princess to rescue. He knew that he was supposed to help them on their quests, but he wasn't sure anymore of his own. Maybe he wasn't supposed to have a quest of his own. Or maybe his reasons were too small. But now, as SueSue looked at him, and as their eyes met and blended, he knew she was asking about something personal, something he had wanted all his life. But he wasn't sure he should say it. Wasn't sure if it was important enough compared to kingdoms, jewels, and lost princesses.

"Your passion, Hamelin. Your longing . . . what is it?"

"But shouldn't I just do what I'm told to do? Isn't that my job—to do what I'm supposed to do?" He remembered the children's home and added, "Like my daily chores?"

She smiled, looked at him kindly, and said, "Yes, Hamelin, all of us must do our work. And certainly what we are rightly and properly told to do becomes our duty, our obligation. But as we grow, what we are justly asked to do and what we deeply want to do can become the same thing. Doing our chores prepares us to achieve the longings of the heart. And as we know our longings, we learn patience in doing our duty. Your duty now is to help Eraina and Lars, but tell me, what do you long for more than anything else?"

Hamelin knew the answer, but the words stuck in his mouth—he was embarrassed, even ashamed, to say it out loud. He had spent all his life at the home not wanting to cry or whine about it. Not wanting the others to think he was a baby. Besides, the eagle had warned him . . . He looked at the fire. He thought for just a moment he saw a hazy figure moving in the flames. It reminded him of the Atrium of the Worlds when he had looked at the crystal above the western throne. He looked again at SueSue, and finally the words came out.

"I want to find my mother and father," he said. His voice was low but clear, and his words, even as he said them, surprised him. He waited, wondering if she would scold him. SueSue looked at him and smiled.

And then more words tumbled out. "I want to know who my family is. I want to know who I am and where I'm from." And then he paused for a moment. "And I want to know my *name*."

"Good. You've said it. You know and admit your passion, and it is not selfish or small. All things matter to the Ancient One."

"But the eagle said there were big things—"

"Yes. It's true. There are. But the eagle doesn't know everything. Nor do I. But I know these big things involve you, Hamelin—your past, your courage, your faults, and your hopes. All of it. The Ancient One has chosen you for his plans to help many."

"But how?"

"It won't be easy—but how you do it is just as important as what you do. You long to find your family and learn your name. This passion will tempt you to turn aside from helping Eraina and Lars, but their quests will prepare you for yours. Besides, you cannot defeat Ren'dal until theirs are done."

"Ren'dal?" asked Hamelin. He suddenly felt in his chest a rush of dread and fear. "The eagle and others have mentioned Ren'dal," he said. "Where—?"

"Shhh," whispered SueSue softly as she leaned toward Hamelin, placed her hands on his face, and looked into his eyes. "You will learn more soon enough. For now, go rest."

Hamelin went to bed, but he didn't fall asleep quickly. He tried to think about Eraina and Lars and their quests, but he couldn't help also thinking about Ren'dal, his parents, and what the path to Ventradees might be.

Chapter 11

The Journey to Osmethan

THE NEXT MORNING, THE THREE FRIENDS LEFT WITH clean clothes, full stomachs, the special gifts from Sue Ammi, and an eagerness, above all else, to accomplish their tasks. SueSue stood on the porch and waved as they walked away. "Just stay on the path," she reminded them. They waved in return, and each felt an almost overwhelming desire to be strong and brave, if for no other reason than not to disappoint the beautiful woman who had given them so much.

She continued to watch them, and Hamelin looked back. He wished he could just stay with her, but he knew he had to leave the comfort of her home—which made him more determined than ever to remember what she had said to him last night. As they headed westward along the base of the mountain range, each of them glanced back one last time, but SueSue was gone. Not even the house was visible.

She had given each of them a day's provision of food and drink and also assured them that they would have enough to make it to Osmethan if they moved steadily and stayed on the path. The path was clearly marked but not well worn. It was uneven and rocky, and it was not unusual for Hamelin and Eraina to slip or stumble. Because of his shoes, however, Lars had no difficulty maintaining his balance. He was in a hurry to go, and on more than one occasion, he sighed impatiently or rolled his eyes if Hamelin or Eraina fell back.

By midday, they were still traveling westward along the base of the mountain range, watching for the pass that would turn north. Lars didn't want to stop for lunch until they got to the pass. Feeling impatient, he said, "Come on, you two, let's pick it up."

"Easy for you to say, Mr. Fancy Shoes," Eraina shot back. "I'm probably every bit as fast as you are without those shoes."

"Oh, yeah?" he fired back.

"Hey," said Hamelin, "I'm tired. Let's sit down and have some lunch."

Lars sighed loudly, but Eraina quickly sided with Hamelin and plopped down next to a boulder beside their path. Hamelin joined her. Lars had no choice, so they pulled out their provisions and ate. There wasn't much talking, and Eraina hardly looked at Lars. But it wasn't long before he was ready to go again, and they all found themselves trudging westward.

It was midafternoon when the mountain to their right started to descend on its western face. "Sure glad we decided to eat before we got to the pass," Eraina said to Hamelin but loud enough for Lars—who was ahead of them, waiting for them to catch up—to hear.

He ignored her sarcasm and said, "I think it's just ahead." When all of them were together again at the same spot, they could see where the path would likely turn north. Their pace picked up. About fifteen minutes later, the path turned northward through the mountains.

But after only an hour, the route had so continuously narrowed that it was just wide enough for them to proceed single file. The real problem, however, came soon thereafter. The path was suddenly impassable. A landslide had caused three sizable boulders to block their only way through.

"Whoa," said Lars. "What do we do now?"

"Why don't you just take your fast shoes and run around the mountain?" said Eraina, whose words looked and sounded to Hamelin like they came from the side of her mouth.

"Funny," said Lars. "Anyway, I could run around it faster than *you* could. But if you remember what we were told by SueSue, we are supposed to work together and stay *on* the path. I could probably climb over some of these boulders, but I don't see any way for all of us to get around them, whether slow or fast."

Hamelin didn't say anything, but he knew what to do. Lars and Eraina had forgotten about his gloves. He had put them back on after lunch. Now, without a word, he walked over to the closest boulder—which was about his height—and tossed it aside. Then the next boulder, though even larger, was likewise no match for him as he got under it with both hands, lifted it above his head, and, with what appeared to be some amount of strain, heaved it to the spot where the other boulder lay.

"Oh my," said Eraina. "Those gloves!"

Now there was room for all three of them to enter the narrow pass, but one more large boulder still blocked their way. This one was too large for even Hamelin to lift, but recalling his experience at the mouth of the cave, he decided to roll the boulder. With a groaning effort, he pushed it forward along the path, and fortunately, the farther through the pass he went, the wider the path became. Once the boulder started moving, it was not difficult to roll it forward enough until the three of them could squeeze around it.

"Wow," said Lars, who could only shake his head in amazement at Hamelin's strength. "Nice job."

Hamelin smiled, while Eraina walked past Lars and gave him a smirk that seemed to say, "See, you're not the only one with talents!"

The crease between the mountains continued to widen, and as they headed north, the way became smoother and descended slightly.

By late afternoon, they reached the end of the mountain pass and came to a flat, dirt plain, where the path continued northward for almost a mile. As they followed it, they could see it led to what looked like a canyon. So far, their journey had matched up well with SueSue's directions.

The path became rocky as it led right up to the canyon before it turned west. They were then able, just a few paces off the trail, to peer into the great east-west canyon that stretched in front of and below them. On the other side of the canyon, which was several hundred yards wide, they could see sparks of light from what was evidently a large city. The rays of the sun, now setting in the west, danced off the rooftops, chimneys, towers, and other surfaces of the city. This was, no doubt, Osmethan.

Each of them felt both excitement and dread while looking at the vast and sparkling city of Tumultor. From their viewpoint, it looked like a great oval, wider from east to west than from north to south, and it appeared well situated for defending itself. On the side nearest them was the canyon.

On its western and eastern sides, the city was flanked by woods. And on its northern side, the three travelers could see another great mountain range far in the distance. All those features gave Osmethan the appearance of a well-protected city built in a strategic spot of mountainous, wooded beauty, safe from attack on every side.

"It looks big," said Hamelin, who had seldom traveled far from Middleton. He was pretty sure, just looking at Lars and Eraina, that they felt the same way—overwhelmed by the size of the city they would soon have to secretly enter.

Chapter 12

The Canyon and the Bridge

T THE SPOT WHERE THE PATH TURNED WESTWARD, THE young people stood looking across the canyon toward the great city. According to Sue Ammi, the path would carry them west around the canyon to approach the city from its southwest side.

"I think we'd better find a place to stop for the night," Eraina said.

"Stop?" asked Hamelin. "But we've used up our food and water. SueSue said she gave us enough to last until we got to Osmethan. We're not there yet, so I think we're supposed to go on."

"I'm not so sure," said Eraina. "I don't think we can make it all the way around this canyon before nightfall. Besides, she didn't say she'd *given* us enough to last until Osmethan; she said we would *have* enough to last to Osmethan."

"What's the difference?" asked Lars. He pointed eastward along the canyon. "Anyway, I think I see something that will solve our problem."

Hamelin strained his eyes to see. Sure enough, though they hadn't noticed it at first, there was something shining and sparkling to their right. As the three of them looked at it, it became clearer that it was a bridge—stretching from their side of the canyon all the way over to Osmethan. The bridge would apparently carry them to the southeastern part of the city. It was high and, judging from the sunlight glancing off the masonry of its great stone arches, also strong and magnificent. It was evidently a broad, main road from this side of the canyon to the other.

"You're right," said Hamelin. "Let's go."

"Wait just a minute!" said Eraina quickly. "What do you two think you're doing? Don't you remember what Sue Ammi said? She said we're supposed to follow the path around the west side of the canyon. She said nothing about a bridge to cross over it."

"Oh, don't be so picky," said Lars. "We know what she meant. She wanted us to go through the mountain pass and get to Tumultor's city. And that's where the bridge will take us. What's the problem if we take a little shortcut?"

"Look," said Eraina, "I know what she said, and I think I also know what she meant. And no matter what you think, I know she said we're supposed to stay on the path and go around the canyon. That bridge is clearly off the path, and it goes over the canyon, not around it. I know you two guys are fast and strong, but for just a moment, would you mind using your heads?"

"Okay, Miss See All and Know All," said Lars, "since you're the one who's supposed to be able to see things, just loosen up that scarf a little, take a look over there, and tell me what you see."

Eraina narrowed her eyes and squeezed her lips together in a look of disgust. Finally, she said, "Okay, I'll take a look and tell you just *exactly* what I see." She paused. "All right, you two," she said, "move a little bit to your right."

"What?" Lars asked.

"Just do as I say," she said. With that, she pulled the scarf around her shoulders and then extended the upper side of it so it reached all the way to her forehead. She then pulled the long ends of the scarf to her chest with both hands.

"A little more to the right, you two. I need to be able to see clearly." Lars and Hamelin moved a little more to their right. Now she appeared to be squinting over their shoulders to the bridge behind them.

"Well, what do you see?" asked Hamelin. She continued to stare, her eyes now glazed and watery.

"Come on," said Lars. "What is it? What do you see?"

"Uhmmm," she said solemnly and carefully. "I *do* see something. It's amazing."

"What *is* it?" they asked in unison.

Eraina quickly stood up straight, pulled the scarf off her head, put her hands on her hips, and said, "I'll *tell* you what I see: two *idiots*! The bridge is east and the path goes west, and *that's* what SueSue said we should take, so that's what we're going to do. It doesn't take a special scarf to see *that*!" She turned on her heels and continued on the path.

"I don't care *what* you say," said Lars in reply. "What I see is obvious. And I don't need some magic scarf!" Then, pointing as he spoke, he shouted toward Eraina, "There is a *canyon* that separates us from the city we're supposed to go to. There's a *bridge* over that canyon. It's *late*, the sun is almost down, Hamelin and I are hungry and thirsty and tired, and

I'm going across that bridge." He turned and started off eastward in a slow jog.

Hamelin paused, stuck in his spot, but looked in both directions, first at Lars and then at Eraina and then back to Lars. Then he yelled, "Hey, Lars! Wait for me. I'm coming too."

Eraina was disgusted. She clenched her fists and watched the two boys jog away, off the path and toward the east. And then she saw something, something she hadn't seen before. The whole bridge flickered, not just in parts, but altogether and all at once. She pulled the scarf back up onto her head and looked again at the bridge. But this time she tried to look not just far, but, as SueSue had said, deeply. She stared, and then, with an expression of horror on her face, she ran toward the boys as fast as she could.

"Wait," she yelled. "*Wait!*"

"Hey," said Hamelin. "Here she comes. Should we wait on her?"

"Naw," said Lars. "She's just mad because we're ahead of her and she's afraid to be left by herself. Serves her right. We'll wait for her on the other side of the bridge."

The two boys kept going. Lars, enjoying his balance and speed, shot ahead of Hamelin, who ran at about half speed and occasionally slipped on the rocks in the path.

Eraina was furiously running after them, but she lagged some fifty yards behind. "Stop," she yelled. "Stop, I tell you!"

But the boys weren't listening. Lars arrived near the bridge first and waited for Hamelin, who soon caught up to him. Then the two of them stood there at the edge of the canyon, eyeing the magnificent bridge in front of them. It was beautiful, almost golden from the rays of the setting sun. It appeared to be some fifteen feet wide and was interlaced with massive wooden girders, supported by arched stone and mortar pillars, with iron rails all around. The path across the bridge appeared truly solid. The rails on the sides were high and wide. It was broad and obviously capable of carrying many people as well as carts and wagons all at once. Hit from the west by the setting sun, the stones and iron of the bridge fairly glistened with a reflected light that told of depth and thickness and strength.

But Hamelin hesitated. It wasn't because he thought any more about being off the path; it was just that even this bridge brought back memories of the footbridge. And however strong this bridge was, it was still suspended hundreds of yards above the deep canyon. He looked down into it.

"Stop," Eraina continued to yell. "Don't get on that bridge!"

Lars smiled at Hamelin and then whispered, "Hey, I think I'll run out there a little way, dance around a bit, and come back, just to annoy her." Hamelin chuckled at the idea and stepped back to watch.

Eraina was wildly waving her arms and was now within fifteen hard running strides of the boys. Again she yelled, but now she was screaming, "*Please, stop! Please!*" This time there was something in her voice so full of fear and pleading that the two boys, ready to tease and show off, couldn't ignore it.

Lars's smile began to flicker at the corners of his mouth. He looked back at her and even retreated a few steps toward her. "What . . . what is it?" he said, trying to show indifference in his voice but unable to hide his concern.

Eraina never slowed down. She rushed up to them, fiercely grabbed the boys by their shirts, and, with an amazing amount of strength, pulled them away from the edge of the canyon.

"*Don't!*" she screamed.

"What are you doing?" Lars asked.

"What's going on?" said Hamelin.

"It's not there!" she screamed. "It's not there! Can't you see? There's no bridge!"

"What?" they both asked simultaneously.

"There's no bridge! I don't know what you're seeing, or what I saw at first too, but it's not really there! Whatever's there won't hold you!"

Eraina cautiously walked to the edge of the canyon, picked up a rock the size of a fist, and tossed it toward the bridge. Instead of landing on the crossbeams of the bridge, however, it simply flew straight through the air as if nothing at all was there.

"What the . . ." said Lars. "Are you kidding me?"

Hamelin and Lars slowly walked to the edge of the canyon. Each could still see the bridge and couldn't fathom why the rock had just passed through it. Lars kicked some pebbles at his feet toward the opening of the bridge, and they tumbled down the side of the canyon. Hamelin picked up a rock the size of a baseball and threw it as hard as he could down the length of the bridge, but there was no sound, no bounce, only a free-falling rock. The only sound they finally heard was the rock hitting the canyon floor far below.

"See?" said Eraina, softer now but still out of breath. "See what I'm saying?" She stared again across the canyon for several long seconds. Eventually her gaze broke, and she closed her eyes but continued to breathe deeply.

The boys looked at Eraina and then back at the bridge, only now they saw nothing. It was gone. All of them quickly stepped away from the canyon.

"What happened?" asked Lars.

"It's not there. It never was."

"What do you mean?" said Hamelin.

"After I called you 'idiots,' and you ran off, I kept looking. I covered my head fully with the scarf, which is how I saw the trap. The scarf let me see that the bridge wasn't real."

"I . . . I don't know what to say, Eraina," said Lars. "I'm . . . I'm sorry. I *am* an idiot."

"Yeah," said Hamelin softly. "Me too. I'm sorry, Eraina."

Just then a cold breeze blew across them, and Lars said, "Hey, let's go. We need to get back on the path."

They moved quickly at first, especially trying to stay back from the canyon, but the sun was now down, and it was getting harder to see the ground. The fear of walking off the edge into the canyon took hold, and their pace slowed to a crawl.

"Look," said Lars, "I know I'm the one who got us into this mess, but, please, let me make a suggestion." Eraina and Hamelin looked at him. "Eraina, put the scarf over your head and lead the way. Use it especially to watch the ground. Hamelin will be in the middle, and I'll stay in the back. Obviously, getting off the path was a stupid and dangerous thing, and I'm sorry. But you can make sure we get back on it."

And that's what they did. Their surroundings were growing steadily colder and darker, but before long they made it back to the path, where it had turned westward to encircle the canyon. They all felt safer, and Lars took a deep breath.

It was now almost completely dark, but Eraina, with her scarf fully engaged, led the way. After a few hundred yards, the path took a slight bend to the south, away from the canyon. There they found a hollowed-out area in the ground, almost like a small basin some twelve feet wide, four feet deep, and roughly circular. The area was not completely smoothed out, but there was some sparse ground covering, and they decided to stop there for the night.

"I'm hungry," said Hamelin, and as soon as he said it, he wished he hadn't.

Lars ducked his head and breathed in deeply. "I'm sorry," he said. "Eraina was right. We should have stayed on the path. We would probably have been at a better stopping place by now and maybe even found some food in the remaining daylight."

"I know what you're saying, Lars, but it's not all your fault," said Hamelin. "I was right there with you. Being hungry is my fault too, but it beats being alone—or dead at the bottom of the canyon."

They were all silent, trying not to think about what would have happened if Lars and Hamelin had run out onto the mysterious bridge. But as they sat in a circle, barely able to see one another in that small, shallow basin, Eraina looked at the two boys and smiled. "If you promise to go slowly," she said, "I've got something for you." She then opened the small bag that Sue Ammi had given her. Each of the boys had received one as well, but Eraina still had a small portion of food left and a little bit to drink. "If we share," she said, "it'll be enough to last us till morning."

The two boys moved closer to her, and the three friends shared the provisions she had saved. Before long, they were all yawning. Hamelin kept his gloves on but gave Eraina his jacket to use as a pillow. The boys encouraged her to keep the scarf around her shoulders, because they wanted her to be able to see whatever was going on.

Soon they were all asleep. That night Hamelin dreamed strange dreams. There were images of the bridge and on it a creature like the last one he had seen in the pond. And beyond the bridge was a city with sad children and a dancing clown. Sometimes the eagle flew across his dreams, and sometimes the snakelike goat was chasing him across some woods and toward a cliff, roaring like a lion.

Chapter 13

The Final Turn toward the Great City

THE NEXT MORNING, HAMELIN, ERAINA, AND LARS WOKE up early as the sun rose from the eastern end of the canyon and stirred them from their uncomfortable resting place. Sleeping outside in that shallow basin with sparse vegetation had not given them a good night's rest. Still, they had been partly protected from the cold winds that blew across the canyon at night. But now a gnawing hunger was grinding away at their stomachs. They stepped out of the basin area, stiff and still tired but knowing they had to make the final leg of the trip to Osmethan.

They silently trudged along the path that led westward around the canyon. They could see that it turned north at the far end of the canyon and from there would lead them into the southwestern corner of the great city.

As they walked, the events—and near disaster—of the previous late afternoon were hanging in their minds, even though they didn't talk about them. The illusion of a bridge leading across the canyon and a fall to the death that might have resulted from it reminded them of the dangerous nature of their quests. They didn't want to retell the episode, but none of them could forget it. Finally, Eraina broke the silence.

"I know we don't need to go over what happened last night," she said. "And I certainly don't intend to make either of you feel any worse than I know you do. But there's something more I need to tell you."

"What is it?" asked Hamelin.

"Well, I haven't really wanted to talk about it . . ."

"It's okay," said Lars. "We'll listen. What else was there?"

"After I spread the scarf over my head, I also saw something else. At the end of the fake bridge, on the other side, I saw a huge brown bear growling on all fours. He was waiting for the two of you. At first that's what frightened me, because I was afraid the two of you would run right into the paws of that bear. But that's when I realized that the bridge was an illusion."

"Was the bear an illusion?" asked Hamelin.

"No, the bear was really there, but it wasn't like any bear I've ever seen. It looked like it was made of lights and shadows—almost like a ghost but brown and with a golden glow. I don't know how to describe it, but somehow I had the feeling that whatever the bridge was, it was flowing out of the bear and couldn't be good."

"Out of the bear?" asked Hamelin. "How—?"

"So what happened then?" interrupted Lars.

"Well, after you both realized the bridge wasn't there, I looked again. The bridge vanished, but the bear was still there, and he was fighting some large bird—I think it was an eagle. He was standing on his hind legs and furiously swatting at the eagle, who swooped all around him and clawed at him. They weren't playing. It looked like a fight to the death. The eagle's attacks finally scared the bear away, and then the eagle flew off." Hamelin thought briefly of the time the eagle had saved him from the strange looking bobcat.

"So the bear and the eagle were real?" said Hamelin.

"Yes."

"What does it all mean?" asked Lars.

"I don't know," said Eraina.

There was a long pause as the three continued to walk. Finally, Hamelin spoke. "I think I may know something about that eagle. If he's the same eagle I know, he's our friend."

"Well, that bear was for sure no friend," added Eraina.

"Tell us more about your eagle," said Lars.

Hamelin quickly retold his story, especially describing how they first met, the two trips to the footbridge, and then how the eagle had pushed him through the pond.

"This eagle must be very powerful and fierce," said Lars.

Hamelin nodded.

"But," added Eraina, "he obviously helped you, and last night he was fighting off that huge bear."

"Oh, yes," said Hamelin. "He is powerful and fierce, but I'm sure he was always *for* me. I've been afraid of him," he added, "but I trust him. He knows a lot about things over here, but it's hard to get him to explain them, though he does talk some . . . when he wants to."

By now the three companions had almost reached the western end of the canyon. It was approaching midmorning, and all three were thirsty and hungry.

"I'm not sure how much farther I can go without water," said Eraina. She said it, but they all felt it. Still, they knew they had to go on.

Then something odd happened. The path turned sharply north. It was no doubt leading toward the southwestern portion of the city, but they weren't all the way around the western end of the canyon, and now it appeared that the trail led directly toward the edge of it. As they cautiously followed it and neared the drop-off, they could plainly see that the path led downward, but exactly where, they couldn't tell. It vanished into some shadows that came from an outcropping on the western end of the canyon.

"Whoa," said Lars. "I don't like the looks of that."

"But, Lars—" interjected Eraina.

"I know, I know! But . . . okay . . . you're right," he said quickly. "I learned my lesson. Better to risk the path than . . . than—"

"Risk getting off it," said Eraina.

"I agree," said Hamelin. "Yesterday, the bridge looked like the easiest way, but it wasn't."

"Well, it sure doesn't look easy here," said Lars. For a second, they all stopped and looked.

"Look there," said Eraina, pointing. "The slope's not extremely steep."

"I just wish we could see more of it," said Lars.

"I know," said Eraina, "but we should go where we know to go, even if we can't see the end of it. Besides, SueSue's path wouldn't lead us off the sheer edge of this canyon."

Calling it "SueSue's path" seemed to help. So, although it was daytime, and the two boys could see ahead for only a short distance before the trail disappeared into the shadows, they started moving down it again.

"I think I see where it's leading us," said Eraina as she adjusted her scarf. "But we have to follow it carefully."

Lars went first, since the shoes gave him not only speed but balance. Hamelin was close behind, in case there were large objects in the way that needed to be moved. But he also reached back to clasp Eraina's hand so that he could steady her if she slipped. Even with Eraina at the rear, however, the boys still depended on her ability to look ahead and warn them of any dangers. Her other hand gripped both ends of her scarf up close to her chin.

In this way, single file, the three went down the canyon's edge—on a trail that sloped at about a forty-five-degree angle and was only about three feet wide. While there was obvious danger—a sheer drop into the canyon just to their right—they were able to descend about thirty feet. Then the path abruptly turned left, and they found themselves following it inside and under a covered opening in the canyon wall.

This crease was a horizontally carved-out area that—as they could see—covered a lot of the western edge of the canyon rim. About seven or eight feet high, it extended some twenty feet back into the wall. The three young people now had no trouble at all walking on the path, since it was wider, under cover, and also several feet away from the sheer edge.

They hadn't walked far when they came across a large, circular, straw-like mat.

"What's that?" asked Eraina.

"It looks like a nest, like a giant bird's nest," replied Hamelin.

"It looks just like an eagle's nest," said Lars. "They often make them on the sides of cliffs and in the inner walls of canyons. But if it is, it's the nest of an eagle larger than any I've ever seen."

"Well," said Hamelin. "It could—"

"Look here!" shouted Eraina. With that, the two boys ran over to the spot where she stood, just a few feet beyond the nest. There, on the ground, they found an almost square patch of smooth rock, about six feet per side. In the middle of it were fruits and berries. And just the other side of the fruits and berries was a small indenture in the rock. It had a shallow, bowl-like shape, and from just above it there was a slow dripping of water, each drop hitting precisely in the middle. The bowl was full, and the water looked pure.

Lars shook his head. "I'm so sorry."

"Why?" asked Eraina.

"Don't you see? If we had kept walking and not wasted time with the bridge, we could've made it just about this far. Or at least gotten here a lot earlier than now. SueSue was right. There were—right here—enough provisions for us."

"Do you think the eagle I saw fighting the bear was here?" asked Eraina.

"Well," answered Hamelin, "if it was the same eagle I know, you can never predict where he'll be and when. But this looks like his work."

"It's on the path," said Eraina, "and it looks like no one else is here, so I say let's eat."

Neither Lars nor Hamelin gave any objection. The three sat down quickly around the fruits and berries and ate their fill. The food was delicious, though a few of the provisions were tart and overripe, as if they had been there too long. The water was pure and cool. All of them—the boys insisted that Eraina go first—drank their fill, and there was plenty left.

The three friends sat there after eating and drinking. They looked at each other with occasional smiles and nods, and it was again obvious to them, without anyone saying it, that their best security lay in following SueSue's advice. They also realized that they needed each other. There was still a lot to do, and the dangers were probably only just beginning, but they were learning a lot as they went.

Chapter 14

Entering Osmethan

AFTER RESTING BRIEFLY, THEY STARTED OFF AGAIN. THE path continued on its course—below ground level and covered by an overhanging ledge—for the remainder of the journey around the western end of the canyon. Finally, when it curved back right and was under the open sky, it immediately moved up the canyon wall.

The three friends slowly ascended together. The way was wide enough for them to crawl on their hands and knees side by side, which they did to remain hidden. When they peeked over the edge, they saw Osmethan—the southwestern corner was less than half a mile away.

"Eraina," said Lars, "I think this is where we need your eyes again."

"Right," she responded, quickly raising the scarf and covering her head. She gazed carefully and thoroughly all across the city, sweeping her eyes from west to east and back again. After several minutes, she lowered her head, and the three of them backed down the path a few feet, out of sight.

"What'd you see?" asked Hamelin.

"Well," she started, "there is a huge palace way over to the right, in the southeastern corner. And as we could tell yesterday, the city is protected on all sides. Other things were what you'd expect to see—bazaars, shops, and many streets and roadways that crisscross the city. Crowds of people are buying and selling in open-air markets, and there is a lot of activity. In fact, the people seem quick and lively."

"What do you mean?" asked Hamelin.

"I mean, it's like almost no one walks slowly, as if everybody is young and agile. The city is mostly full of children and young people—with the oldest maybe in their midthirties. There were hardly any middle-aged or older people.

"I noticed two other things. As I said, there's a magnificent palace on the southeastern side of the city. It's surrounded by great buildings, things like halls of government and courts. I could also see museums, gardens, and theaters.

"But here's the thing—something big is going on, and it's going to happen at the palace. It looks like there are servants, artisans, buyers, and sellers all over the place. There are massive and beautiful decorations. It's obvious they're preparing for some huge event, some spectacular festival or ceremony."

"You said you noticed two things," said Hamelin.

"Yes," said Eraina. "In the very northwestern part of the city, I saw another kind of preparations. It's a very small section of Osmethan, with only a few hundred citizens as compared to maybe a few thousand of the young people I saw everywhere else. And this is the odd thing—in that part of the city, I saw middle-aged people and older. In fact, some very much older. And there was great sadness everywhere."

"What's going on there?" asked Lars.

"Preparations of some kind. But for something much more somber and serious. It looked like there was one special house where people were going in and out, moving very slowly."

"Could you see into the house?" asked Hamelin.

"Oh, yes. I looked into the house, and I saw a very old man lying in bed. Each person would walk up to him and say something. Then he would speak, and they would leave. Everyone looked sad. I would guess that the old man was on his deathbed, and they were maybe speaking final words to him."

"Anything else?" asked Lars.

"I couldn't help noticing that that section of the city is not as impressive as the other parts."

"What do you mean?" asked Hamelin.

"In the rest of the city, the buildings are clean and fresh, and there's a newness to it all. The northwestern section of the city, however, looks drab and plain."

"You looked for a long time," said Hamelin. "Was there anything—or anyone—else you saw?"

"Yes," said Eraina, who paused before going on. "I was also looking for my sister Charissa. We think she was brought here." She looked back toward Osmethan, and her eyes became moist. "Finding her is why I came."

"We'll help you, Eraina," said Hamelin.

They all looked at the city. Then Lars said, "So you didn't see her?"

"No," Eraina replied. "But there are thousands in the city. I couldn't search every face. But I'll find her. If she's in Osmethan, she'll be among the young and the active. Charissa is very beautiful, and she'll be where other attractive people are. I'll have to look more."

"For sure," offered Lars. "So here's what I think we need to do. First, we need to split up. We don't want the three of us to always be seen together. Once people associate us with each other, it'll be easier to recognize us—and watch us."

Hamelin said, "But aren't we supposed to stay together?"

"Not necessarily," answered Eraina. "We certainly have to work together and help each other, but we may need to divide our work for a while and split up briefly. We'll set up a meeting place to report back what we've learned."

"Exactly," said Lars. "Here's my suggestion. Let me go to the older portion of the city and see what that's all about. The way I'm dressed, with my baggy clothes and this hood over my face, I'll be able to move around pretty much unnoticed."

"Yeah," said Hamelin. "If they're preparing for a funeral up there, your clothes should fit right in. Sometimes I can't tell whether you look more like a jester or a priest."

Lars smiled. "Right, and that's generally my idea. Since my clothes are not very colorful, I think I look more like a holy man, so I can pull this hood over my face and mix with that crowd of mourners. Hamelin, I think you and Eraina ought to stay together. Why don't the two of you investigate the other parts of the city, especially the ceremony they're preparing for? Your strength will protect you both if trouble starts. And Eraina's sight should help her find out what's going on—and maybe even find Charissa."

"I agree," said Eraina. She then pulled out a small leather purse. Showing it to the boys, she said, "And I've got a few silver coins that we can use if needed." She handed a few each to Lars and Hamelin. They nodded their thanks.

"Where do we meet up again?" asked Hamelin.

"How about right here?" said Lars.

"Sounds good," said Eraina. "Let's take as long as we need but be back no later than sundown."

With that, the three headed into Osmethan. Lars first and then, about twenty minutes later, Eraina and Hamelin.

Chapter 15

Lars's Trip to the Home of Simannas

IT DIDN'T TAKE LARS LONG TO WALK TO THE SOUTHWEST-
ern gate of Osmethan. That area of the city was just as
Eraina had described it—bright and active and full of
youthful people.

Lars knew that his area of concern, however, did not
lie there but farther north, to the northwest. Therefore, he
slowly made his way along one of the great avenues, which
seemed to have come from the east and provided a loop
around the inner portions of the city. There was a great deal
of traffic on that road—carts, wagons, carriages, and other
means of transportation, including horseback. Lars passed
shops and markets, which bustled with activity, conversation, and commerce. There were so many people up and
down the street and walkways that he found it easy to move
along unnoticed.

As he approached its northwest corner, the city began
to look different. The homes and shops were not run
down—they actually were clean and in good repair—but, as

Eraina had said, they were drab. Lars could also now see for himself that the people there were much older. And almost immediately upon reaching the area, he also saw that the faces and moods of the people were different. Not only were they older, but they walked more slowly and clearly seemed to stay to themselves, away from the bustling movement and the colorful look of the rest of the city.

He followed the general flow of the older folk toward the middle of their part of Osmethan. There was a sadness in their gait as they moved along the streets and walkways, and just as Eraina had observed, people were walking either toward or away from one very old house.

Lars kept his hood over his head, not only to protect himself from the sun but to make sure he wasn't easily noticed. He walked with his head down and his shoulders a bit stooped, trying to imitate the look of the older citizens.

He soon found the place where people were lining up to enter the house. He casually joined the end of the line and waited as it slowly moved forward. He judged, after waiting several minutes and watching the human traffic as it exited from the side of the house, that it would take at least an hour before he could enter it.

Soon there were others behind him in line, and it wasn't hard to catch snatches of conversation. Even though people spoke in hushed tones, an overall quietness allowed Lars to overhear—

"I can't believe Simannas is dying."

"It seems like he's always been here."

"Will there be someone else to lead our kind?"

"Well, he has to die eventually—all of us do."

"We could give him just a little of the water or—"

"No! We couldn't do that! It would be against everything we've committed to! Besides, he wouldn't allow it."

"What's going to become of us?"

"And our children and our grandchildren?"

"Two of our grandchildren recently left for the other part of the city. In spite of all we taught them, they decided to join their friends and drink Tumultor's water."

"They'll regret it. Maybe they'll even come back . . . if they don't stay too long. I just hope they have enough conscience left to realize the mistake they've made."

"I want to die myself . . ."

"You know, he was expected to die yesterday."

"Yes, I heard that too."

"But he's had a look of expectation, as if he was waiting for someone."

"Something is keeping him alive. But the end is surely near."

Lars was beginning to get an idea of what was going on. Apparently this section of the city was the only part that was aging. There were waters that would extend life, but for some reason, Simannas and the people here preferred aging and dying to drinking those waters.

Finally, the line moved forward enough that Lars could step inside the house. He looked around as best he could without drawing attention to himself. The house was sparsely furnished but clean. The room was simple, with a table, a chair, a fireplace, and a small brick oven. From there, the line entered what was apparently the only other room in the house, the bedroom of the revered man, Simannas.

As Lars got close enough to see what was happening, he noted that each person, or couple, or sometimes a group of three or four, would go to the bed where the old man lay and speak to him ever so briefly. He would breathe out a few words as he looked into their faces. Then after a feeble movement of his hand, their heads would lower, and they would slowly depart through a side door.

As Lars got closer, he could see the man more clearly. Simannas's lengthy beard and hair were silver white, and his face was old and worn. The lines and wrinkles, however, did not conceal the hope and peace he reflected. His blankets covered him up to his shoulders, with his arms outside the blankets. His hands were those of a man accustomed to work, with long fingers that, though now weak, had been strong in their day.

He closed his eyes briefly between each group of visitors, as if trying to rest every moment possible. As each small group approached his bed, he would struggle to open his eyes, which were never fully opened, as far as Lars could tell. But Lars could see that the eyes searched each face, as if looking for one last ray of hope or one final face to recognize.

Now it was Lars's turn to go to the bedside. Because he knew no one else and no one else knew him, he walked alone to the right of the dying man. As he approached, Simannas's eyes opened a bit wider. By the time he reached the side of his bed, the man's gaze was clearer than Lars had yet seen. His bony hand moved a few inches to his right and touched Lars's forearm.

Simannas tried to speak, but his words came slowly and with great effort. "Is it you? Have you come at last?"

Lars was silent. He tried to think what to say. Did the old man suppose he was someone else?

"Sir, I . . ." Simannas raised his head and leaned closer, inspecting Lars's face.

"Come closer, son. I want to see you. You're not from here, are you?"

"No, sir, I come from another land."

"Where are the others? Are there not two others with you?"

Lars hesitated. Should he say anything? Was it safe to mention Eraina and Hamelin? He took a deep breath. "Yes, sir, there are. They are searching the other part of the city, seeking to rescue a sister, a princess."

"Ah . . . I *knew* it was you. I've been waiting. I nearly gave up hope. But now it has been granted me, as I was promised, to see at least one of you. Perhaps the days are near."

Then his gaze weakened again, his eyes closed, and his head and shoulders fell back on the pillow. Lars thought he was gone. A few in line had edged closer, as they noticed him speaking more to this stranger than to others. When Simannas slumped back, they too feared the worst.

But Simannas, without raising his body, opened his eyes again. With laboring breaths, he asked, "Tell me, *why* are you here?"

"I seek the jewel that transfers light."

"Ah, yes, then you are Lars . . . son of Elwood. I know what you seek and why, but where it is I do not know. No doubt . . . Tumultor . . . has stolen it . . . just as . . ." His eyes closed again, but this time Lars expected him—judging from the faint rising of his chest—to speak again. Within moments, his eyes opened once more and his voice was even fainter. "That deceiver has tried to steal life as well."

"But how?" asked Lars in an urgent whisper as he leaned closer.

Simannas's breaths were shallow now. "His father, Chimera, diverted the waters . . . of the Ancient River . . . that flow underground . . . near the Forbidden Garden. The waters have touched the roots of life . . . but they cannot . . . all who drink remain young, but . . ."

His eyes closed again.

Lars feared that he couldn't wait for Simannas to open his eyes again, and so, leaning even lower, he said, "Sir, why don't you drink of those waters yourself?"

The eyes opened, almost full again, and, as much as was possible in his weakened state, had a look of defiance in them. "Because, though all who drink remain young . . . they must continually drink . . . and never become wise. I hear there are other waters you drink only once, and once tasted . . ."

"But, sir, if just this time—"

"No . . . I drank Chimera's waters once when I was young, but they only made me foolish . . . His diverted waters . . . make you forget to ask why."

Then in a last, almost ferocious display of strength, Simannas again raised himself a few inches and leaned just a bit to his right, putting weight on his right elbow. His face was near Lars, who leaned in even closer.

"My boy," he whispered, "do *not* drink the waters of the Great Rock . . . and do not let those you love drink them either. To find the light, find Tumultor's bride . . . but the bear is one of . . ." Simannas took a gurgling, gasping breath, and hoarsely forced his broken words. "Don't be deceived . . . the four . . . are not . . ."

As he tried to speak, Simannas's final words had a breathy hissing sound. He coughed faintly and fell back again. All signs of life were leaving his body. His eyes were open but glassy. A second more passed, and they closed. Others nearby, including an older man who looked like his servant, rushed to the bedside. There was a soft shimmer of light that surrounded his body, and, within an instant, he vanished.

"He is gone," moaned a woman in a wailsome voice, clinging to the elderly man.

"He died the death of the good," cried someone else. The line of people waiting broke and rushed to crowd around the bed. Lars moved back a step or two, and others pressed into his space.

"He's left us," groaned a man. And then the crowd began to weep as word passed back through the house.

"Now what?" cried a woman.

"For him or for us?" asked another plaintively.

Lars quickly made his way out the side exit, making sure that his hood was close around his face. He got to the main road and kept moving. He decided to walk slowly around the neighborhood, listening to the conversations of the people on the streets, but he learned nothing more of importance.

As he walked, he tried to gather in his mind what he had learned. Simannas, the leader of these people, had died. And somehow he had been expecting Lars and his friends to come. How did everything fit together? The old man left him with some partial answers, but they created new questions.

Lars continued to walk the streets. He was hungry, but he decided not to attract attention by spending his silver coin. However, an old street vendor noticed he looked tired and hungry and offered him a few portions of food and drink.

"You may have these," the old vendor said, "in the name of Simannas. Today is a sad day for us all, but perhaps not for him."

As the day turned to evening, Lars returned to their hideaway in the side of the canyon. He had a lot to tell.

Chapter 16

Wedding Plans and a Surprise Meeting

AFTER LARS SAFELY LEFT THEIR HIDING PLACE IN THE canyon, and they could see that he made it through the city gates, Eraina and Hamelin climbed out and headed toward the southwest corner of Osmethan. Before long, they too passed through the gate, but once they reached the same main thoroughfare that looped the city, they stayed on it.

Walking eastward along the southern sweep of the city, they occasionally nodded at each other as they looked about. They could see that Osmethan was exactly as Eraina had described it with the aid of her scarf. The streets were full of children and young people moving about briskly. Hardly anyone looked beyond the age of thirty. The buildings and structures were beautiful and obviously newly constructed or else recently redone.

They noticed, however, that with all the busyness and vibrancy of youth in the city, there was something missing. There was noise, a great deal of talking, a lot of words shouted here and there, and the usual sounds of commerce in a great city, but there was no banter, no laughter, and no shouts of greeting or friendship. The people, though young, often had a look of seriousness, sometimes even anger, on their faces. But most of all, they looked puzzled, uncertain, as if they had little experience in what they were doing and no sense of what was going on around them. They were busy and dull at the same time.

Eraina and Hamelin, looking as casual as they could, also worked to pick up pieces of conversation. Whenever they saw a small group talking together, they tried to stand close enough to overhear without attracting attention. They heard some interesting remarks:

"So, another young bride for Tumultor!"

"Why *another*?"

"Who knows? And who cares?"

"Is she young?"

"Young enough!"

"Has she drunk the water?"

"No, fool, not until tomorrow, not until the wedding!"

The wedding. So that was it. That's what the people were preparing for. Now it made more sense.

As they continued to walk toward the palace and the southeastern corner of the city, the human traffic picked up. People scurried to and fro, carrying packages, boxes, and crates that held glasses, plates, and silverware. There were pieces of silver wrapped in linen, great candelabra, and beautiful silver candlesticks by the box load. And there were cartloads of food and drink—poultry, venison, veal, and fruits and vegetables of every description. All being carried toward the palace. There were shouts of anger, vendors jostling for position, and a level of irritation and frenzy that increased the closer they got to the royal castle.

Eraina and Hamelin did their best to look like they belonged, but Hamelin's Texas clothing stuck out, and people began to notice as he passed by.

They reached the outer courts of the palace, where the guards were so busy checking loads and parcels and the crowds were so big that Eraina and Hamelin were able to make their way along the outer edge of one group that had been ushered in—though not without some strange looks at Hamelin.

"Hamelin, we've *got* to find you some different clothes," Eraina whispered urgently. "People are staring."

They made it into the large inner courtyard of the grand palace and rushed along the edges of its wide corridors, staying between the pillars and the walls whenever they had the opportunity, so as to attract less attention.

At one point, Eraina noticed some young men about Hamelin's size and age coming in and out of a room marked "Attendants."

"Hamelin, go in there and see what you can find."

He did, and when he emerged a few minutes later, he was wearing a one-piece garment that was almost a tunic, with a full-length robe that covered his jacket and pants.

"Well, it doesn't look great, but at least now you don't look so strange," said Eraina.

Hamelin frowned. "Whatever you say."

Eraina smiled and said, "Come on. Let's keep moving."

After wandering around the palace for a while, they realized that the flow of traffic in and through the grounds tended to move around three central areas. First, there was a banquet hall, where small carts and large boxes of foodstuffs, linens, silver for table settings, and other decorations were moving in and out.

Second, as they learned from the conversation around them, there was a massive vaulted chamber called the Great Hall of the Rock into which other decorations were going—huge silver-framed mirrors, ornate lampstands, and some beautiful chairs. It was obvious that the wedding would take place here.

With his gloves on, Hamelin grabbed a big crate packed with a large four-by-eight mirror and nodded toward Eraina. "Let's have a look inside the Great Hall of the Rock," he said.

A voice from the side yelled, "Hey, you, be careful with that mirror!"

"Yes, sir!" Hamelin replied without looking at the source of the voice, a man who was obviously a foreman over these proceedings. Eraina picked up what looked like a bolt of linen and followed.

As they moved into the Great Hall of the Rock, they were stunned by what they saw. It was a lengthy, vaulted chamber full of precious stones, exotic woods, granite, and ivory. It was at least twenty-five man-sized paces wide and, as Hamelin counted while moving the crate from one end of the Great Hall to the other, about forty paces in length. At the far end, there was a large, raised platform, almost a stage, some four feet above the floor level and as wide as the entire chamber.

Directly above the front of the platform, a huge ball of crystal was suspended by a thick iron chain wrapped with strands of gold. At the back of the platform, there were large doors on each side. As Eraina saw from a quick look when one of the doors was briefly held open, they led to a beautiful, well-kept garden. High up on the back wall of the raised platform were magnificent windows through which the open air could be seen and the rising eastern sun would shine.

Eraina and Hamelin were overwhelmed by the central feature of the entire room, one from which the Great Hall got its name. At the back of the raised platform, dominating the center and rising to a level of some ten feet, was a massive rock. As wide as it was high, the rock appeared to have a natural spring within it. Water constantly flowed from the top of the rock and streamed down its sides, emptying into a pool at its base. The pool, which was curbed by a wall of granite rising three feet above the platform, was constantly filling and bubbling.

From other decorations, including flowers and candelabra, it was evident that the ceremony would take place upon the raised platform—in front of the massive rock.

"Hey, we haven't got all day!" another supervisor shouted at Hamelin as he and Eraina stood looking around.

"Yes, sir!" Hamelin replied. He and Eraina quickly hurried back to the huge front doors of the Great Hall and out into the large foyer, where the other crates and mirrors had been delivered. However, just before exiting the room, they both turned around and gathered in the full view of the massive chamber.

The layout was simple enough, though the beauty of the place was breathtaking. There was a wide center aisle down which the bride would walk, along with her attendants. But what caught the eye of both Hamelin and Eraina was what other workers and attendants were doing with the mirrors like the one Hamelin had carried in. The mirrors were being propped up and fastened all around the perimeter walls of the chamber, where they were already multiplying the beams of light shining through both the huge windows in the eastern wall and the smaller windows running the entire length of the southern wall.

Eraina and Hamelin looked at each other. Both of them were thinking it was an odd way to decorate for a wedding. They made their way out of the foyer and into the large inner courtyard, where other groups of workers and vendors were hustling back and forth with their wares.

They then moved with some of the crowd toward the third area—in addition to the banquet chamber and the Great Hall of the Rock—that seemed to attract attention. It connected to the inner courtyard and fed toward the north-eastern corner of the palace, especially toward a set of stairs that moved up beyond the vision of those standing in the courtyard.

"Where does that lead?" asked Hamelin.

"Give me just a moment and I'll tell you," answered Eraina. With that, the two of them moved toward the stairs, but back into a smaller, darker corner of that section of the courtyard. Then Eraina, with the scarf pulled around her head again, slowly peered up the winding stairs. Finally, her head was fixed almost straight up from where she stood. She looked, and then she seemed to gaze more deeply. Suddenly a startled expression of recognition came over her face. She quickly pulled the scarf back from her head, placed it around her neck, and turned to Hamelin with a look of shock on her face.

"What is it?" he asked.

Eraina finally swallowed hard and said, slowly and almost in a monotone, "Those stairs, they lead toward a chamber on the fifth level at the very top of this tower."

"What else?"

"That's where the vendors and servants, particularly women, are rushing to, carrying fabrics, shoes, jewelry, and wedding clothes."

"So it's where the bride is getting ready for the wedding?" said Hamelin.

"It is," said Eraina. Her voice fell and her shoulders slumped.

"Well, what is it?" asked Hamelin. "What else did you see?"

"I saw the bride."

"Okay," said Hamelin. "You saw the bride in the bride's room. So what's the problem?"

"The bride is my sister . . . Charissa."

Chapter 17

The Meeting with Charissa

RAINA WASTED NO TIME. SHE SHOOK HER HEAD AND came out of her momentary daze. "Here, come along, boy!" she said loudly, gesturing toward Hamelin. "Pick up those bolts of purple! I've got the linen. Let's go!"

Hamelin immediately guessed what she was up to and grabbed two bolts of purple cloth that were lying unattended on a cart nearby. She strode off toward the stairs, and he followed.

As they made their way up, there was bumping and shoving from each side, as decorators, jewelers, and various wedding organizers moved up and down the stairs. Since the crowd of people on the stairs thickened the higher they went, it took the two of them some thirty minutes to reach the fifth level and, after jostling and pushing with the others, another twenty minutes to get inside the bride's large chamber. It was a room furnished with items of enormous luxury and spectacular beauty. It had mirrors on every wall, and the floors and walls were made elegant by tapestries and rugs of every kind. The furniture was stylish and ornate—an armoire, chairs, and hand-carved side tables, though these were now pushed more toward the walls and covered with lavish items. Open boxes of jewelry, shoes, and cosmetics were strewn throughout the room, all of them available to the bride. Some would be used, others rejected—but all were fit for a queen.

The room was also crowded with attendants and sellers. But finally, as those in front of him shifted their positions, Hamelin got his first look at Eraina's sister, the captured princess he had until then only heard about.

Charissa was tall and beautiful, self-possessed and talkative. She looked at every item that was brought before her but tired of them all quickly. She would hastily say, "Yes, that," and "No, not *that*!" "Yes, I *love* that," or "Oh, *no*, how could you think I would want *that*?" Vendors and their assistants scurried back and forth as she accepted this, altered that, and dismissed things and people summarily. Her brunette hair flowed magnificently to the middle of her back. She was clearly being made up for the festivities of the next day. She wore her bridal dress, though not the veil, while seamstresses and tailors tugged and snipped, altered and pinched here and there as she simultaneously ordered servants to bring, fetch, remove, and otherwise serve her every wish.

And wherever she turned, there was a mirror facing her, radiating back her beauty. In a short period of time, Hamelin saw a lot. Her eyes looked hastily at everything but focused on little or nothing. She was at the same time kind and rude, dismissive and interested, demanding and silly. Once her voice suddenly snapped at those around her, then quickly changed to a loud giggle—her mouth opening so wide that she abruptly covered it with her hand. Eraina had explained to him that her sister's name meant "grace," and in momentary flashes, he could see that quality. But it was all too quickly covered by a sudden and furious tongue lashing that caused its victims and most everyone else nearby to flinch and bow.

After one such outburst, there was a general silence in the room, and Eraina saw her opportunity. Moving forward, she took the place of those immediately in front of Charissa who had stepped backward at her angry display.

"My lady," said Eraina, "have you considered these linens? I bring them from afar, and I'm certain that should your shrewd eye look closely, you will find them both mysterious and interesting."

She spread her forearms with the beautiful white linen draped over them, holding it in front of her. Then she boldly looked into her sister's eyes, as Charissa looked first at the linen and then toward the voice, which she seemed faintly to recognize. Their eyes met.

"My lady," said Eraina softly, "I hope it pleases you that I have brought these from another land." They held each other's gaze.

Charissa's eyes widened, and then, in a flurry, as if the two sisters were playing a game of dress-up as they had so often in their youth, she quickly responded, "Oh, I *love* it! And now you must show me *everything* you've brought! Come! Bring your goods over here to the window in the corner, so that I may see them in a fuller light."

Realizing that Charissa had recognized her, Eraina continued the game. "Here, boy," she said, motioning to Hamelin, "you come too. And bring that purple with you!"

Charissa smiled and, for a moment, seemed like the older sister of years ago, who had played such games with her siblings, happy to join in their make-believe stories.

The two sisters, with Hamelin trailing behind, went to a corner of the room where there was a window and where they were likewise outside the earshot—but not the glare—of the others in the room. They were also outside the direct line of the mirrors.

"Eraina!" Charissa blurted out in a loud whisper. "What are you doing here?"

"Shhh. I know you're whispering, but whisper softer," said Eraina. "We've come to help you escape."

"Escape? Why would I want to *escape*?"

"Because you were kidnapped! Landon's men stole you from our land. And Father is weak and sick. He cries daily for you—Charissa, what's *wrong* with you?"

For a moment, Charissa looked stunned, almost dazed. Her eyelids fluttered, and she shook her head from side to side as if trying to awaken from a bad dream. She looked again at Eraina, and their eyes met. "Eraina," she said. "I . . . I . . . is it really you, Eraina?"

"Yes, Charissa, it is I, your sister. We must escape. You must come with me. Landon has handed you over to Tumultor—and he's forcing you to *marry* him! But, Charissa, we can escape. You *must* find a way to come with us!"

Again Charissa appeared dazed, but now she was looking into Eraina's face and occasionally glancing at Hamelin with a seriousness they had not seen before. "Yes, I . . . I think I remember. They captured me. But I escaped. Oh, there was that huge lion! He led me to a cavern—a pond. I *waited*! I really did. I tried so hard, but it was so *dark*—but they didn't come, and I went to the light and into the pond . . . and ended up here!"

Hamelin's stomach turned when he heard her mention the cavern, a pond, and waiting before going through it. And in a flash he remembered. "She is *waiting* for us," the eagle had said when he had failed to cross the bridge . . . It was *Charissa* . . . waiting for him three and a half years ago. But more—something else he had never connected . . . she was also the one who gave up and went through the pond! Hamelin's thoughts were spinning, but there was no time to explain, or even to apologize.

"Oh, Eraina," Charissa said in a loud whisper, and then a look of horror crossed her face as she came even more fully to herself. "How is Father? Oh!" She looked around the room in panic. "You must get me out of here!"

"My lady!" A woman's voice abruptly cut through their conversation. Charissa's head jerked up as if she were a marionette whose string was suddenly pulled taut.

A woman Eraina had not seen before stood at the center of the room. The woman possessed a stark kind of beauty, but it was harsh, even cold, in its color and appearance. She had black hair, powder-white skin, and dark-brown eyes. She stood almost completely motionless, but her stare and her words seemed to control the entire room, especially Charissa.

"Come here, my lady!" ordered the pale, slender woman. "You must stand over *here* to see these exquisite items."

And then the woman raised a hand-held mirror and pointed it at Charissa, who looked toward the woman. As she did, her face was caught by the mirror, and her shoulders slumped.

"Yes," she said in a soft monotone. "I'll be right there."

"Charissa," whispered Eraina again, "*don't*! You've got to find a way out of here. I don't know what they've done to you, but you're not right. Whoever that woman is, she can't be good." Eraina took a small step and very slightly nudged Charissa, shoulder to shoulder. "When can I come back to get you? When are you ever alone?"

Slowly, for just a brief moment, Charissa turned away from the mirror and looked softly at her sister. Her breathing became rapid and shallow. "Eraina," she said, "I love you, little sister. I *want* to come home, but I *can't*."

And then she turned again, and the glaring eyes of the fierce lady and the light that flashed from the mirror caught her eyes once more. She slowly walked back to the middle of the room, where again the mirrors surrounded her, and she stood pensively. Within moments, the vendors and organizers resumed their work, and Charissa was again the center of a whirl of activity with all her attendants and things of beauty surrounding her.

Then, looking back at Eraina and Hamelin, she lightly, almost with a giggle, said across the room, "Oh, it was so good to see you. Do come again! Perhaps sometime after the wedding, it would be lovely for all of us to get together. You simply must meet my dear prince, Tumultie. He's such a handsome man!" And with that, she turned and never again looked their way.

Eraina and Hamelin had no choice but to go, trying to keep up their image as merchants but not easily able to hide the look of defeat that had fallen over them, especially Eraina. As they reached the exit, they turned once more to look at Charissa, but the pale woman blocked their view. She stared at them, and her look exuded force. Its effect on most people was fear, but Eraina glared back defiantly, and their eyes locked in struggle for long seconds. The woman blinked first, and immediately Eraina stuck out her chin, turned her back, and walked out.

The woman's head trembled faintly before she looked around fiercely and snarled to all those staring at her, "Back to work!"

Eraina led Hamelin down the stairs, pushing aside the vendors in her way. They quickly left the palace and hurried through the streets and back toward the canyon, where they would meet Lars. As they walked, Hamelin could see and almost feel the despair in Eraina's slumping head and fallen shoulders. He was sure that at any moment she would burst into tears. But she didn't.

Chapter 18

Back at the Canyon

Lars was waiting for Hamelin and Eraina back at the cavern below the edge of the canyon. He could tell that both were discouraged. Eraina in particular kept looking down, staring into space, so he offered to begin.

"I came into the northwestern portion of the city, just as we planned. Sure enough, as Eraina saw, it was older—its buildings and its people. They walked slowly—but their houses were okay, showing they had taken good care of them—but everything looked and felt old. I followed the crowd to a house where an old man by the name of Simannas was dying. When it was finally my turn to approach his bed, he got more alert, searching my face for my identity. It was really strange. He gave the impression that he had been looking for us—*all* of us." Eraina lifted her head and looked at Lars but remained silent.

"I heard from others that they expected him to die sooner, but somehow he rallied and was still seeing people today."

"So, he's still alive?" said Hamelin.

"No," said Lars, shaking his head softly. "But he told me several things before he died. He mentioned waters that give a long life to the body, but he had refused them, except for once as a young man. He said those who keep drinking this water don't die, and obviously a lot of people are drinking the water, because the rest of the city is made up of the young. Apparently, those who refuse the water age and die, and that's certainly the impression I got from all those who were in that section of the city."

"Why don't the old people want the water?" asked Hamelin.

"Because they believe that it lets you live, but it doesn't give wisdom or goodness. The older crowd obviously prefer death to stupidity, or maybe to something or someplace even worse."

"Worse?" said Hamelin.

"Yeah, maybe greediness, selfishness, even cruelty. Or other dark places. My father once told me that if you keep living but never get wiser, you could end up truly bad."

"Like Landon and Tumultor," blurted out Eraina. They were all silent for a moment. "So what else did you learn?" she asked.

"Simannas knew my father by name, and he also knew of the jewel, but he didn't know where it is. He told me very pointedly—as weak as he was—*not* to drink the waters, and not to let those I care for drink them either. There was more, but that's enough for now. In the end, the old man—who was obviously loved as their leader—died, right as I stood *next* to him!"

"How did he die?" asked Eraina.

"The death of the good," said Lars.

Eraina nodded and looked down. Hamelin wasn't sure he understood the question or the answer, but he had heard people on his side of the Atrium talk about those who had died, and he knew they sometimes used odd expressions about "passing away," or if it was a baby, that "heaven needed more angels."

"So what happened next?" he asked.

"Everyone started crowding around his bed, so I slipped out, and no one else, I think, overheard what he said to me. But it was very strange."

Everyone was quiet, so Lars paused before asking, "Well, what did you two find when you went to the other parts of the city?"

Eraina remained silent, a faraway look on her face, so Hamelin started their story. "A lot. We learned that the big festival, or ceremony, to be held tomorrow is a wedding. We overheard people in the streets saying that the bride is young and beautiful and that she has not yet drunk the water . . ." Hamelin hesitated as he looked at Eraina. "But she will at the wedding."

"Who's the groom?" asked Lars.

"Tumultor," said Hamelin plainly.

"Go on," said Lars.

Hamelin looked at Eraina, so she slowly picked up the story, but in a soft monotone. "We followed the crowds to the palace, where most of the activity was happening. We saw the rooms, the great banquet hall, and then especially a place called the Great Hall of the Rock, where the wedding will take place in the morning at ten."

Eraina's voice began to gather some strength. "It was being furnished with mirrors all around. There was very little seating at the floor level, but mostly a central, wide-open space for the bridal processional. There were raised galleries, like balconies, on each side. The Great Hall of the Rock runs east and west, and at its eastern end, there's a raised stone platform. At the back of that is a huge rock. From the very top of the rock there is flowing water, and the water comes down the rock's sides into a granite pool at the base. Above the rock there are beautiful windows."

"Now tell me again about the mirrors. What are they for?" asked Lars.

"I really don't know," said Eraina, "because I've never seen a wedding hall decorated like that. I wonder if they realize the effect once the light of the morning sun shines through those huge windows above the rock."

"Any other details?" asked Lars. Eraina's eyes dropped.

"We took a quick look," continued Hamelin, "and behind the end of the hall is a garden. There are two doors to it, one on each side of the rock."

"What else did you find around the palace?" asked Lars. At this point, Eraina began to describe the stairs and the tower at the fifth level, but suddenly she stopped. She took a deep breath and was clearly trying to hold back tears. Lars glanced at Hamelin with his eyebrows up and a "What's that about?" look on his face, so Hamelin took up the story from there.

"We pretended to be cloth merchants and went up the stairs to see the bride. We had to push our way to the top floor, where she was in a very special tower room. Once we made it up the stairs, we were in the middle of all kinds of people who were waiting upon the bride, and others who were selling things. There were mirrors all around the room. She was trying on her wedding dress and looked beautiful.

She's tall with long brown hair, but there's a strange look on her face, and her manners are pretty . . . well, she's pushy."

"She's a *princess*!" said Eraina suddenly.

"Okay," said Hamelin, who knew he was upsetting Eraina but went on. "But most of the time she's just selfish and rude. She seems to care a lot about her beauty . . . and she's *very* talkative."

"So did you find *Charissa*?" asked Lars.

Hamelin looked at Eraina, and Eraina answered with tight lips and no emotion, "Yes."

"You did?" said Lars. "Where is she?"

"The bride *is* Charissa!" said Eraina angrily.

"What?" said Lars, raising his voice. "The bride is *Charissa*? Why is she marrying Tumultor?" At this point, Eraina began to weep softly. Hamelin waited a few moments, then resumed the story.

"Like I said, we pretended to be cloth merchants. We went up to Charissa, and she recognized Eraina when Eraina spoke to her. For just a little while, we talked to her in private, and she changed. She remembered her sisters and her father and that she had been captured by Landon's men and ended up here with Tumultor."

Hamelin paused, thinking about what else Charissa had said about a cavern and a pond, but he took a breath and went on.

"At one point, she even wanted to go with us, but then a strange woman appeared from nowhere. The woman spoke sternly to Charissa, like she was in charge, and held a mirror up to her, and Charissa seemed to go into a daze. Within a few seconds, she went back to the middle of the room and was surrounded by a lot of mirrors again. Then she just went back to being mean to everyone around her. It was like we weren't there anymore. So we left."

"Was there any sign of the jewel?" asked Lars.

"No," said Eraina, regaining her composure. "There were many jewels all around, and Charissa was even trying on some that she will wear tomorrow at the wedding, but no sign of the jewel of Periluna, at least nothing like what you've described."

Lars looked down and shook his head.

"It's obvious," Eraina continued, "that my sister is being controlled, and it's got something to do with those mirrors. For just a few moments—when she was away from them—she recognized me, and it was like we were children again playing a game; but then, when that woman spoke, she acted like she didn't even know me and wouldn't *want* us to rescue her!"

"But at least," said Hamelin, "for a few moments she did."

"I know," said Eraina. "But what's the matter with her *now*?" She raised her hands to the sides of her face and clenched her fists. With eyes closed, she blew out a deep breath. "Oh! I'm so *mad* at her! She's the *oldest*, and more than all of us, she was trained to *fight!*"

"You don't understand," said Hamelin in a firm voice that surprised even him and made Eraina turn toward him and scowl.

"What do *you* know about her?" she said sharply.

"I know there's more to what's happened to her than you know!" said Hamelin in a tone that began to match hers.

"Well, I know she should have tried to *escape!*" Eraina said, raising her voice another notch.

Hamelin started to say something but just lowered his head and swallowed. Eraina glared at him for long moments.

"I think she did," he finally mumbled. Eraina's glare changed quickly into a puzzled look.

"What do you mean, Hamelin?" said Lars. "Is there something else?"

Hamelin raised his eyes and looked at Eraina. "You remember that Charissa said something about a cavern and a pond?" She nodded, and her eyes narrowed.

"I sorta mentioned this to you before," Hamelin said, "when we all told our stories, but there's some parts of my own story that I probably wanted to forget, and some other bits I just kept to myself."

"Like what?" said Eraina.

"Do you remember that I told you I was supposed to come over here about three and a half years ago, when I was eight years old, but I was too afraid to cross the rope bridge?"

Lars nodded, and Eraina's face softened a little.

"Well, the eagle was really mad at me after I gave up, and he said something like, 'She is *waiting* for us.'"

Eraina's eyes widened.

"Then just a few days ago, after I finally got back to the cave and crossed over the bridge, you remember that I told you about a beautiful cavern with a pond, where I was almost captured, and that the eagle finally pushed me through it?"

"Yes," Eraina said, nodding slowly.

"The eagle said something about a girl who was deceived and went through that pond the wrong way, and that maybe one day I could ask her some questions. He also said I was supposed to help somebody—who turned out to be you—find her sister. After I met you, I knew that part of what he said was about Charissa, because you said Tumultor had your sister and you were going to rescue her. But I didn't realize until now that the girl who was waiting and the girl who was deceived and went through the pond the wrong way were the same person. And not only that, but she's also your missing sister Charissa! He must have been talking about her all those times, and I was too worried about myself to listen carefully, so I'm just now putting it together."

"But *why* did she go through the pond the wrong way? Why did she let *that* happen?" asked Eraina with tears filling her eyes again and her voice straining.

"She didn't just *let* it happen. She *waited*. On *me*! Besides, those waters . . . they can overpower anyone. The eagle told me they are the waters of *death* and *life*. I remember they made me feel strong when I was tired and later even healed the cuts I had in my shoulders where the eagle grabbed me with his talons.

"But they are also dangerous! I *know* what happened to Charissa. It was happening to *me*! When you look into that pond, you're tricked by it. You think you're something you're not, and the reflection takes you over. You want to get away, but you can't! You *know* you should, but you can't *do* it. It's like you're filled with yourself, like you're all that matters."

"My sister could be pretty proud and conceited *without* enchanted waters! *That's* what got her caught by Landon in the first place!" But Eraina looked down, shaking her head as soon as she said it, as if wishing she hadn't.

"Eraina," Hamelin said softly, "it wasn't all her fault. I was *supposed* to *be* there. Everybody needs help sometimes. I mean, we're helping each other now."

Eraina was silent.

"And one more thing. You told me that Landon's men caught her."

"Yes."

"But now she's here with Tumultor."

"Right. Like we heard, Landon turned her over to his brother."

"But that's not what *she* said."

Eraina's eyes narrowed as she thought back to Charissa's words. And then her eyes suddenly widened.

"You're right! She said she 'escaped' and 'ended up here' in Osmethan."

"So what are you both thinking?" said Lars.

"I'm thinking," said Hamelin, "if she was in that cave and waiting for me—and remember, Eraina, she also said something about a huge lion who led her there—then sometime or other, after Landon first got her but before Tumultor did, she really did escape."

Eraina nodded her head slowly.

"And when I didn't show up, there's no telling *how long* she ended up waiting. Remember she kept referring to the *dark*? She said she 'tried so hard.'"

Lars and Eraina looked at Hamelin, and several silent moments passed as they all imagined waiting alone in the dark.

"So," said Hamelin, "eventually it must have happened. There was light in the room with the pond, the room the eagle calls the Atrium of the Worlds. She must have seen her reflection in the water, gotten fooled by it, and then gone into the pond, which led to her getting captured again on the other side."

"What about the lion?" said Lars.

"I don't know about a lion," said Hamelin. "But I know there are some powerful creatures over here, and some of them, like the eagle and maybe this lion, are trying to help us."

"So if her reflection in the pond did bewitch her," said Eraina, "then maybe there's also still hope she'll fight with us."

"The eagle told me she *resisted*. I'm *sure* she still can."

"How did you overcome it, Hamelin?" asked Lars.

"I really didn't, at least not on my own. But, like Eraina said, it has a lot to do with the pond's reflection."

"So what changed? What happened?" said Lars.

"At the last second, the eagle stirred up the water and disturbed my reflection. Then I thought I heard someone call my name. I was barely able to turn my back to the pond, and I saw a hazy human figure on the wall. The eagle said later it was something like . . . like my 'true self' being reflected in the crystal but reversed back to my real image."

"Sounds pretty strange," said Lars.

"It was. But there I was, or something like me, above a great throne in the cavern where we were. But whatever happened, it broke the pond's spell. And the eagle pushed me backward into the water."

Hamelin paused and took a deep breath before rushing on. "But because of me, *no one* was there, not even the eagle, to help *Charissa*. So, like the eagle said, she went into the pond deceived and facing in the wrong direction."

"My poor sister!" said Eraina, her voice cracking.

"If all that's true," said Lars, "then it explains why everywhere Charissa is, or is going to be—like the wedding hall!—they have mirrors. They obviously have to keep up the enchantment that feeds on her reflection and her vanity. Like the woman's use of that mirror. So maybe she *can* still fight. I mean, if for a short time she talked to you like her old self, then evidently the spell can still be broken, at least for a while."

"If only we could fight off the mirrors and help her," said Eraina. "But I have no idea how to do that."

"Maybe that's just something we'll have to figure out along the way," said Lars. "For now, we have to do what we know to do." Everyone was quiet until Eraina spoke again.

"There are a couple of things I know for sure. First, we've got to make sure Charissa doesn't drink the water that Simannas referred to. It would only make the spell on her mind worse—maybe even permanent. I assume it's the water that flows out of that rock if it's the water she's supposed to drink at the wedding?"

"That's right!" said Lars. "Just before he died, Simannas referred to 'the waters of the *Great Rock.*' That must be the huge rock you saw in the Great Hall."

"And," added Hamelin, "we've got to stop the wedding."

"That's the other thing I'm sure of," said Eraina.

"But we must work together, whatever it is we do," Lars said. "Like SueSue told us."

"For sure," added Hamelin. "I have this sword, but remember, I can use it only once. We've got to stay together, and we've got to try to stop the wedding, but we can't strike until we know that we can get Charissa *and* the jewel."

"Charissa *and* the jewel?" said Eraina. "But we don't even know where the jewel is! And the wedding's *tomorrow!*"

"Wait," said Lars. "The jewel. Almost the last thing Simannas tried to tell me was something about finding the light *and* finding Tumultor's bride. He was hard to understand, but he did mention them together."

"So we've got to hope that somehow stopping the wedding will help us find the jewel," said Eraina.

"Which reminds me . . ." said Lars, "Simannas also tried to tell me something about 'the bear,' and I think he said 'four' something just as he died, maybe referring to the four thrones, but he never finished."

"Something else to watch out for," replied Hamelin as he and Lars looked toward Eraina, remembering what she had said about seeing the eagle fighting the bear at the illusory bridge.

The three companions continued to talk. They knew it would be difficult to devise a plan until they were actually on the scene. They agreed that they had to find a way to get into the Great Hall of the Rock to see the wedding, but they would have to wait until the next morning to figure out just how that could be done. They would seize whatever opportunities were there. And, above all, they agreed to work together.

They found places in the cavern and finally fell asleep. Hamelin had dreams that he couldn't exactly remember the next day, though he remembered waking up once after dreaming he was standing on the edge of a high mountain, with a strong wind whipping across his face.

Chapter 19

The Plan

THE NEXT MORNING, THE THREE FRIENDS WOKE UP EARLY. To their surprise, something occurred during the night that reminded them they weren't alone. Their supply of provisions was renewed. The small basin on the rock surface continuously refilled, so they had always had a fresh supply of water. But there was a new batch of fruits and berries. They didn't know who or what supplied them, but they quickly drank and ate their fill. This time everything was fresh.

Ready to depart, they again peered over the edge of the canyon toward Osmethan. Eraina pulled the scarf over her head and looked carefully at the movements of people. It was still very early in the morning, and so there were several hours before the wedding would begin, but already the streets were filling up with merchants and traders and crowds gathering outside the palace, hoping to catch a glimpse of the royal couple. Eraina could see that there was extensive security in place. Groups of men who looked like police, soldiers, or elite palace guards were closely monitoring everyone who came into the palace grounds and especially those who approached the Great Hall of the Rock.

As she scanned the situation, she reported to the boys that although the number of guards posted at the entries to the city had increased, they would likely have little trouble entering again at the southwest corner, since the crowds were so large. Though many were turned away at the palace grounds, some were admitted, especially those who had business to take care of for the wedding. However, she added, it was rare to see someone permitted into the area around the Great Hall of the Rock. As a princess familiar with such royal proceedings, she knew the inside seats for the wedding ceremony would be reserved for high-level royalty and other invited officials.

Eraina also confirmed that there were very few chairs on the ground floor of the Great Hall, probably so as not to block the effects of the mirrors along the walls. And she guessed that most of those who were prestigious enough to be invited were going to be seated in the upper galleries on the south and north sides.

After she described what she could see, the three of them moved back into the cavern to discuss their options.

"We obviously don't have invitations," began Eraina, "and we certainly don't have any inside connections to give us special permission to enter the palace grounds, much less the Great Hall."

"So what do we do?" asked Hamelin.

"Hmmm," said Lars. "Have you looked everywhere, Eraina? What about the garden area at the back of the Hall, to the east?"

"That's a thought," she said. "I spent most of my time looking at the obvious ways of entry. Let me look again."

She went back up, unfolded her scarf, and surveyed the area Lars mentioned. Within a few minutes, she scrambled back down.

"There may be something there," she said with energy in her voice. "It's amazing. With all the security that's being provided, it seems they just assumed no one would come in through the back."

"That makes sense," said Hamelin, "because the garden has a big wall around it, right?"

"Yes," said Eraina. "There is a wall, and it goes around the entire garden. The garden is as long as the Great Hall and slightly wider. I'm judging that those walls are at least fifteen feet high and probably five feet thick."

"That's not too bad," said Hamelin. "We can climb over that with the help of the gloves and shoes. I mean, if you're willing to be boosted and maybe tossed around a little, Eraina."

"Please," she said, "it's too late now to worry about my dignity."

"How much security is back there?" asked Lars.

"Not much," she said. "They have two guards posted around the outside of the garden wall, one at each of the two corners farthest from the back of the Great Hall."

"What about inside the garden?" asked Hamelin.

"There's only one person stationed just inside the garden. I think he's controlling entry through those two doors that lead into the Great Hall, right onto the stone platform next to the Rock. And just inside those two doors, there's another two doors, one on each side, that lead into narrow stairways going straight up to the galleries. And even better, the end of each gallery is right above the stone platform. If we could get to the southern gallery, we'd be right above the Rock and have a great view of the ceremony."

"I wonder why there's only one person guarding those doors," said Lars.

"Actually," said Eraina, "he doesn't even look like a guard. He looks more like a priest. From what I can tell, those two back doors and the two inside stairways are used by the guardians of the Great Rock, the priests and their helpers. I'm sure no one else is even expected to be back in that area, what with the high walls and the two soldiers at the outside corners."

"Okay," said Lars, "then that sounds like our best option. We've got to get into the city, reach the outside walls of the garden, figure out how to avoid those two soldiers, get over the wall, and then make it past the priest who guards the two doors from the garden side."

"Perfect," said Eraina. "If that's all there is to it, what are we waiting for?"

Lars rolled his eyes. Hamelin smiled, Eraina patted him on the shoulder, and they all laughed.

Hamelin, Lars, and Eraina together slowly emerged from the canyon. At that point, they decided that it was too late to worry about being seen with one another. The moment of truth had come, and they would walk right into Osmethan, side by side.

Chapter 20

The Wedding Crashers

AS THEY MADE THEIR WAY TOWARD THE SOUTHWESTERN gate, the three friends saw a great press of people coming from the countryside and realized that it wouldn't be difficult to get inside the gate. The guards had apparently been told to let as many people come in as possible, since it would be a great day for buying and selling throughout the city. So Hamelin, Eraina, and Lars blended in with a small group of country folk who had come to see the sights on the big day. By avoiding the eyes of the guards and acting like they knew what they were doing, they made it through the gate.

They then walked east along the wide avenue leading toward the palace.

"So far, so good," said Hamelin.

"Yes," said Eraina. She repeatedly looked around, pointed, and smiled, giving her best impression of a sightseer. "Our next job, though, won't be as easy. We need to get to the back of that garden and over the wall."

"Right," said Hamelin, "but if we get that far, I'm not worried about getting over that wall—just what we do once we're there."

"I know," said Eraina, still smiling and looking around with wide eyes. "We've still got to figure out what to do with the priest."

"Hey, Hamelin," said Lars, "remember when you said my clothes made me look like either a holy man or a jester?"

"Yeah."

"Well, maybe it's a little of both. Maybe I can start off like a jester . . . but I'll tell you my plan later. In the meantime, look for a vendor. We need to buy some rope."

It wasn't hard to find rope, though the price was higher than expected. Merchants of every type were all over the city, buying and selling trinkets, sweets, fruits and vegetables, clothing, and tack of every sort for handling livestock. They ended up buying far more than Lars thought they would need, but for the sake of time, he took the rope in the length the merchant had already cut and wrapped for quick sale, and they headed on. It was easy to hide it under his baggy clothing.

They soon reached the eastern portion of Osmethan, where the road forked. To the right was another massive gate, which led in and out from the southeastern side of the city, and to the left the avenue angled northward toward the palace area. The three moved to the right, as if they were going toward the city gate, but instead of exiting, they turned and blended with those who were entering from the southeast and had already passed the guards at the gate.

Since the guards were watching those who entered and not what was happening immediately behind them, the three quickly moved on farther east, off the road but still inside the city wall. They were in an open area and kept expecting to be stopped, but no warning shouts came, so they kept going.

"Just keep strolling," said Eraina, "and don't look back."

They did just that. The city wall continued farther eastward and from Eraina's description would eventually turn back north. It was from near there that they hoped to gain access to the garden wall.

Fortunately, not very far east along the city wall, they approached a wooded area. The woods didn't reach all the way to the wall, but a lightly forested area did occupy a small stretch of the otherwise open land that led eastward from the city gates, and they used it for cover.

They then headed north through the woods and reached an area that faced the southern wall of the garden behind the Great Hall. There they paused and thought about their next moves. Eraina once again took out the scarf and concentrated especially on the movements of the two soldiers at the eastern corners. She also checked again inside the garden to see if anything had changed.

Everything was the same. She saw only the two soldiers outside the garden walls and the one priest inside the garden. Between their hiding place and the garden was about fifty yards of open space.

"Okay, Lars, you said you have a plan. Let's hear it," said Hamelin. Lars quickly explained it, and Hamelin and Eraina nodded.

"So," he said, "I need two short strips of this rope, maybe three or four feet each." He pulled the rope from beneath his baggy outer shirt. Hamelin took out his pocketknife and cut off two lengths of rope. There was still a lot left, and Lars put the rest of it back beneath his shirt.

"Okay, Hamelin, now it's up to you to get us over the wall." Hamelin took a deep breath and nodded.

The three friends crouched in the woods and waited for their chance to dash across the open space between them and the garden wall. They waited for what seemed like a long time, but it was still a good hour before the wedding would start. Finally, their opportunity came. The guard stationed at the southeastern corner apparently grew bored. His fellow guard, whose post was more on the northeastern corner, was out of the sight line of the three companions but was, according to Eraina, still standing in place. The guard closest to the three soon began looking north and was evidently talking to his fellow guard. Before long, he had turned his back and had sauntered a few steps around the corner and in the direction of the other soldier. This was their chance. They made a break and dashed across the open ground to the southern wall of the garden, close to the southeastern corner.

They paused at the wall, crouching low, before their next move. Eraina again unrolled her scarf, but she now looked inside the walls to see whether anything had changed. They had to make sure the priest inside wasn't looking their way, but they also had to scale the wall before the guard got back to his corner and could see them.

"Eraina, what's up? Hurry. I can hear the guard yelling to the other one. He may be coming back," Lars whispered.

Just then, the priest inside was summoned to the side door closest to the northern gallery, at the opposite corner of the garden from where the three were crouching.

"Okay, now!" said Eraina. "He's not looking our way."

Hamelin quickly gave Lars a strong boost up, propelling him into the air but being careful not to throw him high enough to be spotted by the guards. Lars made it. With his balance, he easily landed on the wall and flattened himself on his stomach.

"Okay, Eraina, now it's your turn. This may hurt."

"I can do it," she said firmly.

Hamelin pushed hard and tossed her straight up. She grabbed Lars's hand and pulled herself the rest of the way.

Then Hamelin, making his own finger holes and gripping the stone wall with his powerful, gloved hands, not only quickly scaled the wall but was the first one down the other side into the garden. Fortunately, the shrubs and trees in that corner were heavy enough for him to duck behind. Lars let his whole body dangle over the side of the wall, gripping in between the rocks and mortar with the inside edges of his shoes, and then pushed away softly with his hands and feet and dropped down. Hamelin caught him to soften his fall.

Now it was up to Eraina to trust them. She sat with her back to the boys and gave them one last look. Lars nodded at her, and she rocked backward and dropped. The two boys caught her in the cradle they formed with their hands and arms. The two guards outside the wall didn't notice a thing.

Still following Lars's plan, Eraina and Hamelin tied his hands loosely in front of him and did the same with his feet. He could easily have freed himself from the soft knots they made, but he had the appearance of being tied up. Then they rubbed some mud on his face. By now the young priest was back in the garden, still standing between the two doors, looking bored.

With Hamelin and Eraina crouching behind the shrubbery, Lars went into his act. He hopped quickly into the open area in the middle of the garden and, with his hood pulled over his face and mud rubbed on his cheeks, cried out, "Sir, sir, please help!" He hopped even closer to the priest.

"What . . . who are you?" yelled the startled priest, taking a few steps forward. "What are you doing here?"

Before the priest could summon help, Lars fell down on his knees before him and said, "Oh, sir, please help me! I'm the prince's court jester, and his guards have abused me terribly all night long. They had a drunken party at my expense, they tossed me around and made fun of me, and now they've left me tied up in my master's garden, certain that I'll be caught and whipped for foolishness. Please, sir, *help me!*"

The priest looked skeptical at first but then, upon hearing the plea for pity, came forward to help. While he bent over to loosen Lars's ropes, Hamelin sneaked up behind him and placed his gloved hand around the back of his neck. He had no intention of hurting the young man, but the sudden, firm pressure immobilized him. Then, as Hamelin knew would happen if he applied pressure to both sides of the man's neck, the priest began to lose oxygen to his brain and fainted. The three of them dragged him behind some bushes in the garden, pulled his frock off, and tied him up. Then Hamelin, who was almost his size, put on the priest's garb.

"So much for the jester," said Lars, wiping the mud off his face. "Now I'll do my best to look like a holy man."

The three of them then walked straight to the back door on their left and—after a collective deep breath—brazenly walked in.

Hamelin entered first and, bowing and using his hands, acted as if he were granting permission for the others to enter. He then opened the stairway door leading up to the southern gallery and stood to the side, nodding for Lars and

Eraina to go in. First went Lars, with his hands folded, bowing toward Hamelin. Then Eraina—remembering her training as a princess and acting very royal—quickly entered the
stairwell. Hamelin followed.

Once they had climbed the steps, there was no turning
back. They opened the door that led into the southern gallery, and Hamelin once again played the part of the priestly
usher. He insisted with a few motions of his hands that those
in the closest row make room for Eraina and Lars. He then
stood guard at the door with his hands folded, giving any
and all who glanced his way the look of someone in charge
of the situation. They had made it.

All of that had taken longer than they expected, and it
was obvious from the activity taking place below that it was
nearly time for the wedding to begin. The three friends carefully glanced at one another. Lars felt around his waist for the
rope. Eraina adjusted the scarf around her neck, and Hamelin felt the handle of the invisible sword, which he wore on
his left side. Their eyes met again. With slow nods, they all
confirmed that they were as ready as they would ever be.

Chapter 21

The Wedding

ROM THEIR POSITIONS IN THE GALLERY, EACH OF THEM
had a perfect view of the scene below. Just beneath were
the Great Rock and the pool of water that surrounded
it. The ceremony would take place at the front of the Rock
but still on the raised stone platform. To their far left was the
entryway to the Great Hall, and from there, Charissa would
proceed in her bridal march, ending up just below them at
the front.

To their left, the floor level of the Great Hall was quickly
filled with two rows of a dozen trumpeters. With a loud flour-
ish, they sounded the beginning of the ceremonies. It was then
announced that Prince Tumultor, son of Chimera, was entering. With blaring fanfare, a strong and majestic figure entered
in dazzling royal apparel—a golden crown and a dark-blue
cape that stretched from his shoulders to the floor. He walked
with the confidence of a man for whom this was not the first
wedding and, upon reaching and ascending the elevated platform, turned with a sneer as he waited for his bride to enter.

As large as the Great Hall was, it now looked even more expansive since it was lined with tall mirrors. Benefiting from and adding to the effect of the mirrors, the morning sun was pouring into the Hall, and its rays were multiplied in brightness and force. The trumpeters then announced in softer tones the bridal party, with flower girls and maids of honor slowly processing to the front and taking their places at the floor level below the prince.

Then through the corner door just opposite Hamelin and his friends—which also led to the garden—emerged a holy man dressed in splendid regalia with a robe of scarlet, white, and gold. Obviously of high religious status, he took his place next to Tumultor. As with all the people in this part of the city, citizens and royalty alike, the priest was younger than expected for a man in such garments. He looked hardly beyond the age of thirty, but he was older than most in the Great Hall.

He raised his hand in what seemed to be some kind of sacred gesture, and then from the far end of the room, a boy who looked to be about eight years old slowly walked forward to soft musical accompaniment. He had cradled in his arms a pillow, and on that pillow lay a wooden box with beautiful golden ornamentation. About nine inches square and at least six inches deep, the box apparently contained a ring of great size and beauty. The boy proceeded all the way to the front and handed the box up to the priest, who in turn handed it to Tumultor.

And now the fanfare sounded again, with tones mightier, brighter, and louder than ever. It was time for the bride to enter, and the massive wooden doors were once again thrown open.

Eraina gasped. There stood Charissa, and she captured every eye in the room. She had never looked more beautiful.

Her stately posture, her radiant smile, her flowing hair, and her milky eyes—Eraina wondered if they were glistening with tears—all worked together to make her the picture of youth, power, and beauty. She carried herself with a self-possession that challenged every other youthful beauty in the room.

Her dress was magnificent, crystal and white in every detail, long and flowing. It was made of cloth so brilliantly luminous and silky that it shone and radiated different sparkles of light with her every step. But there was one strange, almost distracting feature to the dress—a semicircular neckpiece that was attached to her shoulders and extended around to the front of her face. Made of what appeared to be a brilliant glass, it projected outward from below her neck, almost horizontally, to several inches beyond her chin line. This unusual piece, almost like a collar, seemed to catch every ray of light in the room and then reflect it upward into Charissa's face, robbing her skin of its natural color.

As she entered, the sneering Tumultor, seeing her beauty, leaned over and spoke to the priest. Eraina could read his lips as he mouthed, "Make this quick." The priest gave a pious nod and beatific smile.

Sure enough, the opening portions of the ceremony, undertaken after Charissa ascended the platform and stood beside Tumultor, took little time. The priest intoned words from a strange language that no one seemed to understand. Then Charissa and Tumultor both nodded to the priest, allowing the ceremony to proceed. Regardless of how long the ceremony was intended to take, however, Lars, Eraina, and Hamelin knew they couldn't wait much longer.

The prince then reached into the ornate wooden box to take out what all expected to be a magnificent ring. As the rest of the audience oohed in wonder and admiration, Lars and Eraina gasped in shock when a massive jewel the size of a man's fist was lifted from the box. It was attached to a golden chain. Lars knew immediately that it was the jewel stolen from Periluna. Then as Charissa dutifully kneeled before Tumultor, he placed it around her neck—which extended just above the mirror collar. The jewel was so magnificent that all other precious gems in the room grew dull by comparison. And the people in the galleries instinctively moved their hands to their faces to deflect the glare of the mirrors and the jewel as Charissa stood.

But Lars was one of the few who knew that the jewel also had power, the power to absorb and then regenerate the other lights in the Great Hall. Even the light that shone from the mirroring collar around Charissa's neck was now deflected by the greater glory of the gem itself. Throughout the Great Hall, sun rays that had poured from the eastern windows were altered. What had been an almost blinding glare was now bent and absorbed into the greater light of the spectacular jewel of Periluna.

And Charissa's face, which earlier was made pale by the constantly mirroring effects of the collar and the mirrors around the room, began to change. Lars knew the properties of the jewel, and Eraina knew the face of her sister. Without speaking to each other, they nonetheless could see—Eraina aided too by the scarf—the effect the jewel was beginning to have. The jewel's power to draw light was absorbing the mesmerizing, enchanting work of the mirrored lights on Charissa. Her face became richer and fuller, her skin more like her natural color than the false whiteness produced by the mirrors. Her eyes, which before had stared out from a milky glaze, now grew deeper, taking on a clarity that matched the growing beauty of the living hues of her cheeks and the natural brunette richness of her hair.

Charissa, apparently affected by these changes, looked around quickly, taking in the room and her surroundings. She looked at Tumultor, then the priest, and then back at Tumultor, as if recognizing them for the first time after waking from a dream. Eraina could see a look of alarm move across her face.

But in spite of the changes on Charissa's face and in the light in the Hall, the ceremony continued. The priest reached back with a large chalice of silver into the flowing water behind him and offered the dripping, overflowing vessel to Tumultor, who drank from it and then returned it to the priest. The priest smiled a broad, toothy grin, and his eyes widened as he handed it to Charissa.

She took it in both hands and gazed into the cup. The water, touched by the dancing light, seemed to bubble up toward her. She took a deep breath, which was accompanied by a discernible lifting of her head and shoulders, and a questioning look crossed her face that suggested she had begun to change her mind.

Eraina could see it coming. The hesitation Charissa showed at drinking the water was also increasingly evident to Tumultor and the priest. Then as long seconds passed without her raising the silver cup to sip the waters of the Great Rock, whispers and awkward coughs could be heard passing through the galleries.

Eraina looked at Lars as if to say, "Do something!" and at the same moment, Lars saw his opportunity. He jumped on top of the railing that ran along the length of the gallery with a shout of "Ho!" Then like a tightrope walker, he spun to his left and danced along that railing to draw all eyes to himself and away from the proceedings at the front. It worked.

There was a collective gasp from the crowd as all eyes stayed on him. Eraina saw her chance and quietly moved from her seat, slipped through the corner door, and made her way quickly back down the steps. Meanwhile, Lars, acting every bit the circus acrobat with his jaunty steps and an occasional faked fall, walked on the rail the entire length of the Great Hall until he reached the far end of the gallery closest to the main entryway.

Then with all eyes from the galleries above and the attendants below looking at him, he raced at top speed back down the length of the rail, retracing his steps toward the front. So spectacular was his speed and so amazing his balance that few noticed when, as he reached the other end, he pulled the gathered rope from beneath his shirt and dropped it at Hamelin's feet. At that same moment, like a broad jumper hitting the take-off board at the moment of his highest speed, Lars launched himself at an angle toward the top of the flowing Rock behind the priest.

The crowd loudly sucked in its collective breath as he flew through the air and, landing feet first, caught himself at the top of the Rock. There he remained balanced on two feet, with his arms stretched wide, like a performer who has just completed his finest jump.

The ceremony had already come to a complete halt, and the wedding guests were staring in silent shock. The priest shouted at Lars, "*You*! What do you think you're doing?" At the same time, the soldiers stationed in the room were signaled by Tumultor and rushed from their positions near the entryway toward the stone platform.

But Lars was not done. With a standing two-footed jump from the top of the Rock, he soared directly at the priest and landed on the man's shoulders, sending him sprawling on his back. Lars retained his balance and was now standing next to Tumultor.

Before the prince knew what was happening, Lars had, with one more jump, brought his feet to the chest of the startled prince and with a powerful kick sent him sailing off the platform. Charissa, still holding the silver chalice but now fully herself, raised the vessel overhead with her right hand—spilling some of the water on her head—and simultaneously ripped the glass collar from her neck with her left. She then threw them both at Tumultor as he lay on the floor. The neckpiece just missed his face, but the chalice caught him in the lower abdomen, producing a dull groan.

At about the time Lars was making his jump toward the shoulders of the befuddled priest, Hamelin had picked up the rope, unwrapped it, quickly knotted one end, and thrown it around the chain that suspended the massive, round crystal fixture hanging just over the front of the platform. The force of his throw was so strong that the knotted end of the rope wrapped itself several times around the chain.

Hamelin then swung down from the gallery and landed on the platform next to Lars and just in front of Charissa. By this time, Eraina had made her way down the steps and was now rushing to the side of her sister. Charissa looked at her, and the recognition was immediate.

The bridal party, musicians, and wedding guests fled in a chaotic rush out the doors while Tumultor's soldiers were fighting their way through the crowd to get to the platform. Tumultor, trying to stand, pointed and shouted hoarsely, "Seize them!"

Hamelin knew what he'd have to do next.

Chapter 22

The Fight above the Fight

BY THE TIME TUMULTOR GAVE HIS GROANING, BLUSTERY order, the holy man had crawled away on all fours and escaped through the corner door. The two dozen soldiers now on the floor near Tumultor looked up to the platform and saw Lars, Hamelin, Eraina, and Charissa, who clutched her sister's hand.

Eraina turned to her right and muttered, "Good plan so far, boys, but now what?"

Hamelin grabbed the frock he was wearing, tore it from top to bottom, and threw it away like a boxer tossing away his robe before the fight begins.

But if the guests who either stayed to watch or were still trapped in the galleries expected only a brief scuffle before the soldiers subdued and captured the intruders, what they saw was different from what anyone could have anticipated. With his right hand, Hamelin reached to his left, and for the first time since it had been entrusted to him by Sue Ammi, he drew the sword and held it above his head with both hands. The sword and its sheath and belt became visible.

And before the soldiers had time to leap up to the platform or Hamelin could draw the sword back to strike, it began to whir and glow. Hamelin could feel it vibrate with energy, an energy that flowed from the sword into his hands and grew stronger and stronger, making the sword feel lighter and lighter. The vibrations combined with the sword's increasing glow to produce a blend of sound and sight, high tones and bursting radiance, with rolling, almost musical explosions connected to flashing bolts of fire.

The soldiers who were poised to strike hesitated at the spectacle of the sword and then were knocked to the floor by its nearly blinding light and nerve-penetrating sounds as it began to whirl in an ever-widening arc above Hamelin's head.

"Go!" yelled Hamelin, and Lars started quickly, but Charissa, with Eraina still holding her hand, stood there.

"Charissa, let's go!" said Eraina.

Charissa tried to move but couldn't. The jewel was elevating away from her body. It was still attached to the gold chain around her neck, but it was pulling up and away from her, and it held her in place.

"Charissa! We've got to go!" Eraina said again but this time added, "What's wrong?"

Charissa reached for the chain with one hand and grasped it.

"Don't pull it off!" yelled Lars. Charissa looked at him, took a deep breath, and leaned against the pull of the jewel and the chain.

Eraina looked at her and the jewel and then beyond it, in the direction it was pulling—toward the vaulted chamber.

Hamelin also looked up, at first to see the sword, but then he saw objects and rapid movements high and above. It was something his eyes could see, but he knew immediately that it was beyond his normal vision. There, in the upper spaces of the Great Hall, above even the heads of the remaining spectators in the galleries, a battle was raging—the Great Eagle and a giant brown bear were in furious combat. The bear was standing on two legs, pawing and swiping at the eagle but achieving only glancing blows. The eagle, in spite of his great size, was moving almost as nimbly as a hummingbird, with flapping wings and clawing talons thrashing in fury at the bear. They were covered by a shining mist of cold blue light that filled the room above Hamelin's head. Hamelin sensed—because no one else was looking up at them—that while others could hear and see the sounds and sights created by the sword, they couldn't see the pitched battle above them.

And then he saw more. The cold blue light was actually flowing from the bear. His roars shot the light toward Hamelin and the others, but the jewel around Charissa's neck was absorbing it. She wasn't harmed by it, but neither could she move.

The soldiers still lay on the floor, shielding their eyes and covering their ears from the glaring sight and piercing sounds of Hamelin's sword. But then Hamelin felt the sword beginning to get warm and even heavy in his arms. He remembered—or did he hear?—the words of SueSue: "You must not delay in using it. You must strike and immediately let it go, for it will bring death to those it wounds, but also to you if you cling to it while the power is present."

As the sword grew heavier and heavier, the battle above him grew fiercer and fiercer. Hamelin then heard a sustained shriek from the bird when a swipe from the bear's flailing paws caught him just below his left wing and drew blood. The sword was still arcing and turning, whirling and whirring around Hamelin's head, faster and faster. But where should he throw it? At the soldiers? At Tumultor? He looked up again at the eagle and bear, and it looked like the bear was moving closer to the wounded bird to strike again. The bear stood near the bird and roared, and the blue light erupted even more in volume and speed. Hamelin knew what to do.

With one last revolution of the sword above his head, he then added the strength of his gloved hands to the speed of the sword. The handle had grown hot, and though he could scarcely hold on to it, it was at the same time difficult to let go. But timing one last turn of his hands around his shoulders and throwing his body in a full circle, with a quick back step and a driving pivot off his right foot, Hamelin let go and flung the sword upward toward the battle above.

The sword, in a radiant streaking sweep of white and red, flew directly toward—and then through—the great bear, striking his head just between his right eye and ear. With a loud, roaring wail, the bear disappeared in an explosion of light and fire, while the great bird took flight, though slowly at first, straight toward the peak of the chamber and disappeared. The blue light vanished, and the jewel fell back on Charissa's chest.

"It's gone!" said Eraina as she pulled on Charissa's hand again.

"Now! Go!" yelled Hamelin.

Lars and the two sisters dashed through the side door and out of the Great Hall into the garden.

The sword, however, remained visible and was still flashing, spinning, and whirring as it continued upward even after striking the bear, before turning tip down and falling back toward the stone platform. The point of the flaming sword plunged into the top of the Great Rock and lodged up to its hilt. The water that flowed from the Rock bubbled and gurgled momentarily and then ceased entirely.

One of the soldiers sat up, pointed at the Rock, and yelled, "Look! The *water*. The water has *stopped*!"

A look of shock, followed by despair, covered the faces of all, especially Tumultor. Hamelin turned immediately and ran out the same door his friends had taken. He could hear the crowd in the Great Hall wail and shriek.

Chapter 23

Fleeing
Osmethan

N O SOONER HAD HAMELIN DASHED OUT THE DOOR THAN
he saw trouble in the garden. A heavyset soldier had
apparently been repositioned inside the walled area
during the ceremony. Now Hamelin could see that Lars,
Eraina, and Charissa were being held at bay by the soldier,
who was barking orders at them to stand still and jabbing
his spear at Lars, who was closest to the soldier and making threatening moves. Charissa, recognized by the guard
as Tumultor's bride, was standing to the side. The guard was
confused by her presence and had assumed she was being
kidnapped.

As Hamelin started running toward them, the soldier's
attention was diverted, and in that split second, Lars made
a quick move to try to shove the point of the spear away
from the small group. The guard, momentarily off balance,
nonetheless regained his composure and stepped back. Seeing Hamelin coming, he jabbed once more at Lars, but Lars
quickly sidestepped and grabbed the shaft of the spear. The

two then struggled, pushing and pulling, with each of them gripping the spear with both hands.

Hamelin was now rushing to them, and the burly soldier gave one hard yank and wrested the spear from Lars's grip. However, as the soldier lunged at Lars, Charissa stepped forward and was just in the process of yelling, "Stop! Back up! These are my *friends*." But it was too late. As she stepped between the soldier and Lars, the point of the spear, which was intended to strike Lars, hit sharply and deeply in her left side and ripped her flesh. She went down on her knees, gripping her side, with blood oozing around her hands.

By this time, Hamelin was upon the group. It took him hardly a moment to give the shocked soldier a good shot to the chest with one of his gloved fists, downing him immediately. He then took the spear and snapped it as if it were a twig. Lars gave the soldier a hard kick in the abdomen, and the dazed man crawled and then stumbled off toward the back of the Great Hall.

Meanwhile, Eraina kneeled over Charissa and was doing her best to attend to her as the red spot from her wound constantly widened on her white gown.

"Lars," said Hamelin, "we've got no time to lose. They'll be after us any second."

Eraina yelled, "No! Wait!" But it didn't take much for Hamelin to give Lars a boost up the garden wall, since Lars had the ability to use his toes in the grout of the wall to walk himself up. Next was Eraina.

"I can't *leave* her!" she cried as she leaned over her sister.

"I promise you, we won't," said Hamelin. "But all of us will be caught if you don't go *now*!" And though Eraina couldn't bear to leave Charissa for even a moment, there was no other choice.

"Hurry!" yelled Hamelin as shouts went up back to their left. They both could see that the doors behind the Great Rock were open and soldiers were pouring into the garden, running toward them. Hamelin grabbed Eraina and unceremoniously tossed her up to Lars, who caught her as she grabbed him around the shoulders and, with his balance, held them both on top of the wall. Now for Charissa.

She was in pain, but Hamelin had to act. Grabbing her with his right hand and cradling her against him, he reached as high as he could with his left hand and pinched his fingers into the wall, creating his own handhold and pulling them both up several feet off the ground. Then with Charissa facing the wall, he quickly shifted his right hand under her left leg and, with Lars and Eraina waiting at the top, pushed her upward. Each of them leaned down and caught her arms and pulled her up.

Charissa screamed in pain as blood flowed from her side and splattered on Hamelin's face. The soldiers were getting closer, and he quickly pulled himself up to the top of the wall. By the time he did so, Lars had already deftly used his toes against the wall to climb down the other side as fast as he could and then braced himself as he had to jump the last seven or eight feet. With his balance, he had no problem.

Hamelin then told Eraina to stay on the wall and, when he was on the ground, to drop Charissa into their arms. Eraina nodded in agreement. After he quickly climbed down, Eraina pulled Charissa into a sitting position and then quickly pushed her over. The boys caught her and laid her on the ground. Eraina, still standing on the wall, had no time to see if the boys were ready for her. A spear whizzed by her head.

"Catch me!" she yelled while she jumped, arms and legs flying. They did.

Because the garden wall was built to keep people from breaking in, it also kept people from getting out easily. The soldiers couldn't climb over it, and they had no other choice but to run back inside the Great Hall in order to get outside and then circle the walls to take up the pursuit.

By then, however, the four young people had the advantage, in spite of Charissa's weakened condition. In addition to the extra distance the soldiers had to cover, by the time they charged back into the Great Hall, the entire place was in chaos. The press of the panicked crowd was so dense that it was impossible for them to exit quickly.

It took the soldiers several minutes to push, shove, and shoulder their way through the crowd just to gain the main entrance to the Great Hall. Then they had to rush across the enclosed courtyard of the castle and race southward another thirty yards to exit the castle itself.

They turned east and circled around the garden. However, Hamelin and his friends were nowhere to be seen—the four had moved in the opposite direction around the castle.

Lars and Eraina led the way, and Hamelin helped Charissa walk fast, her arm around his neck. The four headed northward as soon as they could and then went west on the great avenue. Crowds of onlookers were still present along that northern loop but were not as numerous as on the southern portion. As the four moved along, however, one of them in a bloodstained white gown, they attracted stares.

Eraina grabbed a large blue cloth as it hung from one of the nearby shops, quickly tossed the merchant a silver coin, and yelled back to him, "I hope you don't mind, but one of the bridal attendants is very sick, and we need to get her home to lie down." She then took the cloth, wrapped it around Charissa's shoulders and upper body, and covered not only the bloodstain but also the jewel and some of the white dress as well.

With all the confusion, members of the palace security and soldiers from other portions of the city all rushed toward the palace grounds. In the chaos, Hamelin and his friends soon realized that their best strategy was simply to get out of the way. They took shelter just inside one of the open-air shops and waited while more and more of the clamoring crowd flowed by, heading toward the palace grounds.

Hamelin wiped the blood off his face as best he could. A few moments later, they emerged, helping Charissa and walking slowly so as not to draw any attention. They made their way toward the northwestern part of the city.

They hoped it would be the area of the city where Tumultor and his men would look last. Lars also hoped to find a friendly face there.

Chapter 24

A Brief Respite

CHARISSA WAS GETTING WEAKER AND WEAKER, BUT THEY had to press on. Lars led the small band back to the area of the city he had come to know the previous day. By the time he and his friends reached the home of Simannas, the streets were less crowded.

Unknown to most residents of the city, especially those caught up in the excitement of the great wedding festival, the people of the northwestern quarter were just returning from a ceremony of their own. They had solemnly gathered to remember the life of Simannas and were now returning to their homes. As Lars and his friends approached the house, the looks of desperation in their faces caught the attention of the man whom Lars remembered as Simannas's manservant.

The servant recognized Lars and sensed immediately that he and his friends needed help. He quickly ushered them into the house, and there they laid Charissa on the bed where only yesterday Simannas himself had lain.

Hamelin gently helped her lie down. As he did so, the empty scabbard on his left side brushed her wound, and she let out a sharp cry of pain.

"I'm so sorry, Princess Charissa!" he said.

"It's okay," she mumbled in a breathy voice as she lay back slowly. Hamelin took the scabbard off in case he had to lift or move her again. But she lay there still, eyes closed, breathing in short, rapid breaths.

Eraina motioned to the boys to leave and, with the help of Simannas's woman servant, removed Charissa's gown, washed and gently dressed her wound, and stopped the bleeding. The old woman found a plain dress that fit Charissa. Then with her sister's permission, Eraina removed the gold chain that held the jewel around her neck and took it to Lars.

"You should take care of this," she said. He solemnly took the jewel and nodded to her—knowing that it may have cost Eraina and Charissa dearly to get it back. He placed the chain around his neck and hid the jewel under his baggy shirt.

They all ate something and tried to rest, hoping that Charissa would be able to move again soon. But they couldn't wait very long.

Word had spread about the events in the Great Hall of the Rock. What had people in a panic, though, was that the Rock no longer produced water—the same water that had given the city ever-enduring life had been stopped by a strange sword that was now implanted in the top of the Great Rock and could not be pulled out.

Chaos in the streets had also severely hindered Tumultor's ability to muster a fighting group. His soldiers were more concerned about the failed water flow than chasing the intruders. It was hours before Tumultor could get his servants to outfit him with his horse and armor and still longer before he could regather a force of men to join him in pursuit.

Hamelin's group didn't know at first of the advantages they had gained. Nonetheless, reports of what had taken place began to circulate even into the Quarter of the Aged, the customary name of the northwest portion of the city. Simannas's two servants described to Lars, Hamelin, and Eraina what was going on in Osmethan. They reported that Hamelin's sword had stopped the flow of water from the Great Rock, the city was in chaos, and Tumultor was screaming for soldiers.

Hamelin and his friends knew they didn't have much time. By late that afternoon, they decided they would not spend the night there.

Charissa had taken some food and drink and was feeling somewhat better, though her blood loss had been significant and the pain in her side was still sharp.

"Oh, Eraina," she said, "I am so sorry. All of this is my fault."

"Shhh," her little sister replied. "Just get better. It's going to be all right."

Eraina exchanged her clothes for the plain, less fashionable styles of that area, taking her scarf and small moneybag with her. Lars kept his usual clothing since it protected him from the sun. Hamelin borrowed some simple items to wear over his jacket and blue jeans, but realizing he would need to support Charissa, he handed the leather belt and empty sheath to Simannas's manservant, who promised to care for them. He kept his gloves in the pocket of his jacket. At the last second, he felt the small hammer he had found in the Atrium in his pants pocket.

"Just a second," he said to the manservant. "I don't need this to weigh me down." He dropped the little hammer into the sheath and was ready to go.

Before they left, Lars told Simannas's two servants, the man and the woman, what their master had said to him just before he died. They seemed to understand something of Simannas's last words, but they offered no interpretation of them, and Lars didn't have time to ask them to explain.

Before leaving, Eraina pulled the scarf over her head and stood at the door of the house, looking all around. She quickly reported back to the others that there was no sign of Tumultor or his men. So with hasty farewells, the four left.

With Charissa limping only slightly and the others doing their best to look as if everything were normal, Hamelin, Lars, and the two sisters made their way toward the south-western gate of the city. After leaving Osmethan, they walked slowly for the first two hundred yards, trying to appear only as weary travelers heading home at the end of the big day. As the sun began to set, however, they left the main road and quickly rejoined the path that Hamelin, Lars, and Eraina had taken that morning. They made their way down the slope of the canyon and into the small cavern.

They expected to find provisions again in that small rocky hideaway. But things quickly turned from bad to worse.

Chapter 25

Disappointment Turns to Despair

AS THEY ENTERED THE CAVERN, TWO HUGE DISAPPOINT-
ments struck them immediately. First, the bleeding
in Charissa's side had resumed, and she was getting
weaker by the moment. Eraina attended to her the best
she could, but there was not a lot to do. Second, the place
where they had found provisions on two previous occasions was empty. The shallow stone basin for water was full,
but it was filled by the dripping from above. Whoever, or
whatever—Hamelin still thought he knew—had provided
their food earlier had not returned to the cavern.

He was surprised that nothing was there waiting for
them. He knew that the food was a gift, but he still expected
it. Hadn't they done all they were told to do? Weren't they
promised provisions? But now Charissa was hurt, and
they had nothing to eat. They would need food before long,
especially if they were to take care of Charissa and manage
the long journey back to the home of Sue Ammi. Assuming,

of course, that they weren't tracked down by Tumultor and forced to flee another way.

The small cavern opened to the east, and though it was only about thirty minutes past sundown, it was already growing dark. Eraina came to Lars and Hamelin and whispered that Charissa had become feverish. They looked at the darkening skies, and Eraina folded her arms in front of her and squeezed her shoulders together. The night air was obviously growing colder, and Hamelin took off his borrowed clothes so she could use them to cover Charissa.

Eraina returned to her sister, and Hamelin and Lars remained in the opening. The skies were darkening with every passing moment.

Finally, Lars whispered to Hamelin, "Even if we can get her strong enough to move again, then we've got to worry about how to avoid Tumultor and his men. By now, even with all the confusion in the city, Tumultor has probably gathered enough men to come after us, no doubt on horses."

"Yeah," agreed Hamelin. "And don't forget that he knows we've got Charissa *and* the jewel. He'll be coming hard."

"Besides," Lars continued, "that was more than just a wedding we broke up. Tumultor knows that two of the kingdoms Chimera has stolen are now at stake."

Hamelin knew he was talking about Periluna and Parthogen. He wanted to add—but didn't—that he had things riding on this as well. He knew from both the eagle and Sue Ammi that his hopes for learning his story and finding his family were connected to the other kingdoms.

"If only the eagle was here," said Hamelin. "Where *is* he? And that empty nest over there . . . I *know* he built it." He then remembered the explosion when the sword hit the bear. "What if the eagle—?" He stopped himself—he didn't want to consider the possibility.

Lars turned back to check again on Charissa and Eraina, and Hamelin, looking into the deep-blue darkness of the eastern sky, felt despair coming over him like an iron shirt he couldn't throw off. His chest felt heavy and his throat tight. He knew they had to leave, but they'd never make it with Charissa. She'd never last the whole trip. He had never seen someone die . . .

Hamelin hadn't felt this way in a long time—at least not since the first time he tried to cross the footbridge—but he could feel himself giving up. He felt himself falling, deeper and deeper into the darkness, as if he really had fallen off the bridge into the hot blackness below. He waited, eyes shut. Then he remembered. He *hadn't* fallen. And though he didn't make it the first time, he did the second time. The Great Eagle had been with him. His first failure wasn't the end of the story.

Slowly, something started building up inside him, and he felt it growing stronger. The words of a letter from Layla years ago fluttered through his mind: "Keep waiting and keep hoping." He opened his eyes.

He looked up into the dark night skies one more time and refused to accept the empty answer they were giving back. He walked out of the cavern opening and back up the path and peered over the top, first north, toward the growing lights of Osmethan, then westward.

In the west, there was still some light lingering, trapped on the horizon in a small cloud the size of his outstretched hand. And then, for just a moment, he thought he saw a dark speck rise just above the cloud, though it quickly disappeared. What was that?

Hamelin closed his eyes and shook his head to clear his mind. He looked once more, and there it was again, but this time, instead of dropping from sight, the black speck moved slightly to the right. The longer he watched it, the more he realized that it was moving in a circle that grew wider and moved higher as the speck itself grew in size. Whatever it was, it was coming closer.

Hamelin's hope stirred, and he knew. Even before he could clearly see—in fact, even as the sky grew darker in the west—he knew it was the Great Eagle.

Circling, soaring, and perhaps even patrolling the area, the great bird came closer. Hamelin rushed back down to the inner recess of their small cavern and saw even there a few good signs. Eraina had dipped her scarf in the waters of the rock basin and was bathing Charissa's forehead. Lars kneeled at her side, looking at her closely for signs of renewed strength. Then a very slight breeze blew into the cavern, and Charissa stirred and opened her eyes.

In that same moment, they all looked up at Hamelin, and he said, "There's still hope."

Chapter 26

A Change of Plans

WITHIN MOMENTS, THEY COULD ALL FEEL AND HEAR the chopping winds that flooded their small rock hideaway just before the Great Eagle landed.

Charissa lay there, still weak but alert enough to see the huge bird. Eraina and Lars froze in their places but quickly looked to Hamelin as if to ask, "Is this the eagle you've told us about?" One look from Hamelin, with a nod and a wide smile, confirmed that this was indeed the great bird.

The eagle had swooped into that cleft canyon with a large white cloth, gathered at its four corners in his talons and obviously holding something within its folds. When the bird dropped the cloth, the four corners spread out, and there on the smooth rock surface were new supplies for the weary group. There were fruits, berries, nuts, and bread.

Then the eagle spoke. "I regret that I was delayed. I was sent much earlier, but Chimera's beast detained me."

Hamelin wondered whether the eagle and the bear had continued to fight. He had hoped the bear was dead. Then he saw what may have slowed the eagle down—a wound in his side. It looked to be where the bear had struck the bird with his paw. The eagle's eyes caught Hamelin looking at his side, and with a half flex of his wings, he covered the spot.

"My friends here, sir," said Hamelin, pointing to Eraina and Lars, "are the ones you told me I'd meet. And there," he said, pointing to Charissa, "is the one who waited and entered the pool . . . well, you know." He couldn't bring himself to say "wrongly."

The eagle acknowledged Hamelin's words with a blink of his eyes. Then the great bird spoke again. "You must all leave tonight. Eat enough to last you for now, and the rest you may gather up and take with you for the journey. Tumultor will make every effort to track you. We must hope that Chimera does not summon his oldest son, Ren'dal, from the north. Tumultor is evil enough, but Ren'dal is cruel, a master of tricks who deceives too much to be easily fooled himself."

There again were the names Chimera and Ren'dal, spoken together, but there was no time to find out more about them, especially Ren'dal.

"There is no time for delay," the eagle continued. "If you leave now, you'll have some advantage, but it will still be a close race for you to reach the home of the Hospitable Woman before Tumultor overtakes you. Even then you'll probably need help. If you make it to her house, you will be safe at least for a while, and she can give you your next instructions from the Ancient One. But you must hurry."

But that's impossible! Hamelin thought. He had known all along that he and Eraina and Lars would have to make that journey and that it would require speed, but what about Charissa? He looked at the eagle and could not bring himself to speak, but neither did he move. The eagle stared back and, with eyes that widened at Hamelin's failure to react, spoke again, "Did you not *hear* me? I said you must leave and leave quickly."

Hamelin could not believe what came out of his mouth next: "But, sir, we know that we must leave, and we know that we'll be chased. But surely you can see that Princess Charissa can't possibly make the trip in her condition. She's weak and has lost a lot of blood."

"I know," said the great bird. "Those are consequences of her own folly. She likely will not survive, but there is no other choice. You must take her with you to the home of Sue Ammi. There, if all of you make it, she can rest and perhaps be restored and her quest, along with Eraina's, fulfilled."

"No," said Hamelin. "It's not possible! She can't make it the way she is now, and you yourself said that the success of one of us depends on the success of *all*."

"But she cannot stay here," said the bird, "and there is no other place for her to go for rest and healing."

Hamelin stood silent for a moment, thinking, and then he burst out again. "But there is! The waters. They're dangerous, but they're also waters of life and *healing*. My shoulders were torn by your claws, but after we made it through, they were healed. We could take her back to the outside pond!"

The eagle's chest expanded, and he stood taller, apparently surprised by Hamelin's forcefulness. He pulled his wings in tighter and settled back before responding.

"The waters do not work that way. Yes, you were healed because, though you were initially deceived, you *turned*," said the bird, "and you went through those waters *rightly*. But *she* did not, and now she lies weak and bleeding as a consequence of her own will and her own deeds."

"I know," said Hamelin with obvious impatience in his voice. "But can't she be forgiven? I've heard her say how sorry she is for what she did. She was deceived, but she also refused to drink from Tumultor's cup, and she came with us. Her wound, just like yours," Hamelin dared to say, pointing at the eagle's side, "was a result of bravery."

The eagle paused. He didn't answer at first. Then slowly shaking his head, he said softly, "Of course there is room for forgiveness, but justice must be served as well."

"But she *has* paid. And her last drop of blood will soon fall on the ground." Hamelin looked toward Charissa, whose head was lying flat again, her eyes half closed.

"Yes, yes," said the eagle softly, "she can be forgiven later, in the end. But now . . ."

Hamelin saw the eagle's hesitation. "But why not *now*? Is there no help *now*?"

The eagle spoke slowly, as if unsure. "Yes, perhaps it is possible," he said. "But there is great risk."

"To us?" asked Hamelin, looking at Eraina and Lars.

The bird looked him in the eye and said, "To you."

"But if I can't succeed without her, and she can't make it without help from me, then where's the risk? We are risking *everything* if we *don't* take the risk to save her."

And then the eagle, as if in a moment of impatient frustration, said with a low, screechy voice, "But you don't know what you are asking for! There are other problems to consider in all of this . . . but now . . . all of this arguing . . . there is no more time! Take the provisions! Eat what you can, and carry as much of the rest with you as you can!"

Then the great bird turned, apparently trying to figure out how to do what he was allowing to happen. He abruptly turned back to face Hamelin and said, "Place Princess

Charissa on this white sheet and wrap her tightly. Hamelin, you must carry her in your arms, and I will carry you. Even if we can get her to those waters again, I do not know how . . . but for now . . . it is enough that we do what we can."

He looked at Eraina and Lars. "But the two of you must find your way to the home of the Hospitable Woman by the mountain path. It will not be easy, and Tumultor will surely pursue you. Make haste and be gone!"

From that point, the three companions moved quickly, each knowing what he or she had to do without saying a word to the others. Hamelin and Lars moved the provisions off the white cloth. They stuffed a few handfuls of food into their mouths while they worked, and Lars packed up as much of the rest as he could carry for himself and Eraina. Eraina attended to Charissa, feeding her as much as she could and insisting that she drink as deeply as possible.

Hamelin and Lars spread out the white cloth and gently laid Charissa across it diagonally. The cloth was as long from corner to corner as she was tall. They took the other two corners and wrapped them across her middle, tucking them together underneath her as tightly as they dared. Hamelin then put on the gloves, picked up Charissa, cradling her in his arms, and turned to the eagle.

"We're ready," he said. He took one last look at Eraina and Lars, who by this time were also packed up and ready to go. "Good-bye," he said softly. "We'll see you at the home of Sue Ammi."

They nodded, and Eraina, unable to hold back her tears, looked at Charissa's face, now barely showing through the swaddling cloth in Hamelin's arms, and said, "I love you, my sister." She tried to add "good-bye," but the word was choked with a sob.

Holding Charissa, Hamelin took a few steps toward the edge of the drop-off just outside their little hideaway. The eagle, with a short hop and a flutter of his wings, lifted himself behind Hamelin and used his legs to pinch the sides of his torso just below his armpits.

Then the eagle stretched his wings, and after one stroke, the bird, Hamelin, and Charissa plummeted off the cliff. Eraina and Lars ran quickly to the edge and looked over. There they saw the great bird and his human cargo, falling precipitously toward the bottom of the canyon. They saw the eagle fighting the wind with his powerful wings and, more gradually than they would have hoped, slowly gaining control of the currents. Then, reversing their descent from somewhere in the darkness near the bottom of the canyon, the eagle soared back to the level of the edge where they stood, continued upward, and disappeared off to their right, heading toward the mountains to the southeast.

Eraina and Lars, holding what food they could in the pockets of their clothes, left within minutes, heading southward. Eventually they emerged from the canyon and picked up the path that would lead them to the mountain pass. It was dark, and the air had grown cold, but they marched forward, heads down, into the night.

Chapter 27

Two Journeys, One Night

ERAINA AND LARS PUSHED THROUGH THE NIGHT, BUT even with her scarf, they were slowed down by the darkness and their weariness. As they walked, they occasionally nibbled on small bits of the foods they had brought along, but they kept on at a steady pace. The bread and nuts filled their stomachs, and the fruit and berries were a good substitute for water.

It was approaching midnight before they reached the pass through the mountains. As they moved through the wider portions of it that would eventually lead to the narrow, vertical crease at its southern end, the weather changed dramatically. What started off as gentle snowflakes soon became a hard, driving snowstorm.

The walls of the mountain pass kept them on track, as did Eraina's now almost constant use of the scarf, which she pulled over her head for warmth as well as sight. At first Lars found himself leading Eraina, but then, as the snowstorm became blinding in its force, it was Eraina who led the way as Lars clung to her elbow.

"I just hope there hasn't been another rockslide," he said. "This time, we don't have Hamelin to lift the boulders."

"That's for sure," she said.

In spite of the storm, they maintained a relatively steady walking pace, though it was not uncommon for Eraina to slip on the slick and icy rocks that covered their path. They made a good team: Lars from behind, holding on to Eraina's elbow with his left hand and supporting her in the small of her back with his right, and Eraina guiding their way.

Just past daybreak, they came to the narrowest stretch of the pass, and the snowfall had not let up. They both feared the worst, but though great drifts had gathered there, they were able to push, stumble, and high-step their way through. It was hard going, but no new rockslides had occurred to block their way.

They continued to press forward. The snow was letting up some, but now it turned to sleet and made the path even more treacherous for Eraina, who slipped and slid left and right, held up at times only by Lars's balance and support at her elbow and back. Lars could see almost nothing because of the sleet and, in any case, only seldom lifted his head because of the pelting cold on his face. Eraina, on the other hand, had to keep her head up to see. She held both ends of the scarf under her chin with her left hand and attempted to guard her eyes with her right as they continued to trudge forward.

Though she was bitterly cold, Eraina's temperament grew hotter and hotter. All she could think about was Charissa—finding and rescuing her but then seeing her stabbed in a scuffle. Now they were separated once again, and she didn't know if Charissa was alive or dead. And the lack of sleep and the icy conditions made her frustration worse.

"Why does this have to happen *now*?" she blurted out angrily. "We've been on the road for days and it's been perfect weather. But when we need it most, we get snow and wind and sleet instead! I don't understand it! Just when we think we've done everything right, Charissa is wounded, the provisions weren't there—and when they were, we hardly had time to *eat*!—and now we're here, up all night, fighting our way through the pass over these rocks and in these conditions. *Why*?" she yelled out loud to no one in particular, though of course Lars could hear.

"I wish I could do something about it," he said back rather sharply, "but at least *you* can *see*. I'm having to keep my head down and can look only at the ground beneath my feet."

"Don't complain to *me*," she shot back. "With those shoes you've got, at least you don't slip and fall. I've hit the ground a dozen times, and I've got the bruises on my elbows and scrapes on my knees to prove it! And if your balance is so great, why are you holding on to me?" she yelled.

"Because I'm trying to keep *you* from falling!" he said. He let go of her, but a fresh biting wind whipped and whistled through the pass, and he instinctively reached out to steady her. They both fell silent and trudged on.

By midmorning, they had made it through the pass and were again heading eastward along the open space at the base of the mountain. The ground was rocky and frozen, which made them take short steps to help Eraina's balance but also made it harder to step around the rocks, all of which added to their difficulties. Still, they dared not leave the path—it was the only sure way to Sue Ammi's house. They pressed on.

———————

The journey for the eagle, Hamelin, and Charissa was even harder. The wound in the great bird's side slowed him down and made almost every stroke of his powerful wings feel like a fresh cut. Charissa lay unconscious in Hamelin's arms, and when he occasionally placed his cheek against her forehead, he could tell that she was burning with fever. She stirred restlessly—which sometimes was the only way he knew for sure that she was still alive—and Hamelin did all he could to hold her close to his chest, trying not to jostle or in any way stretch the side of her body. The wound continued to seep blood, but the freezing cold slowed the loss.

They had no protection against the elements. The cold winds and snow that hit Eraina and Lars slammed hard into Hamelin and the eagle, though at the higher altitude it felt even colder. The flight would get them to their destination more quickly than Eraina and Lars would reach theirs, but the bitterness of the cold was beyond anything Hamelin had ever experienced.

And his arms ached. Not even the strength of his gloved hands could stop the dull pain that ran from his wrists up to his shoulders and into his chest and down his back. It was agony, but he held Charissa close and did all he could to protect her. He felt so sorry for the beautiful young woman who reminded him occasionally of Layla. She must have suffered greatly after being captured by Landon. And how had she managed to swim through the pond in the Atrium, especially with all those underwater creatures? She had mentioned escaping and being led by a huge lion, then waiting—and then it hit him again. Her pain and struggles were all because of his failure to cross the bridge that first time.

Hamelin kept reconstructing her story—and his own—in his mind. All the pieces fit. She was first captured almost four years ago, according to Eraina, and about six months after that, he had failed to cross the footbridge—exactly when, just ahead in the Atrium, she was waiting.

How long had she waited . . . in the dark . . . for him? So much of her pain was his fault.

The eagle flew on through the darkness, continuing in a southeasterly direction. Once they crossed over the mountains, Hamelin could see that the Forest of Fears was approaching from the south on the horizon.

Then in a surprise move, the great bird began to glide downward into the open field between the Forest and the mountain range. Why? Was the eagle giving up?

They landed as softly as Hamelin could have expected. As he saw the ground approaching, he instinctively lifted his legs as high as he could and stretched them forward, while the eagle found a way to slow down as much as he could. Hamelin let his left arm drop and his gloved hand touched first to cushion the landing. He then found himself seated on the ground, Charissa still in his arms, and the great bird standing at his side.

The eagle panted and with breathiness between his words said, "We . . . must . . . rest."

Hamelin was glad for that, as he wasn't sure how much longer he could have held on. They had made their way through the night and the storms, and now, though it was still dark, the sky to the east began to exchange its black for a very dark blue.

After only about fifteen minutes, the great bird stirred. "We must go again," he said. "And now there can be no further stopping until we reach the waters. Are you ready?"

Hamelin, relieved to hear they were still going to the pond but exhausted beyond anything he had ever felt in his life, nodded.

The eagle then grabbed him and told him he would need to help, running while the great bird made his first powerful strokes. Hamelin thought how strange it would look to his friends, or the Kaleys, back at the children's home to see him cradling a young woman in his arms while running underneath the body of a huge eagle, trying to take off. He ran like a child trying to launch a kite, and the eagle, holding him from behind, stretched and beat his mighty wings, and they gradually lifted off the ground, Hamelin's legs still pumping a few seconds after they rose. The eagle slowly gained altitude and soared above the first trees they encountered in the Forest of Fears. It was still dark, and now they flew due south.

Chapter 28

Back at the Pond: Hamelin's Ordeal

AS THEY SOARED HIGH OVER THE FOREST OF FEARS, Hamelin could see lighter shades of blue in the east. He had insisted that the waters could restore Charissa, but now he wondered how it would really work. He distinctly remembered that it had been important for him to go through the pond without looking at his reflection. He also needed the light from the rising sun to see a true image as he looked into the crystal—but now there would be no wall of crystal, no true image, and she wasn't conscious enough to see things anyway. The waters were the same, but they would be at the other pond, where Hamelin had exited, the one connected underground to the pond in the Atrium. Thoughts of what lay beneath it brought other memories, dark ones, and Hamelin tried to push from his mind the images of the hideous creatures that had appeared under the waters.

He began hoping things would be easier this time. He imagined himself laying Charissa at the pond's edge and then, with both his hands, gently splashing water over her wound. He also saw himself cupping the back of her head in one hand while slowly allowing her to drink the healing waters from the other.

The pool came into sight, and soon they landed near it. The eagle stood at the water's edge, and Hamelin kneeled beside Charissa's prone, unconscious body, trying to help her drink. He put the water on her lips, but she could barely swallow.

The eagle looked at Charissa and said, "A few small sips are not enough to reverse her condition. Her wounds are deeper than the one in her side. She has traveled the wrong way—full of vanity—through the waters. And now she is too weak to fight back—even if it were permissible for her to go through them—of her own will."

"But," said Hamelin, "I *know* these waters can heal her. She's already paid for her mistakes, and for mine! She's really sorry—I know it. Surely she can have another chance for these waters to heal her this time and not hurt her."

"But there are many risks here," said the bird with a sadness in his voice.

"But you said she could be *forgiven*," said Hamelin.

"Forgiven, yes, but she needs healing and restoration. For that, she must fully enter these waters and do so willingly. I have no doubt that she would—"

"Yes," interrupted Hamelin, "I *know* she would."

"But," continued the eagle, "she hasn't the strength to fight what she will face down there."

"I'll take her," said Hamelin. Then, after a pause, he added, "I've known all along I would have to."

"But you *can't*," said the eagle. "You can only go through these waters rightly once, and you've done that."

"But I wouldn't be going for myself," said Hamelin. "I'd be going for Charissa. I'll take her through myself."

"You . . . can't," said the eagle, but even as he did, he tilted his head to one side, as if unsure of his answer.

"But why not? *You* came to my rescue when I was captured by my image in the waters."

"But that was different," said the eagle. "That was before—"

"And you said we'd all have to succeed *together*," insisted Hamelin. "I'm willing to take the risk. I know I'm just doing what Charissa herself would do if only she could open her eyes and speak. I'll take her!"

"But *she* has to choose!"

"Maybe she *is* choosing. Inside. We don't know what she's thinking," Hamelin fired back.

"But she can't physically enter."

"Well, if she wants to do it but can't, then I'll do it *for her*!"

Then without waiting for the eagle to respond, Hamelin stood Charissa up and balanced her on her feet with his left hand still at her back. He leaned her forward just slightly and quickly stepped in front of her so that her body weight fell against his back. He reached behind him, took her hands, and put them at his waist. He felt a faint squeezing from her forearms. He then bent forward even more and reached back with his hands and grasped her behind the knees. From there he hitched her weight up higher on his back, and leaning forward, he stepped toward the pond.

"O young man, you can't," screeched the Great Eagle. "It'll take great strength to hold her to you, and if you do that, how will you pull yourself through the water?"

"I've still got the gloves," Hamelin said, looking down at the water. "I'll hold her with one hand—"

"But even if that can be done, how will you fight the creatures below? The risk is all yours, Hamelin! She's almost
gone, but you're alive, and perhaps there are other ways to
fulfill your quest. If you go in again, even for her, it won't be
like last time. This time they will *fight* you!"

"Then *let* them! I failed her once before when she waited
for me in the dark! I'm not abandoning her again!"

Now the eagle was silent. The sun was breaking through
the eastern horizon. Hamelin took another step closer to the
edge of the pond, his right foot wet up to his ankle. He then
bent again at the knees, preparing to jump. Before he could
move, however, the eagle screeched louder than Hamelin
had ever heard before. This shriek had as well the agonized
sound of a trapped animal in it. He turned to look at the bird.

Suddenly the Great Eagle took a mighty leap into the air
and, clawing through the pain of his own side wound, shot
upward explosively. Then with a twisting pirouette, he plummeted toward the pair. Hamelin feared the eagle was going
to do something to stop him, as he had done once before
when he had faced the pond. But just as Hamelin bent his
knees to hurry his jump, the eagle, with full flying force—
his wings outstretched and his talons forward—dug his long,
pointed claws into Charissa's back.

For a split second, Hamelin thought the great bird
intended to rip her like prey away from his grasp. But instead
of pulling her away, the downward force of the eagle's blow
propelled them all powerfully forward, and Hamelin knew
immediately that the great bird had joined his efforts to save
Charissa. Together, the three allies plunged, face first, into
the waters of death and life.

Charissa realized her mind would apparently be the last thing to die. She knew she was dying, but she also knew she was not yet dead, though her body had mostly given up. Her will still lived, so she could think. But it too was fading. Her body was freezing, though her head was burning. And inside the heat that filled her head were images dancing like flames, vague memories of protecting her sister and her sister's friend just outside Tumultor's Great Hall. Stepping in front of the spear was one of the few things she had left to be proud of in these final moments.

Her mind told her the harsh truth—for many years her needs, her wants, her beauty had been everything. And she was dying because of it.

Yes, it was her vanity that caused her to be captured from the beginning. It was her vanity that made her isolation in the dark pit useful to the stern woman and later made her vulnerable to Tumultor. And it was her vain staring at her reflection in that pond that had pulled at her. Never had she looked so beautiful. She had leaned toward herself and gladly plunged into the water, and then she was swept and drawn through the depths of the pond to the other side, which led to her final captivity.

The beautiful creatures she had seen as she went through the pond had waved and smiled at her and invited her forward. Swimming slowly and easily through the water—by her own power, she thought—she had surfaced full of energy and proud of her accomplishment. Never before had she felt so full and alive as when she emerged from the pond on the other side. Her complete self-absorption had made it easy for Tumultor's men to recapture her.

Tumultor had welcomed her and wooed her for three years, and though she had resisted, she had finally given in.

The stern woman's use of mirrors, weakening her will with constant images of her beauty, had tempted her to ignore her memories of her family and all they stood for against Chimera and his sons. These appeals to her vanity were filled with repeated promises of a lavish wedding and the hope of again being treated like royalty. But it had all been a self-loving dream. Never had she been so empty. So her mind, in its last flickers of life, told her.

And now she knew herself to be dying. For hours she had slept deeply in a bitterly cold wind. She dreamed she was flying. Now it was warmer, but she could feel herself falling asleep for the last time. All she needed was one last step, and this step, freely chosen, would be death, her final surrender. But still, along with the death that she knew lay but one step before her, she had that one last pleasant memory—seeing her dear sister Eraina again and putting her own body in front of a spear for the sake of her sister and her sister's friends.

Her eyes were closed, but she could imagine what was happening. The dream was real, and her mind was telling her what she could still barely feel and hear. But wait! Others are here! Is it Tumultor trying to make her drink the water? Yes, but here come her sisters to help! She is being hoisted on someone else's back, like the game of piggyback they had played when they were children, though in those days, she, being the oldest, had carried them.

But who is this carrying her? Is he a friend? Is he stepping in water? Oh, just below her feet is a glassy pool. But no! It looks just like the one she saw years earlier, the one that led to her final capture! Stop! She did *not* marry Tumultor! They couldn't make her drink the water! Her sister and her friends came at just the right time, and now Tumultor and the woman can't make her look again at her reflection in the pond! If they push her in and she drowns, she will at least die in her purity, with a new dress, not Tumultor's gaudy wedding gown, still on her. They can force her body to submit, but not her mind. She will die knowing who she is, a daughter of Carr. If they force her into this pond, the beautiful creatures who greeted her the last time, friends of Tumultor, will surely not welcome her as before. But even if they kill her, she will not again be their ally.

What are those sounds? Voices. One screechy, one young. Are they arguing? Over her? Over who gets her dead body? What is that terrible burning that is tearing into her back? And now, something from behind pushes her forward. The water splashes on her face as they plunge into the watery abyss! No time for a deep breath.

So this is what dying feels like . . .

The pain in her back sent a shock through Charissa's body, but in her weakened state, she could only groan—though the sound was quickly muffled by the water. She partly opened her eyes. The force of the eagle's pressure on her back simultaneously pushed her into Hamelin's back, so he didn't need his hands behind her knees to hold her there—she was pinned between him and the eagle. And the strength of the great bird drove all three of them through the water.

An onslaught from the watery creatures started immediately. It reminded Hamelin of his previous plunge, but now the monsters lunged and flew at him more numerously and furiously than before. All the old images were there in their strange combinations of long, slithering, and slashing fishlike bodies. The faces of rats and the masks of monsters constantly loomed before him, teeth and tentacles snapping and grabbing, claws and paws swiping and snatching.

Hamelin remembered that in his earlier passage through the waters, the monsters of the deep had rushed at him with snarling intent, only to vanish just as they reached him. But this time, as the eagle had predicted, they didn't disappear just before they struck. The first beast that swiped at him drew blood from his right shoulder. He not only felt the pain of that blow but now understood that he would have to do more than hang on—he would have to fight.

So Hamelin struck back fiercely. His gloved hands and his thrashing legs and feet punched, jabbed, and otherwise kicked and pushed the beasts as they attacked him from every direction. Even under water, he could hear the gurgling snarls and roars of these sea monsters as they flew at him. Mixtures of men and mammals, reptilian birds with sharkish thrusts, and creature after creature—crazed and frenzied by the evil that propelled them—all struck at him in a squidlike rush from every conceivable angle and with unexpected speed, faster than before.

But the deeper they plunged, the more Hamelin felt Charissa's life stirring in her body and the more he—with the desperation of someone who had nothing to lose and the hope of everything to gain—found strength to fight. His vision was clear; his blows were direct. Like a trained fighter who has practiced the arts that come only from discipline, struggle, and pain, he fought back and one after another repelled the monsters surging at him and Charissa within the watery pit.

The direction of the eagle's thrust now reached its lowest point, and he began to push up. His mighty strokes were stronger than ever as the waters, Hamelin assumed, were also starting to heal the wound in the great bird's side.

Then the onslaught stopped. Hamelin relaxed just briefly, but suddenly he felt pressure around his shoulders and legs. He twisted and was about to break free when he realized that it was Charissa—her arms and legs in their own strength wrapping themselves around him!

The eagle was still propelling them upward through the waters, and Hamelin glanced quickly just above him to see that there was a great light shining above the surface. He looked around one last time, and too late he saw the last hideous creature, same as before—part lion, part goat, and part snake—slithering toward him from his left in a final rush.

He knew immediately that his punch would be too late. But as it opened its maw wide and closed in, Charissa's long left leg shot out and delivered a kick to the creature's throat. The monster's rush was stalled, and the extra split second allowed Hamelin to give him a furious backhanded strike with his closed fist. The creature tumbled away at high speed in a fog of cold blue.

Hamelin then felt Charissa aiding the eagle in reaching the surface, using her arms and legs to stroke and provide more upward thrust to the bird's momentum. A moment later, Hamelin's face broke the waters, and all three—Hamelin, Charissa, and the Great Eagle—exploded into the air above the pond inside the Atrium of the Worlds. They were facing west, and while still in midair, Hamelin and Charissa both immediately saw—because of the morning light that now filled the room—their true figures shining back at them from the crystal sea above the western throne.

In that split second of vision, Hamelin wondered if he had also seen another figure in the midst of that cloudy crystal glory. It had the likeness of a man but quickly vanished as the princess, the boy, and the eagle fell dripping and gasping, but exhilarated, at the edge of the pond.

Hamelin and Charissa lay on their backs, spewing water, panting for air—and laughing with joy. The great bird screeched, and Hamelin was pretty sure it was a cry of triumph.

Charissa, her eyes and face now full of life, sat up and said, "I remember this place. I was here before. And that pond . . ." She quickly looked away from it to Hamelin and then the eagle and said, "That's the pond that drew me in and led me—"

"But I didn't get here in time," interrupted Hamelin quickly. "I was supposed to be here to help you three and a half years ago . . . but I failed." He looked away in shame.

"Oh," she said thoughtfully. She looked at the eagle and then back to Hamelin. "*You* were the ones I was waiting for? Well, the lion did say 'an eagle and a boy'—"

"But it was my fault," said Hamelin, "not the eagle's."

"Enough," said the great bird.

"I agree," said Charissa. "You're here now and that's what matters. Oh, Hamelin, Eraina's friend, and Sir Eagle, I thank you both." And even with the water still dripping from her face, Hamelin could see the tears that filled her eyes.

The great bird nodded, and if eagles can ever have a gentle look on their faces, the Great Eagle did at that moment.

Charissa smiled, but then her expression quickly changed again. "The water is so amazing, but the creatures . . . They welcomed me before, but this time they attacked."

"They were the same creatures each time," said Hamelin. "What you saw the first time was a lie. You were under some kind of spell and not your true self. They were friendly because they wanted you to be captured by Tumultor." He looked at the eagle. "Right?"

"Yes," said the eagle, looking directly at Charissa. "They are the waters of death *and* life."

"I know they can heal," said Charissa. "But how are these healing waters also the waters of death?"

"As life, they heal. As death, they deceive," said the eagle. "Forty-two months ago, you were entranced by the reflection of the water, and the creatures took advantage of your weakened, deceived mind. What we all saw this time is the way they really are. They are not good, but they can disguise themselves to pretend they are."

Charissa sat quietly, with her eyes closed, in deep, painful thought.

"I was such a *fool*," she said. "I—"

"Enough," said the eagle. "You said before that you were wrong, and now you have confessed it again. It is enough."

They all sat silently for long moments, still breathing deeply.

"I feel so strong," said Charissa, interrupting the silence. "So full of life. And my side!" She touched the spot where the wound had been and now saw only a small scar. "It's healed! Oh, thank you, Hamelin!"

But Hamelin didn't look at her. He could only look at the Great Eagle. Charissa also turned to the eagle, who looked at her and then at Hamelin.

And then she remembered. She looked at the eagle's great talons. "My back . . . you . . . it hurt so, but . . ."

Hamelin looked at her back and said, "Your back looks fine, but . . . I can still see some marks where the talons held you. Maybe the scars will go away."

"I don't care if they don't," said Charissa as she continued to look at the eagle. "I thank you, kind sir. I hope the scars stay. It hurt terribly . . . but it was a kindness I'll never forget."

The room was becoming warm with the light from the morning sun now exploding through the hole high up in the eastern wall. The eagle could allow no more talking, so he said quickly, "Come, there is still much to be done. Grab hold—we must go."

He suddenly propelled himself upward five feet with rapid strokes of his great wings and suspended himself. He then stretched out his powerful legs so that Hamelin and Charissa could each grab one of them. Then the bird rapidly continued his ascent through the Atrium, perched momentarily at the hole in the eastern wall, and flew out the opening, with Hamelin and Charissa hanging on.

Even though their weight swung downward and pulled at the eagle's feet, the great bird was hardly slowed, continuing to climb higher. The waters had healed him as well. He climbed quickly into the heavens and with speed and power flew furiously back toward the Forest of Fears.

Hamelin and Charissa clung to him as they soared above the clouds, with Hamelin occasionally adding a gloved hand of support to Charissa. Off they flew, shouting and laughing all the way to the home of the Hospitable Woman.

Chapter 29

The Reunion

I T WAS NOW WELL PAST MIDDAY AS ERAINA AND LARS fought their exhaustion on the last leg of their journey back to Sue Ammi. The sun was breaking through the heavy clouds, and from the base of the mountains, they thought they could see smoke rising from a chimney in the distance. Though still a good way off, they hoped the end of their journey was near.

With the aid of her scarf, Eraina continuously looked in all directions, but especially behind them, to see if Tumultor's men were in sight.

Just as they both thought to themselves that perhaps the worst was now over, the storm clouds regathered, and the brief sunshine they had seen after the sleet storm now turned into a downpour, a deluge of rain that brought rivulets down every part of the mountains and further soaked the ground at their feet. Eraina found herself once again slipping and falling as both of them slogged through heavy mud.

"I can't believe this," she complained. "Just when you have a flicker of hope, something worse happens. Why?" Beneath her angry words was the fear that her sister had died.

Though Lars previously had responded sharply himself, he now spoke with a softness in his voice. "Eraina," he started, "I've been thinking about that too. You know what I think?"

"I'm sure you're going to tell me!" she said.

"I am. And I think you may even like what I say."

"Hmpf," she muttered.

"Really, Eraina, I mean it. Listen for just a moment. Please." Eraina looked at him. She didn't speak or even nod. Lars continued, "Look, all the trouble we've gone through on this journey back—I know it's been really hard on us, but it has to have been hard on Hamelin and Charissa too. And the eagle didn't look all that strong himself."

"So I'm supposed to *like* that?"

"Please. Let me finish."

Eraina's face softened just a bit. Lars continued, "And all the bad weather we've had—the cold wind, the snow, the driving sleet, and now these miserable flooding rains—as hard as it's been on us, can you imagine how hard it's been on Tumultor and his men, especially on horseback? And didn't you expect them to have caught us by now? The eagle said we'd probably need help. Well, maybe all this trouble is the help we needed."

The thought almost stopped Eraina in her tracks. She looked at Lars and suddenly broke down in tears. "I'm just so frightened. Not for me, not really. I've been scared before, like I was in the Forest of Fears when the wolves were coming, but I really haven't been scared for you or me all this past night and morning. I'm afraid for Charissa. She suffered so much. And then the wound from the spear—she looked so bad.

"But really, what's bothered me most has been how one jab did so much harm—she just stepped in front of the spear! Why did it have to happen? We had her! We were almost free!"

"I know," said Lars softly, "but she stepped in front of it for me, and I'm grateful for that. I'm terribly sorry she was hurt, but maybe there's a reason for that too."

"Maybe," said Eraina as she looked away from Lars. "She was so weak and feverish. What if she's dead?"

"I don't think she is," said Lars. "I don't know why I feel that way, but I just think Charissa is alive, and Hamelin too. That eagle is a powerful bird. And did you see how strong Hamelin was? And not just because of his gloves. He was courageous, standing up to the eagle, arguing that they take her to the pond. I've still got hope.

"And besides, think again about Tumultor and his band of idiots. Can you imagine them in the snow trying to get through that mountain pass, slipping and sliding in the sleet, and now this downpour of rain with mud up to our ankles? I'd rather be walking than on horseback!"

"Yeah, me too. Even without special shoes," she said with a tiny smile as she looked at Lars's feet. He smiled.

They walked on, and the downpour stopped almost as quickly as it started.

With her scarf down over her eyes, Eraina took one last look all around but saw nothing. Even if Tumultor and his men had followed, they had no drive, no heart for the chase. They were young and strong, but they weren't tough.

Eraina then turned back with her scarf still over her head to look for the home of Sue Ammi. It suddenly came into view.

"There it is!" she said. "SueSue's house!" At the same moment, her eyes caught a glimpse of a strange sight in the sky to the southeast. She turned directly toward it, and Lars could hear her sharp intake of breath followed by a scream of joy.

Eraina immediately knew what she saw, but she could hardly believe her eyes. It was the great bird flying with powerful strokes toward the home of Sue Ammi and two others swinging beneath him, alternately holding on with one hand and waving with the other. Occasionally one of them, the boy, reached out to hold the girl.

"Look!" she cried to Lars, who looked up and even without the scarf could now see them. They broke into a dead run, racing toward the great bird and his two passengers.

The Great Eagle landed in front of Sue Ammi's cabin, and it didn't take long for Eraina and Lars to catch up. All four of the young people ran to each other, laughing and yelling. Eraina jumped shoulder to shoulder into Charissa and threw her arms like ropes around her neck. Hamelin and Lars laughed and slapped each other on the back.

And just then Sue Ammi opened the door and walked out, smiling, with her arms open wide to receive her guests.

Chapter 30

Joy and Next Steps

I T WAS A REUNION LIKE NONE OF THEM HAD EVER EXPERI-enced. The two sisters, still hugging and jumping, laughed and cried till they had almost no tears or shouts of joy left. The two boys shook hands but then placed their hands on each other's shoulders—and hugged as well. Soon they were all swept up into the arms of Sue Ammi, like children who had come home again after a long time away.

SueSue then moved over to the Great Eagle, stooped down on one knee before him, and extended her hands, palms up, with her head bowed just a little lower than the great bird's. When she looked up, their eyes met, and she said, "Thank you, noble guide and warrior." The eagle looked at her, blinked, nodded, and suddenly took off straight upward above their heads, soaring faster and faster up the sheer side of the mountain while everyone watched.

Hamelin figured the bird would ascend higher than the peak of the mountain and from there disappear northward over it. But he was wrong. The bird was for sure near the top, but he vanished so suddenly that Hamelin could no longer see his mighty profile against the clear sky. The bird was gone, but as far as Hamelin could tell, he hadn't gone over the mountain. Hamelin was puzzled and looked quickly at SueSue.

She smiled and said to him quietly, "He has a spot up there, a nest. This is one of the many places he patrols and guards."

Disappointed and wishing he had thanked him, or at least said good-bye, Hamelin went into the house with the others. Just as he crossed the threshold, he glanced to his left. For a fleeting moment, he saw bare feet vanishing up the steps. Probably, he thought, the girl he had glimpsed on his first visit.

Just entering SueSue's house was a relief, which made them quieter, though no less happy. They were also tired and hungry, but the Hospitable Woman knew how to remedy that. She sent them upstairs to the bedrooms, where, as before, they could bathe. Charissa was sent to SueSue's room.

After bathing, they found new clothes laid out for them. They dressed, and hearing SueSue call their names, they walked down the steps and to the table, which was set magnificently for a late lunch surpassing any they could have hoped for.

They ate, they talked, they relived their experiences, and they also at times grew silent, content to look into the faces of one another and nod and smile. When the meal was over, Hamelin, Eraina, and Lars were sent upstairs to rest, but SueSue asked Charissa to stay behind. No one knew the details of their conversation, but for Charissa, they were words she would never forget. Though much later, she did tell Eraina one thing. SueSue had told her that if one day, at the end of her life, her story was ever recounted by others, she must strive now to be remembered as not the most beautiful queen who ever lived but the humblest woman her subjects ever knew.

After resting all through the afternoon, the four of them came downstairs again in the evening for supper. They dined again to the full, enjoying each moment, every look and snatch of conversation, in the presence of their friends. SueSue, at the head of the table, quietly smiled, and for just a moment, Hamelin thought he could see in her face a faint reminder of the light that had shone from the eagle when he had led him through the cave.

They got up from the table and, after clearing it, took time to enjoy the night sky. The passing of the storms left the air crisp and the stars bright. SueSue served them all a special hot drink that none of them had ever heard of. It had the color and smell of chocolate to Hamelin, with the faint taste of coconut and vanilla, but there was something else he couldn't identify. Eraina guessed there was maybe some clove and cardamom spice in it.

SueSue called it "candosheen" but just laughed when they asked what was in it. She then grew quiet while they all stirred and sipped their drinks. At times, she hummed while everyone sat and thought. For a moment, Hamelin wished she were his mother, but then he realized that he shouldn't be selfish and that, besides, he had a mother and a father he longed to find.

Finally, SueSue sent them all to bed. She hadn't asked them any more about what happened, but she seemed somehow to know a lot. They slept soundly. Their dreams brought them again not only the moments they had shared but also images and feelings of things they had gone through.

Lars dreamed of leaping from the rail in the Great Hall. Hamelin again felt the sword in his hands. Eraina could see

the pale face of Charissa in the cavern as she bathed it with
cool water. And Charissa could feel the eagle's sharp claws in
her back, always followed by cool water and the face of her
sister Eraina. Alongside all the images that passed through
their minds, there were scenes of happy endings. They could
still feel the peace and contentment of the successes they
had been granted.

The next morning, they awoke to the songlike sounds
of Sue Ammi calling them downstairs. Hamelin noticed
his blue jeans, shirt, jacket, and sweater were all clean and
folded, so he put them on. The breakfast had something for
everyone—fruits, cheese, bread, butter, jam, hot cereal, and
eggs. The meal ended all too quickly, and everyone wanted
to help SueSue clean the table and do the dishes. Hamelin
wondered if he was the only one besides her who had ever
done dishes, but this wasn't like the chores at the children's
home. They all wanted to help, and mostly they wanted to
be with each other and to stay near SueSue.

They were surprised to learn, however, just as the dishes
were washed and put away, that they had to leave.

"I wish you could stay, but rest and happy times also prepare us for our work. And all of you have tasks to complete."

They quickly gathered up their things, and SueSue led
them out to the front of her house again and pointed south
toward the Forest of Fears.

"This time my instructions are simple, but the outcome
still uncertain."

"Uncertain?" asked Hamelin. "Is Tumultor chasing us?"

SueSue paused. Her eyes narrowed as she seemed to be
thinking. "Who or what you will encounter I cannot predict.
But you must go into the Forest of Fears again and then find
the path that will take you to its western side. There you'll

find a road that will lead you through some open country before it forks near the kingdom of Lars's father, Elwood."

"I know that road," said Lars.

"Yes," she said, "you do."

"Good," said Eraina. "So by then we'll be past the Forest of Fears?"

"Yes," SueSue said with a small tilt of her head. "But fear is not always bad and trouble not always where you expect it. The road is a good one, but you'll be in the open, so watch, and stay on the lookout."

The four young people all silently nodded.

"Lars, you'll keep the jewel with you. Your friends will travel with you, but then, where the road forks close to Periluna, you must continue on by yourself to your father's kingdom to restore the jewel. It may be harder than you expect.

"Then," she said, turning to the other three, "you, Hamelin, must escort Eraina and Charissa from there back over open country to the southwest." She then looked especially at Eraina and Charissa. "Eventually you will come to the encampment, just outside the city of Parthogen, where your sister Sophia and your father are waiting for you. You must use what you've learned as daughters of a king. And—listen carefully now—when you are home again, you must attend closely to the words of the prophecy, which tell you to 'pay heed to the words of wisdom' and that when 'the living heirs of the king are reunited and the four thrones filled, the evil creatures will be overcome.'"

All of them nodded solemnly at SueSue. With extra hugs and many thank-yous, more deeply felt than any of them could put into words, they left the sanctuary-like home of Sue Ammi.

Chapter 31

Between
Locusts and
Horses

T HE FOUR FRIENDS BEGAN THEIR JOURNEY SOUTH BACK
toward the Forest of Fears. Their instructions were to
travel under its cover and then, emerging from the Forest on its western edge, to continue toward Periluna, where
they would part from Lars near an aboveground entrance
to the city. They walked at a hard pace. Lars was eager to
get the jewel replaced, and all of them felt sure that Tumultor had not given up.

Once they reached the Forest, it was midday, but they still
had a long way to go. From the northernmost edge of the
Forest, they found a path that struck a direction southwest,
which would allow them, as instructed, to exit at its western
edge and from there pick up the path that would lead toward
Periluna.

They knew they wouldn't be able to make it all the way
through the Forest before nightfall, but they had to cover all
the ground they could. The Forest was a fearful place, and
when Eraina mentioned the possibility that Landon's dogs

might show up from the south and Charissa expressed her fears that Tumultor was likely behind them in pursuit, their anxieties increased.

It was past sundown and getting dark quickly when they found a good spot for making camp, one with enough clearing on the ground and a canopy of trees overhead. Being a newcomer to the Forest, Charissa was leery of staying there during the night, but the others assured her that they had been through it before and that they would make it through the night without incident. Their words had more confidence than their feelings.

They first made a small fire, then laid out the foods Sue-Sue had provided. They spent the evening around the fire, quietly telling stories of their families and their lives growing up. As the night wore on, they became more relaxed and animated, especially as they began to relive their most recent adventures.

The boys were dramatic storytellers, especially Lars, as they competed to tell Charissa all that happened from the time they had first met. But Eraina wasn't shy about interrupting the boys in their stories to correct or add details from her point of view. She especially enjoyed, when the boys got too exaggerated about their feats, reminding them of the bridge and how Lars was going to just run out there and "dance around a bit." Lars rolled his eyes, but he also smiled sheepishly. It was obvious he regretted those words.

The story of the wedding proved to be a particularly favorite memory for them all, as they each relived it from their own perspective. Hamelin finished his recounting of it by describing the eerie battle that had taken place in the upper chamber of the Great Hall. The others were hushed when he told of the upward flight of the sword, which struck the bear before it fell to its final resting place in the Rock.

He looked at Eraina. "You saw it all too, didn't you, with the scarf?"

"Yes, I saw the fight, and I'm sure it was the same bear I saw at the bridge. And the light that spewed out when he roared came all the way down to us. Maybe he was trying to kill us again. But the jewel was taking in the light and not letting it out. That's why Charissa couldn't run away. Until you threw the sword."

"I wondered why you had thrown the sword upward," said Lars. "I just thought either it slipped or your aim was terrible!" Everyone laughed.

"No," said Eraina. "His aim was amazing! Hit the bear right in the side of his head!"

"So that's what released the pull on the chain?" asked Charissa.

"Yes," said Eraina. "Someday I want to ask SueSue more about it, but that's what I saw. The eagle was in a struggle that was invisible to most everyone but probably saved us all."

"And Hamelin maybe also saved the eagle," said Charissa softly.

Everyone fell silent and stared into the fire.

Minutes later, Eraina took up much of the rest of the storytelling, especially those parts that Charissa had been too weak to see.

Most of the stories ended up with laughter, even when the girls sometimes combined their laughter with tears and hugs.

But then, in another quiet moment, Lars asked Charissa about her story. Admitting what she had done, especially to these new friends, not to mention her little sister, was hard—even humiliating. She told her story with tears and shame but left nothing out, from the time of her embarrassing capture by Landon's men, to her fears and loneliness in the darkness of the cellar, to her escape and journey to the Atrium of the Worlds with the help of a massive mountain lion, to finally her vain plunge through the reflecting pond when her two helpers didn't show up as the lion had said.

Charissa never looked at Hamelin when she referred vaguely to her "two helpers." Everyone was silent.

"It's okay to say it, Charissa," said Hamelin. "I've already told them that you were waiting on the eagle and me, and that I was the one who was afraid to continue."

He then reminded them of the story of how he had failed to cross the footbridge, and he ended by saying, "That's when I should've been there the *first* time, three and a half years ago." He then looked at Charissa. "I'm sorry, Charissa."

"No, Hamelin. Please. There's no need to keep apologizing. Certainly I forgive you, but my guilt is greater. The lion knew my weakness and warned me not to go near the pool when it was light."

"But if only I had arrived in time," Hamelin said as he put his hand on his forehead and shaded his eyes.

"But your failure was . . . well, in the end, it turned out to be fortunate for us both."

"Fortunate? How's that?"

"First, I've learned a lot about myself. Back then, even after my first escape from the woman, my vanity still controlled me—and that's why the lion led me to the Atrium and the pond."

"I don't understand," said Eraina.

"Well, I now know that I needed the pond, not just to heal my body, but to heal me. I was afraid of the darkness, mostly because I remembered the cellar where the woman kept me and how terrible it made me look. So when I saw myself in the pond, I let myself be deceived."

"What happened then?" said Eraina.

"The woman came to Osmethan and gained control of me again, but even her use of darkness and mirrors for these past three-plus years did not completely extinguish the memory of my home and family. I learned to remember, to wait, and to try to hope. But just when my vanity had won out and I had finally agreed to marry Tumultor, you came back."

"But still . . ." Hamelin said as he shook his head and looked down.

"No, Hamelin. Please. No more regrets," said Charissa. "The waters you took me through have begun to heal me, and I'm determined to be different.

"And as for you . . . well, it was your failure that later made you so determined to take me back through the pond. That saved my life and changed my heart, Hamelin. It worked for good, for you and me."

Charissa paused and shook her head, apparently remembering a dark time. She poked the fire with a stick and continued. "Yes. All of it has been used. Nothing wasted."

They sat silently. Finally, Eraina hugged her sister. Even the boys leaned in, and all four embraced.

When the fire finally burned low, the boys established an alternate watch, and the girls slept near each other to keep warm and also to whisper some sister talk.

Hamelin heard occasional howling in the distance, and even though it didn't sound near, he was glad when Lars stayed awake with him during most of his watch, so he wouldn't be alone. And Lars, with the jewel around his neck and the embers of the fire glowing into it, took comfort in the presence of his friends while they slept, in spite of his dislike of the dark.

They got up before dawn, washed as quickly as they could using the dew of the ground and small amounts of their water supply, and broke camp. With their early start, it was only two and a half hours before they emerged from the thicker part of the woods and found the trees thinning before them. Within another thirty minutes, they had cleared the western edge of the Forest of Fears and were now traveling west on the path that, after it forked, would lead to Periluna. Though they didn't say it out loud, they were all amazed: the place that had caused them all so much fear was far behind them, and nothing bad had happened.

Getting through the Forest of Fears gave all of them a shot of confidence. None of them would admit how fearful they had been last night. Even though they had enjoyed reliving their stories around the campfire, there had been a cloud of anxiety that they had been unable to shake.

But now their fears evaporated with the morning mist. They were talking and laughing, teasing one another, and enjoying the freshness of the new day. In fact, they were all so relieved that no one thought it necessary to ask Eraina to use her scarf to see if Tumultor's men were still following them. Tumultor had probably either given up the chase or lagged so far behind that he would never catch them. They also figured that he and his men were as fearful of staying in the Forest of Fears as they had been, maybe even more.

———

Tumultor was in fact furious that it had taken so long to gather his forces to pursue the three strangers who had humiliated him by disrupting his wedding. But he was espe-cially enraged over Charissa and the jewel. The blocking of the flow of water was bad, but surely his father, Chimera, could remedy that. But losing the jewel was an outrage. And he would make the pretty daughter of Carr pay for her treachery. He should never have believed her professions of love!

But first, the jewel. Fortunately, chasing one would recover the other. But the snow, sleet, and rainstorm had dramatically slowed the progress of his men and their horses. They finally made it through the mountain pass and then tracked their prey a short distance eastward along the mountain range, but the chase was not going well. His men might have mutinied if he had forced them into the Forest of Fears by night, so instead they camped near the mountains. Then as soon as the morning sun was up, they resumed their pursuit. The horses had slept, and the storms had passed, so Tumultor was intent upon closing the gap between him and his quarry. They moved slowly until they picked up the trail of Charissa and her three rescuers early that morning, and now they were crashing through the woods at an aggres-sive speed.

Though the day had started fresh and sunny, the four friends soon detected a change in the weather. They noticed that winds from the northwest began to blow as they made their journey westward. The winds were not harsh, but there was clearly a stirring in the air. They traveled through lands more familiar to Lars than to Eraina and Charissa, while the entire landscape was new to Hamelin. To the north, they noticed a rolling, grassy plain, and far in the distance, there appeared to be some dark-green patches in the landscape.

Lars explained, "That's a lightly wooded area, and a river very important to my father's kingdom flows through it—the River Starfall." He told his friends that the river began just south of the mountain range they had gone through to get to Osmethan.

"The river is formed from the many small streams that flow down from the mountains. Just where those green patches are, the streams combine to make a shallow river that flows southwest."

He pointed out with a sweep of his hand how the river flowed from those green patches to an area just over a small rise in the path before them. "There we'll find a lake. It looks like a big lake, but it's really very shallow."

"Why's that?" asked Hamelin.

"Well, the river flows down into the lake in a beautiful waterfall. Directly beneath the spot where it hits the lake is a hole that allows the water to drain and become an underground river that flows down into my father's kingdom. It supplies much of our water. Around that hole, the basin of the lake is shallow."

"Oh," said Charissa, "Eraina and I heard all about this waterfall in our geography lessons growing up, but we never knew that it flowed underground into Periluna."

The four friends were eager to see the waterfall, and while they looked toward the area that Lars indicated, they noticed two other things. First, the wind was clearly picking up, and there was a coldness in it as it now blew into them even harder from the northwest, making their walk more difficult. Second, on the western horizon, a dark cloud began to emerge. It looked like a coming rainstorm. In fact, it looked like it was going to be a hard rain, because the cloud was very dark.

They began to pick up their pace. And now, perhaps because the conditions had changed, or perhaps because they no longer felt quite as comfortable as they had at the beginning of the morning, Lars suggested to Eraina that she pull her scarf over her face and look around.

"Take a look at that approaching storm and see if there's any lightning or hail in it, and if you want, you could glance back one more time to make sure Tumultor is still nowhere near."

"Tumultor?" she said. The very mention of his name seemed to surprise Eraina and clearly bothered her. So instead of checking on the storm, she pulled the scarf over her head and immediately looked back toward the east.

"Oh, no," she said sharply. "He's there! I see him!"

"Where?" asked Hamelin.

"Is he coming through the Forest of Fears?" asked Lars.

"No! Worse!" yelled Eraina. "He and his men are already through the Forest of Fears, and they are in a full gallop right toward us!"

"What?" yelled Lars. "How did they—?"

"It's all my fault," groaned Eraina before Lars could finish. "I should've been looking!"

"We *all* forgot," said Lars.

"There's no time for regrets now," said Charissa quickly.

"We can't stay here!" yelled Hamelin. "Where to?"

"There's only one way to go now," yelled Lars. "We've got to stay on this path and make a run for it! Come on! If we can get to the waterfall, there may be some places we can hide. At least we'll be closer to Periluna!"

With those words, the four friends broke into a full sprint. But it wasn't long before they had to stop to rest.

"Look," Lars said. "It's too far to the waterfall for us to try to sprint all the way. We'll have to try a steady run, maybe at half speed for now. Eraina, keep checking to see how close Tumultor and his men are. In the meantime, at least until we can see them with the naked eye, we'll know we have a little distance on them."

"Yes," said Charissa, still panting, "but they've got horses, and I know Tumultor. He's fierce and vicious, and I promise you we don't want to get caught."

"And Hamelin's sword is gone now," added Eraina, "and even with his strength, it's only four of us against all of them, with their horses and weapons."

So the four friends started to run again, and though they had said they would go at half speed, their fears pushed them forward faster and faster.

But Tumultor was not their only worry. The dark cloud that had been forming in front of them had grown. Eraina used her scarf and quickly realized that it wasn't even a cloud. As they got closer, they all could see it too—the mass above them had no light or billowy edges to it like a rain cloud. It was a huge, ever-changing shape, like thousands of black dots held together.

Then they realized it was more like a massive swarm, maybe of bees or locusts. The swarm rapidly approached them from the west, coming even faster than Tumultor and his men. They all still knew they had to run away from Tumultor. But what were they running toward?

Chapter 32

The Mad Dash

THE FOUR SPED TOWARD THE MENACING CLOUD, WHICH
blotched and spread in the sky before them. They still
couldn't make out the creatures that formed the swarm
or what they could or would do. Still, since Tumultor was the
immediate threat and they knew what he was capable of,
they kept racing westward, into the oncoming swarm.

Finally, after running at near top speed for a long time,
they had to stop. They were all out of breath and their legs
burned—except for Lars, who had been slowing himself to
stay at the others' pace. He waited for everyone to catch their
breath and regather their strength.

Eraina, still panting, quickly pulled her scarf around her
head and looked back eastward. "Oh no!" she yelled. "He's
so close now you can probably see him for yourselves."

As soon as she said that, Lars yelled out, "I think I see
him—and his men—right there!" Lars pointed. Sure enough,
Charissa and Hamelin soon quickly made out the small,

dark dots of horses and the cloud of dust behind them. It wouldn't be long before Tumultor's men would catch them.

Though three of them were still breathing heavily, they all knew they would have to start running again soon. They stood for just a moment longer, taking a few more deep breaths.

Then Eraina looked to the west.

"What is it, Eraina?" asked Hamelin.

"Well," she said. "I thought I'd try to get a closer look at whatever it is that's in that cloud."

"What do you see?" Lars asked quickly.

"It's the strangest thing I've ever seen . . ."

"What *is* it, Sister?" said Charissa.

"Thousands of locustlike creatures. It's . . . it's a huge swarm of locusts, but they're not really locusts. They have bodies like locusts, but there's something about them—as if they're wearing armor—that looks like they're ready for battle. Their tails look like scorpions' tails, and I'm not sure, but they're in some kind of formation like they're war horses."

And then a sound, low at first but growing, came from above them.

"What is that?" asked Hamelin.

"I hear it too," said Lars. "It's something humming."

A memory shot into Hamelin's mind—of the sound he, Bryan, and Layla had heard at the mouth of the cave, like thousands of wings beating at once. He then remembered the creatures that had flown out of the cave.

Lars's sudden shout cut through his memories. "We've got to run!"

"But those things are headed our way!" yelled back Eraina.

"We've got no choice!" Charissa answered. "I *know* what's coming behind us, and whatever it costs us to go forward, we've *got* to do it!"

Without another word, they were off and running again, Tumultor's men coming behind them at a hard pace and the swarming creatures now at most only a few hundred yards in front of them.

About then, Tumultor and his men spotted their prey in the distance, and so they whipped their horses to top speed. It was a race between life and death, and to the four young people, what lay before them, though unknown, appeared as dangerous as what was chasing them. But still they raced forward on the path as fast as they could possibly go.

Lars could have gone much faster, but he knew he had to stay with the others. He worked to stay at a speed that was just fast enough to keep him in front of the other three, hoping to draw them along at the fastest pace they had. They were all healthy and had good foot speed, but Charissa, because of her captivity, was not used to being outdoors and active.

"How much farther to the waterfall?" yelled Hamelin.

"It's not that far!" yelled back Lars between big breaths. "See that brake of trees just ahead? The trees surround the riverbed on each side! Right where those trees come to an end is where the river drops off . . . just to our left!"

"Where are we going to hide?" yelled back Eraina. "It won't do us . . . any good . . . to go into the trees to hide . . . Tumultor can already see us!"

"I've got an idea," he yelled back. "Just trust me and follow close! You've got to do whatever I do."

At just that moment, Charissa tripped and fell.

"Go on!" she screamed to the others.

"Are you kidding?" said Hamelin as he ran to her. "We didn't come this far to leave you!"

"I need just another second," she said.

Now the three friends were huddled around Charissa as she sat panting on the ground.

"So what's your plan, Lars?" asked Hamelin.

Lars looked around at the anxious faces staring at him and said, "We've got to jump."

"*Jump*?" the other three said at the same time.

"Yes! Look, we've got to get to the middle of the river, which I know is shallow enough. And then we've got to run downstream for all we're worth and jump right off into the waterfall."

"But I thought you said the lake was shallow," said Hamelin.

"It is—but if we position ourselves right, we could hit right into the deeper area beneath the waterfall, the one that leads to Periluna. The opening is deep enough there so we won't hit the bottom."

"But what about the hole at the bottom of the lake?" said Charissa, her eyes wide.

"Won't we get sucked in?" asked Hamelin. He knew Charissa was thinking—as he was—about the underground waters they had traveled.

A look of doubt came over Lars's face. "Well, I'm counting on your strength to protect you and the girls."

"You call that an idea?" said Eraina.

"There's no other way!" answered Lars.

Suddenly something buzzed by their heads.

"What was that?" Lars asked while looking around.

Then all at once, they knew. While they had huddled around Charissa, the swarm had come closer. But strangely enough, it had now almost stopped, hovering like a giant swatch of black wool. It seemed to linger just over the spot ahead where Lars said the lake was. But now, some of the locustlike creatures had broken away from the swarm and were buzzing and diving toward them at high speed. One crashed into Lars.

"Ow," he yelled suddenly. "That hurt!"

"Did he sting you?" said Hamelin.

"No," replied Lars. "Not a sting, but it sure felt like a bite or something really hard sticking me in the back."

Another one dove into Eraina. "Ow!" she yelled. "Me, too! One of them just hit me!"

"I think they're scouts," yelled Hamelin as all of them jerked around in search of any other diving creatures from the mass that flew close.

Charissa glanced back at Tumultor and his men and got to her feet. She looked west and nodded in the direction of the swarm. "We've got to run toward it," she said.

"I don't know," said Lars.

Eraina shook her head and yelled, "So what else are we going to do? Sue Ammi said to go through the Forest of Fears and follow Lars as far as Periluna. It may sound stupid, but *that's* the way to Periluna," she said, pointing west. "We *have* to take it!"

No one, especially Hamelin and Lars, could disagree with that. "Let's go!" yelled Lars. They ran as fast as they could, straight toward the biting swarm.

Chapter 33

The Clash and the Jump

B
UT JUST RUNNING WASN'T ENOUGH. CHARISSA WAS severely winded, and the girls' dresses weren't made for running. It became obvious they weren't going to make it to the lake before Tumultor and his men reached them.

Hamelin suddenly had a thought and decided that, even if he wasn't as fast as Lars, at least he was faster than Charissa and probably Eraina as well. He quickly ran toward Charissa, who was just a few paces in front of him, and with his left hand grabbed her right leg just above her knee and, with one motion, lifted her up to his left shoulder and held her there with his hand.

"You, too, Eraina," he yelled. And somehow he managed to bend down and, using his right hand, boost Eraina to his right shoulder. Using the strength in his hands, he held the two girls so that their weight really didn't slow him down.

"Why didn't I do this before?" he yelled.

"Doesn't matter," said Lars, "just keep going!"

The two sisters held hands above Hamelin's head to help their balance, and the race continued. But still it was going to be close. Tumultor's men were closing in on them rapidly, and they had at least two hundred yards still to go.

To make matters worse, more and more of the locusts began to break off from the great swarm and dive toward the four. Lars was doing his best to stay in front to protect them, trying to swát the creatures away, but he wasn't stopping many of them.

"Eraina!" he yelled. "Give me the scarf!"

"What? No!"

"Why not?" yelled Charissa.

"Because SueSue said I should never give it to someone else!" Lars groaned and swatted another locust.

Charissa suddenly grabbed the scarf off Eraina's neck and, with a quick flick of her wrist, tossed it to Lars.

"No!" yelled Eraina. "SueSue said—"

"It's okay!" yelled her sister. "You didn't give it to him; I *took* it! Besides, he's just borrowing it!"

Eraina remembered other occasions of her sisters borrowing her clothes. "I better get it back!" she yelled.

Meanwhile, Lars took the scarf, folded it over lengthwise, and gave it a twist. Holding the two ends with one hand and running in front of his three friends, he waved it back and forth like a floppy club, using it to swat away the buzzing locusts. He was partly successful, but many of the creatures still made it through his flailing perimeter. Hamelin had no way to protect himself since his hands were full holding the two girls. Each of the girls was holding the other with one hand and using her free hand to swat away as many locusts as possible. The experience was torturous—something more physically painful than anything the four had ever endured.

More locusts were now coming directly at them—not the entire swarm, but dozens were breaking away from the greater, overhead mass and flying toward them, biting their faces, arms, and bodies. Hamelin could hardly see. All he could do was follow Lars's feet just in front of him. All of them were yelling, sometimes at the biting locusts, other times just out of pain.

It was a nightmare. Running directly into that swarm was the only way forward, since the lake and the waterfall seemed their only hope of safety. But from the sound of things behind them, Tumultor's horses were thundering closer with every second. The horses' hooves and the clanging swords and shields behind them now sounded so near that Hamelin almost broke his stride to give up. The girls looked at each other in shock, and both knew that they would never get to the river before Tumultor's men overwhelmed them. But Hamelin had learned from the footbridge and the pond, and he refused to stop.

Then something changed. An abrupt alteration in the sounds above and behind them made them realize that something different was happening. The same locusts that were tormenting their race forward suddenly stopped buzzing and biting them. Instead, they flew around them, past them, and over them, and were now zooming toward Tumultor and his men.

Almost instantly, the massive cloud of locusts hovering overhead surged forward and was suddenly behind them, engulfing Tumultor's onrushing forces. The chaos resulting from the collision of the locust army with the mounted army created screams and wails from both men and rearing horses, mixed with the strange smashing of helmet and sword, breastplate and shield against the armored hosts of swarming locusts. Men hollered and horses whinnied as the locusts stung them with their scorpion-like tails. The locusts were now instinctively engaged in full battle maneuvers, diving, breaking off, reforming into smaller swarms, and attacking again.

Hamelin and Lars stopped and quickly turned to see the furious, slashing engagement.

But there was no time to stop and stare. Hamelin, still holding the two princesses, and Lars, still slightly in front of them all, resumed running. Soon they had made it to the trees. The girls slipped down from Hamelin's shoulders, and the four ran quickly through the narrow strip of woods that surrounded the river, jumped into the water, and headed downstream almost to the point where the gently flowing river abruptly crashed over its final rocky point into the lake below.

By now, most of Tumultor's men and horses were completely in disarray, either on the ground, injured, or in panicked flight in all directions. Tumultor was thrown by his horse but was quickly picked up by one of his best soldiers. The two of them, the prince in back, saw their human quarry run off, and together they rode after them, pursuing with a vengeance. Tumultor and his rescuer charged into the woods and quickly made their way to the river. When they saw the four young people in the water, they spurred the horse into the shallow river and steadily moved downstream toward them.

"Okay," said Lars to his three friends. He handed Eraina's scarf back to her. "Here's where we separate."

"Separate? What do you mean?" asked Eraina as she also quickly grabbed her scarf from Lars's hand and loosely tied it around her neck.

"Here's the plan," said Lars. "As much as he wants Charissa, it's the jewel he wants even more. I'm going to distract him. Hamelin, when I draw him away, the three of you have got to make a run for it. Head straight down the river, and jump right at the waterfall."

"Are you sure? What if—"

"I'm telling you, jump straight off. And hang on to the girls. If you jump from the center, exactly between the two side banks, you should be directly over the opening at the bottom of the lake! But watch out for the pull of water into the opening!"

With that, Lars yelled at Tumultor, who was about forty yards upstream but steadily moving toward them, "Hey, you big fool, look what I've got!" He held up the great jewel, which still hung around his neck.

Sure enough, seeing the jewel completely changed Tumultor's focus.

"Give me that," he demanded, "or I'll kill you all!"

"Sure you will," Lars yelled back, "just like you got us back at the wedding! But first you've got to *catch* me!"

Lars then took off running back upstream in the knee-high water toward Tumultor. Just as he got within ten yards of him, however, he quickly shot off to his left and ran past them at high speed. Tumultor's soldier jerked the horse's head upstream toward Lars.

Hamelin saw their chance. He looked at Lars.

"Now!" yelled Lars. And with that, Hamelin and the two girls ran straight downstream, high stepping in the shallow water. Just as the three of them, with Hamelin in the middle, came to the very edge of the waterfall, he grabbed the two girls around their waists. They pulled their legs up as he raced to the edge and jumped with all his might.

Lars glanced at them, and as the heads of his friends disappeared over the river's edge, he could hear a long, shrill, three-person yell, until the scream itself was swallowed by the crashing sounds of the waterfall.

"Well, well! So *that's* your plan? Suicide?" said Tumultor. "That just saves me having to take care of them myself. They'll never survive that jump. And now for *you*."

The two riders charged toward Lars, but with his speed and agility, he jumped this way and that, right and left, came toward the horse, and then suddenly backpedaled in every direction.

The horse was at first spooked by the boy's speed, but soon he got a feel for the game. Like a cutting horse that shifts his front legs, catlike, to isolate a calf from the herd, the stallion worked to keep his head constantly in front of Lars's every feint and move. Snorting and neighing, jumping and turning, the muscular charger was staying with Lars. But the powerful animal proved to be too spirited, though not for Lars—for his riders: after one especially quick jump, both men were thrown off balance and into the river, first Tumultor off the back of the horse and then the soldier sideways. The water was shallow, so they were bruised but still conscious and even angrier.

Lars had now accomplished all he needed with his foot games and tore off downstream as fast as he could. All Tumultor could do was yell. In a futile fit of temper, he stood up, pulled his knife, and threw it, but it fell pitifully short, as Lars, now at high speed, quickly reached the river's edge at the waterfall and jumped. His speed made it easy for him to jump farther than his three friends, and he did it intentionally, hoping not to land on top of them.

A minute before, Hamelin and the two sisters had hit the water, but he had held their bodies upright with his hands and had yelled at them to point their legs down. They entered the water with a loud splash, but, thanks to him, were not slapped by it. Down they plunged, but Hamelin still held on to the two girls so all three of them would stay together. However, as they reached the bottom of their underwater plunge—and before they started back up—he could feel the powerful pull of the opening below. He thrust his legs as hard as he could and simultaneously gave the girls a push upward in the small of their backs. They went up, adding their own leg and arm strokes. Hamelin, with his hands free, then furiously pulled the water toward his sides and propelled himself upward.

As soon as he broke the surface, he looked for the girls. But the river of falling water crashed all around him, and the girls were nowhere in sight. Then he saw out of the corner of his eye something falling. It hit the water with a loud boom, as though a rock had landed about ten feet to his side. Was Tumultor throwing boulders at them?

Suddenly he spied the two girls, who were paddling and gasping for air as they also tried to fling their hair out of their eyes. Hamelin quickly swam toward them to make sure they made it to the muddy shore.

He nervously looked around for Lars, and though it seemed to take longer than he thought it should, Lars's head suddenly exploded above the water's surface. His fast feet aided him in paddling, and he quickly joined the others, who were lying wet, muddy, and exhausted on one of the shallow sides of the lake.

"We can't stay here," Lars said in a loud whisper. "Tumultor thinks the jump is deadly. We don't want him to look down and see that we made it."

So Hamelin, Eraina, and Charissa dragged themselves up and followed Lars. They slipped and slogged behind him around the water's edge and, though stumbling from fatigue, made their way first to some slightly drier ground and then hurried around the side of the waterfall. They then ducked behind it, under a rock overhang, just in time.

They sat there, huddled together, cold and tired, but for the moment safe under the shadow of the rock. Within a minute, they heard the voice of Tumultor above them. Raging like a wounded beast, he apparently was standing in the shallow river above them, near the edge of the waterfall, as he screamed in fury into the basin of the lake below. His voice carried in spite of the roar of the waterfall.

"Don't think you have escaped me, you fools! When I return with more men and dam this river, we'll drain the lake and find your bloated, fish-eaten corpses. Then, my dead bride, I'll yank the jewel from your friend's neck with my own hands. And I'll spit on your once pretty face!

"And if we don't find you, then I'll know that you can hear me now, wherever you four are, huddled and whimpering. This I swear: I will go to Ventradees, to my oldest brother, the powerful Ren'dal, and together we will track you from Ventradees through all the Land of Gloaming. And when we find you, you will be flogged within an inch of death. But then we'll force you to drink the water from the Rock so you will be kept alive. You will then be chained as my slaves in Osmethan, working all day and sleeping on a bed of maggots at night, until you beg to join Ren'dal in Ventradees!"

Finally, Tumultor and his man mounted the horse, went back to gather up as many of his scattered and injured men and horses as they could find, and limped back to Osmethan.

The four friends heard every word of his threats. Charissa shivered and trembled at first, and Hamelin expected her to burst into tears. But all he finally heard was a deep breath followed by an explosive outward puff of her lips, as if she had spit—and her shivering stopped. They huddled together for warmth and waited, while the waters of Starfall roared and crashed around them.

Chapter 34

Reaching Periluna

T HE FOUR FRIENDS WAITED CLOSE TO AN HOUR BEHIND the waterfall. They put cool mud on their arms, faces, and wherever else they had suffered from locust bites, which helped some. Eventually, although stiff and tired, they knew they still had to move on. Eraina led them from behind the waterfall, making use of her scarf along the way. She looked in every direction near and far and was able to report that Tumultor and what was left of his men and horses were already a good distance off and moving away from them.

They found a way up the side of the basin of the lake, which was made easier by their special gifts. The strength in Hamelin's hands and the balance in Lars's feet kept all of them on a path that led back up to the level of the river. When they reached the top, Eraina put her head above ground and with the help of her scarf again confirmed that Tumultor and his men had fully retreated.

"Where are we now?" said Charissa.

"The path to Periluna is right beside the lake," said Lars, pointing just ahead of them.

So with shaky legs, they continued the journey. At first they didn't talk much. Charissa was in deep thought—looking very determined—and just stared ahead. And Hamelin kept thinking about the name Tumultor had used—Ren'dal. What had he said? Ren'dal was his older brother? In Ventradees? The eagle of course had mentioned Ren'dal. And Sue Ammi had said something about defeating him when she talked to him about finding his family. What did Ren'dal have to do with his parents?

But Hamelin's thoughts about such things were interrupted when Charissa suddenly spoke. "I've spent a lot of my life—especially after I told our father a few years ago that I wanted no more training in archery or the tactics of war—selfishly avoiding all discomfort and hardship. And, in the end, that's what got me captured, when I had to have my special bath that evening. But now my training has begun again—with a spear, the eagle's claws in my back, the pond, and things like running toward the locusts."

Eraina hugged her sister and rubbed her back softly for a few moments. "What I don't understand about the locusts, or whatever they were," she said, "is that they attacked us, but then attacked Tumultor's men."

"Yes," said Charissa, "but they saved *us*, though painfully."

"And ruined *them*," said Lars.

"Exactly," said Charissa. "The same trouble, but a different result. I should have learned more from my other pains in life and not just tried to ignore them or avoid facing them. The death of our mother, the appearance of Landon . . ."

The four continued to walk along in silence. They were tired and still hurting. They felt safer, but Eraina used her scarf almost constantly to watch for enemies, especially Tumultor.

They also realized they would soon part. Lars was almost home, but the joy of replacing the jewel wouldn't be as sweet without his friends. No one said it, but all of them dreaded the moment when he would depart and their band of four would be broken.

Within another hour, they reached exactly that point. Periluna now lay due west, and Lars could see, though his home city was below ground, some familiar aboveground landmarks. "Just over there," he said, pointing to a few small, rolling hills and another lightly wooded area. "That's where, just underground, my father's kingdom begins. There's a secret spot where I'll drop below. I wish you could come with me, but SueSue's words were clear . . . we'll have to separate."

The fork in the road was suddenly upon them. They all stood there for a few seconds looking at each other. Eraina especially found it hard to look at Lars, now that she had to part with the friend she had argued with and complained to but also endured many hardships with. Charissa first and then Hamelin hugged Lars, but when Eraina and Lars hugged, it was different from the others—it was briefer though closer—but then Eraina quickly let go and turned her head. Lars promised, with a coughing sound in his throat, to see them all again.

"If you ever need me, I will come, and I'll bring the strength of my father's kingdom with me to help for any cause. For now, I must take the jewel to my father. But I promise, you *will* see me again." With one last shy look at Eraina, he turned and left.

The three stood at the fork in the road for the next fifteen minutes and watched as Lars journeyed on down his path.

They waited, and every few minutes, Lars would turn back once again to wave and smile until he was but a small figure on the road, and then suddenly, with one last wave, he dropped underground and out of sight. Hamelin, Eraina, and Charissa turned southwest along the road that would lead to Parthogen and the girls' father, King Carr. Eraina sniffled as quietly as she could while they walked on.

After dropping into the opening, Lars covered the entry spot from below. It was one of several such points of access to Periluna, and their locations were closely guarded secrets, known to very few even among Periluna's leaders, which made Lars wonder again, as so many had, how Tumultor had managed to steal the jewel.

The opening was just above a wide, underground boulder, which is what Lars stood on once he was below the opening. There were a few notches in its side, chiseled in as footholds for anyone climbing it. Lars's special shoes made going down a lot easier than climbing up the boulder had been when he first left Periluna. But before going any farther, he had one more thing to do.

Near the boulder was a closet carved in the rock wall, where he found his underground clothes just as he had left them. After yanking off his baggy clothes and stuffing them in the closet, he quickly dressed in his normal clothes, a heavy linen shirt and trousers that were light in weight but made from a tightly woven wool. He placed the jewel in a leather bag and strapped it around his waist and under his shirt. Now he was ready to run.

He lit a torch and moved quickly to a long, steep flight of stone steps that would take him a hundred yards down to the main level of Periluna. He descended the steps rapidly but paused at the floor level to take in the air and sights of his homeland. Something was wrong. What should have given him pleasure was absent. The familiar, musty, clay-like smells of home were missing—no, they were there, but different. And the walls of earth at the borders of the kingdom looked odd, misshapen, as if they were crowding him. The air of Periluna was always cool, but this was colder than it should be, and the walls—what was it? And then he understood.

With only the light of his torch, it had taken longer to see, but now he realized it. The walls were closer, except they weren't really the natural rock walls of the caverns of Periluna. What he was seeing were mounds, tens of feet high, of freshly deposited soft, moist dirt. And the air *was* moister and colder. He then remembered what his father told him could happen if the jewel wasn't quickly returned. The absence of the jewel and its refracted, diffused light would make their underground world cool by several degrees. The air and all the inner walls would also lose the drying power of the light, and Periluna would become habitable—once again—by the Giant Earthworms That Never Die.

Long years ago, or so the stories went, when Elwood's forefathers had fled underground—why they did so was part of their ancient history—they had placed the great jewel at the top of Periluna's dome, and the light and warmth it produced had driven away the Giant Earthworms. It was said the Worms That Never Die had migrated to Nefas, the inner realm of the kingdom of Chimera, and there lived by the Burning River.

Losing the life-giving light of the jewel would itself have produced a slow death for Periluna. But if these mounds of dirt were the deposits left by the return of the Giant Earthworms, then Periluna could already be devastated. Panic pushed Lars to a top speed. He ran through the winding tunnels and shafts of Periluna farther westward and then somewhat south toward his father's palace, around rocks and across rough, cavernous terrain, as fast as his shoes and his desperate fears could carry him.

Chapter 35

The Giant Earthworms That Never Die

"**P**RINCE! PRINCE LARS!"

Lars had been running so fast, with so little attention to anything but the path, that only a sharp turn, which made him pause long enough to verify his direction, allowed him to hear the voice calling his name. It belonged to a member of his father's palace guard.

"Jander, what are you doing here?" said Lars as he kneeled over the seated form of the middle-aged man—who appeared weak and exhausted.

"Forgive me for not rising, oh son of my king. I was sent to guide you. You can't go this way," he said, pointing in the direction Lars was heading.

"Why not? It's the way to my father's house. I have the jewel! I must get it to my father."

"You have the jewel? Your father was right." Jander lowered his eyes. "He's the only one who still thought you'd come. The rest of us had given up."

"So why are you here?"

"On your father's orders. He wants you to know there's no time for you to bring the jewel to him and then to the priests. You must take it directly to its place in the dome yourself."

"But no one but the First Holder knows how—"

"There is no time! The Worms That Never Die have returned. They have already sent their leading Borers. And we believe more are on the way. They could eat through and into Periluna at any time. The first few have already dug their way to the palace. Their mounds are everywhere, blocking roads and passageways."

"Then give me your sword. I'll *fight* them."

"Don't be foolish. Don't you think your father's soldiers have tried? Only the jewel and the light can drive them away now."

"So how do I get there?"

"The old road. It goes to the original temple."

"But the old temple is abandoned," said Lars.

"Yes, but it used to be the place where the Keepers of the Jewel stayed. And it's right below the high spot in the dome where the jewel is placed."

"So there's a road up to it?"

"Yes, though it's not used much since the new temple near the palace was built."

"So how do I get there?"

"The old road runs along the river, and somewhere past here it goes up to the temple. But you have to cross the river, and the only bridge over it that the Borers haven't destroyed is back toward the northeastern opening you used."

"Then I'll swim it. I've done it before near the city."

"But not out here. No one can swim that river this side of the dam. The flow from Starfall is too powerful to swim."

"Then I'll run to the city past the dam!"

"You'll never make it. The Borers are blocking everything on the city side. And that's where the fighting is. You'll have to go back to the bridge."

"But that's too far!" said Lars. "There's no time. Where's the closest point of the river from here?"

"Just a few hundred feet past those three boulders on your left. The river is just around the last large boulder, another fifty feet or so. You should have heard it when you came by there. But it's too wide and too strong. You'll have to go back."

"Perhaps," said Lars, who was already standing to go but then paused. "But what about you? I can't leave you, Jander."

"You must, my prince. And do take my sword. The whole land of Periluna depends on you. If you succeed, I may recover. If you don't, it won't matter."

Lars shook the hand of his father's trusted servant and reluctantly took his sword. Within seconds, he was gone.

He found the river quickly, and it was a rushing torrent. There, on the other side, was the old road he needed. He stood there, torch in hand, trying to figure out how his gifts of speed and balance could help him. He knew he could get up a lot of speed and use it to jump a large distance. But he wasn't sure he could go fast enough to jump far enough to cross the river—which appeared at least a hundred feet wide. It was easily twice, maybe three times, the distance he had jumped in the Great Hall of the Rock. And the space available to build up speed was limited by the surrounding cavern walls.

Lars knew he didn't have much time to think. If there was no way across the river here, then he'd have to do what Jander said and go all the way back near the opening. But then he heard a gurgling sound. Something in the softer dirt along-side the river was stirring the ground near his feet. Suddenly a circular area of dirt about four feet wide sank a few inches, and more gurgling sounds emanated from below it. Then the dirt rose and lowered again, and the area of dirt grew with each motion. The mound came thrusting up again, and now there were also sounds of air being pumped and pushed.

And then something tore out of the mound of dirt. It was the head of a Giant Earthworm, its toothless mouth chewing the open air. Lars jumped back quickly as another pump, gurgle, and thrust brought the worm several feet out. Lars backed up even more and, almost without thinking, used his speed and balance to run up the side of a massive, twenty-foot-high boulder near the water's edge.

If a mouth four feet wide was any indication, this creature was going to be huge. And its emergence now made him realize that Jander's words about more on the way were true. At this point, there was no time to go back the long way. As the creature stretched and pushed itself farther out of the ground, it became obvious to Lars that it would soon have him in range of its enormous body.

After a few more thrusts, the head reached all the way up to the boulder's edge, its slimy mouth sucking at Lars's feet. He could have used his balance to climb higher up the wall next to the boulder, but it was evident that even at the top of the cavern, the Giant Worm, still emerging from the riverbank, would soon be long enough to reach any point in the cavern. Lars wedged the torch several yards behind him in a cleft of the wall and now stood on his toes, sword drawn, ready to fight.

But wait. What had Jander said? It wasn't fighting the Giant Earthworms that would defeat them; it was replacing the light. And it was the absence of the jewel's light that brought them back anyway! How foolish could he be? He smiled at the thought that Eraina might have used the word *idiot*.

Suddenly the worm's head came into view again, and this time it was five feet taller than before and even higher than the boulder. The jerking, thrusting head slapped down at the boulder, and only Lars's speed and balance allowed him to sidestep the creature's blow. The head and open mouth pulled away and stretched up and back. Lars put up his sword and grabbed the torch. The head slowly came forward in an almost dreamlike wave. Lars suddenly moved toward the Giant Earthworm, the torch in both hands, and held it close to the creature's head.

The head and all of the upper body moved slowly away. Lars moved closer to the very edge of the boulder, stretched out the torch with one arm as close to the head as he could, and the creature moved away again but then resumed its flopping and thrusting maneuvers in directions away from Lars. But still the worm was stretching and pulling itself out of the moist ground below.

Well, that's good for now, Lars thought. *But the torch won't last forever.* He couldn't help asking, almost out loud, *Where's Hamelin's eagle when I need a friendly creature to carry me across the river?*

The Giant Earthworm continued to stretch and sway, push and thrust itself, almost always away from Lars, at least not within ten feet of the boulder and the torch, but always higher and longer. *I need more light*, Lars thought, and then he was almost sure he could hear Eraina's voice when she had called Hamelin and him "idiots."

This time Lars did laugh out loud, as he reached for the jewel hidden in the leather bag at his side.

Chapter 36

The Jewel, the Torch, and the River

ARS'S IDEA—AT LEAST THE FIRST PART—HE WAS PRETTY
sure would work. He would have to create enough light
to drive the creature to the other side of the river. At
least make it stretch a good distance in that direction. And
then . . . could he use the Giant Worm as a bridge?

He once again wedged the torch in its spot in the rock
wall behind him. He then took the jewel out and, holding it
securely in both hands above his head, kept his back toward
the torch. Immediately the great jewel of Periluna began to
display its amazing properties.

The light from the torch's flame flickered and danced
off and around the edges of the wall where the torch was
suspended. The jewel, still held above Lars's head, began to
draw the light of the torch to itself, but not the flame, which
continued to dance and move at the same strength from its
source. At first, for a few moments, the great jewel itself flickered from within while showing streaks of light and color,
lightning-like fissures of radiance that came first to the very

edges of the jewel. But then, without warning, bursts of light fired out in jetting streams that filled the nearest walls, ceilings, and floor spaces of the cavern.

The worm reacted immediately. It flung itself away from the jewel and Lars—slapping its body against the upper waves of the river, seeking the cool and cover of the spray and the darker regions of the cavern across the river.

The worm's lower body was still underground, but its stretching and pulling became more urgent as it fled the jewel's light. Lars knew it was time to make his move, while the creature was stretching and extending itself across the river, but before it came out of the ground completely. So he jumped off the boulder straight toward it.

He knew his balance was remarkable, but what it would be on the back of a giant, slimy worm he wouldn't know until he landed. He made it. He was able to catch himself and hold his balance, but he knew it wouldn't—couldn't—last long, because he still held the jewel, the very thing the creature was fleeing. One part of Lars's mind told him, in a split second of fear, that his plan was impossible to execute. But in the same half moment, he knew timing was everything, and he no longer had time to think, only to do.

The plan was to put the jewel back in the leather pouch before the creature's head instinctively jerked away from its light. But he'd also have to use the jewel as long as he could for light to allow him to run along the massive worm's back and gain enough speed to jump the rest of the way to the other side. Part of the jump would have to be made in the dark after the jewel was covered in the bag.

Lars sprinted down the back of the outstretched Giant Worm. He had to get the jewel covered before he got near the light-sensitive parts of the head. He judged the length as he ran, stuffed the jewel back into the bag, and, just where his memory told him the Giant Earthworm's neck would be, planted his left foot and took off like a long jumper in the track-and-field games he had played as a boy.

At the last split second of contact with the worm's body, he felt the massive creature push itself forward, and Lars flew through the dark. His feet hit water first, but the last thrust of the Giant Worm had propelled him the few extra feet needed to land him waist deep at the river's edge. Anything shorter and the violently rushing river would have carried him away. As it was, even landing that deep made him throw his upper body forward, and it took several powerful, high-speed kicks to get safely to shore. Somersaulting forward, he felt for the jewel, then his sword—both were still there. He took the jewel out again, and it continued to light his way forward, drawing from any source of light encountered along the way.

Lars ran along the old road with abandon. He had been on it once as a boy but couldn't remember exactly when or why. A wedding? A ceremonial trip with his family to the old temple? No matter. He ran until he reached the capital city.

Just as Jander said, the old road avoided the heart of the city and moved up a massive, steep underground hill. There were torches at regular spots now to light his way, and the great jewel added splashing bouquets of color as he held it aloft in one hand and raced up the hillside.

Lars hardly had time to enjoy the sights of his home city, but others, especially the poor in the smaller houses on the edges of the city, began to notice him. And the light.

"Look! It's the jewel! He has the *jewel*!" a boy of about ten yelled out as he tried to run with him along the path. Lars, however, was too fast for him.

People came out of their houses and lined the road as he continued. They cheered the racing prince who brought the light, but he didn't have time to acknowledge their shouts. He knew time was still short. Signs of the earth eaters were clearly visible, even from that distance. Mounds of dirt and debris marred the landscape and skyline. He pushed himself harder.

The old path continued sharply upward and was now a narrow ledge, more fitting for mountain sheep. And soon he could see the ruins of the old temple, which had been carved out of the cavern walls high above the city and near the spot in the upper rock ceiling where the jewel was placed. He reached the top of the winding, narrow path. It moved inward toward an old rock-walled pavilion, a space with a smooth stone floor that led into what must have been caves where the old priests stayed.

Lars saw movement. "Who goes there? Show yourself."

Out of the shadows walked a young boy, maybe eight years old. He was barefoot and dressed in simple cloth pants and an animal skin shirt.

The boy spoke in a soft, clear voice. "The old priest said you may replace the jewel yourself. You have recovered it, and he assigns you the duty of restoring it to its place."

"Where?" said Lars.

"Up there," the boy said, pointing to an adjacent sheer rock wall just outside the pavilion, where a rope ladder was hanging from a rectangular opening very near the top of the wall.

"The Old One also said, 'Be sure to wear the robes.'" The boy turned and walked back toward the darkness. But in the shadows of the cave, he stopped and spoke one last time. "When you do this, you will learn the secret of the jewel. Those who cover the jewel know the secret. You must keep the secret until the time to tell it." And he disappeared into the shadows.

Lars knew there was no point in trying to find him. And there was no time for solving riddles if he did. He put the jewel back into the bag and rushed for the rope. Though the rope ladder was intended to deter access, Lars climbed it easily and was immediately in a small, dark area inside the rectangular opening. He instinctively felt inside the bag for the jewel, making sure he still had it. Light shot out from the partly opened bag. Then he remembered that the jewel not only reflected light but could also store it for periods of time.

He pulled it out and could see his surroundings. He was in a very small space some six feet square and maybe seven feet high. In the far corner to his left was a small opening in the ceiling. Small toeholds helped him get up the wall and through the opening, and now he stood in a long, narrow hall that angled back to his left, some four feet wide but extending at least ten feet above him. Somehow this long space had light, and not just from the jewel. Lars looked up, and in the ceiling above him were occasional pinpricks of light.

The hall ended within a hundred feet, but at its end, more light entered, and the jewel shone brightly. The area widened, and Lars could see a closet containing robes. He took off his shirt to change but stopped. With a quick flick of his wrist, he threw his shirt down but then dismissively waved his hand at the robes in the closet.

There's no time for priestly ceremonies. I've got to hurry, he thought. *Everyone and everything depends on getting the jewel back in place.* He looked around and saw another opening just above him.

In the ceiling was a door that apparently led to the next area. Lars put his left foot in a notch in the wall and stepped up, balancing himself and grasping the door's handle with his left hand. He held the jewel in his right hand.

He pushed. The door was heavy, but it moved a little. He pushed the weight of his body upward using both legs—which now spraddled and pressed against notches in opposite walls—and the door in the ceiling swung outward and opened fully on its hinges. There was an explosion of light. Just then Lars realized, as he lost his toeholds in the wall, that he had opened a hatch to the outside upper world.

The blast of light from the sun, which was then multiplied by the jewel in his right hand, knocked him to the floor. The full force of the sun, absorbed and transformed by the jewel, poured into his eyes and onto his exposed skin, stunning and overwhelming him.

He lay on the floor, dazed. The light of the sun beat down from above. His skin began to turn pink, and he trembled in pain. He breathed deeply, almost gasping. His right arm twitched, and the jewel rolled away next to the shirt he had thrown on the floor, its light now partly covered. Lars lay still on the floor. In his head, the world pitched and turned. Then he saw a face and heard a voice: "For just a moment, would you mind using your head? Stay on the path!" It was Eraina.

His eyes opened.

He crawled slowly to the closet and, nearly staggering, put on the robes. He covered the jewel and put it back in the leather bag. Then he pulled the hood of the robe over his eyes, took a deep breath, waited another moment to regain some strength, and climbed out.

Lars stood outside. *Of course,* he thought, *the jewel rests between the light from above and Periluna.* He realized that he would be replacing the jewel from the outside.

From here, there was no obvious direction to follow. But there had to be some clue, or at least some reason for going one way and not another. *Think,* he told himself. *Okay, what do I know? I know the jewel is in the middle of the dome. So from out here, I should be looking for a rise in the ground and someplace in the open.*

From where he stood, it appeared that the ground to the north and east was uneven and bushy. Also, he had a gut feeling—unless he was turned around—that he would have to go a little more west to reach the crest of the dome.

So Lars walked west. Maybe his feet, with their sensitive balance, could help him determine which way. He walked slowly and tried to feel the pitch of the ground. It rose slightly.

And then he saw something. The rays of the afternoon sun made something on the ground give off a momentary flash, like a piece of glass twinkling at a certain angle. He walked toward it and came upon a gently sloped mound, several feet across, where a shallow layer of loose dirt had been spread over a small area. There was another flash. He looked closer and saw a tiny, uncovered spot right where he had seen the glint. After he brushed the soil away, he uncovered something like glass, but thick and opaque. It resembled a dull crystal and was about the size and shape of a large dinner plate turned upside down.

He dug some more around its edges and found enough space, about an inch deep, to be able to grip the sides of it. He pulled on it, gently at first, thinking it might just flip over. But it was more intricately crafted than that. The plate moved upward as Lars pulled, but it required a hard, steady pull to keep it coming.

Underneath the plate and attached to its perimeter was a cylindrical wall. The hole that held the cylinder and plate was itself reinforced by a carefully designed, rounded metal apparatus built into the ground. The cylinder was open at its bottom and rested on a framework that was supported by rods extending horizontally—there was no telling how far—into the layer of rock that started just inches below the top soil. It looked almost like an iron mesh bird's nest and was obviously the product of a skilled worker. But in the middle of it was an opening through which Lars could see right down into a deep cavern. Periluna! He quickly realized that the opening was perfectly shaped to hold the jewel.

He reached with a trembling hand into the leather bag and took out the fist-sized jewel. Holding it in broad daylight created a powerful glare that made him instinctively close his eyes, but he was a split second late. He immediately feared he had blinded himself. But though his eyes ached, they didn't burn. Still, he kept them closed. Turning his head to the side and feeling the contours of the jewel, he matched it to the opening and quickly—barely cracking one eyelid—replaced the plate and cylinder and stood back.

Almost immediately, Lars heard a single shout from below, followed by a tidal wave of cheering. He filled the inch-deep opening around the cylinder with dirt but left the dull crystal uncovered. As he did, he felt something hard to one side of it. He opened his eyes fully and saw another plate, this one rectangular and metal, embedded in the rock surface. It had writing, and he moved around to see it. The script was older than he was used to, but he could make out the letters and then the words, though they were placed closely together. It read:

Hide the jewel the light comes
Cover the jewel the light stays
The Image comes bring the jewel

He read it several times. Was this the secret the boy had referred to? Lars said it to himself, again and again.

—————

He retraced all his steps and, in the restored light, got to the bottom of the narrow ledge and raced toward his father's palace. As he ran, the cheers around him were deafening, and the people were shouting his name, his father's name, and his name again.

Then he heard the noise of swords and the shouts of armed men in battle. He could still hear the airy pumping sounds, but now the Giant Earthworms were in full retreat. He drew his sword, ready to fight, but then he saw his father's house and his father running toward him, shouting, "Lars! My son! You're home! You found the jewel! You've saved us all!"

And then Lars found himself in his father's arms and feeling his father's tears on his neck as they hugged. His eyes and skin felt hot, and then he collapsed.

He was out for many hours. He dreamed of a huge bear, biting locusts, and the Giant Worms. But mostly his mind was filled with scenes of the Great Eagle, a boy who held a sword with powerful hands, a bride with the jewel around her neck, and a beautiful princess with a soft name—a name like falling rain—who kept hugging him and scolding him while he ran and ran and laughed.

Charissa, Eraina, and Hamelin had walked well more than an hour when they felt a rumbling in the ground. At first they thought it might be a tremor from an earthquake. They instinctively looked to the north and, at that very moment, saw a brilliant arc of light shoot from the ground. Then they heard something below. Not falling rock or earthly fissures but human sounds—a wave of roaring, cheering, and shouting. Lars must have made it to Periluna, and now the glorious jewel was restored to its rightful place.

They stopped and gazed to the north, and holding their hands up high, the three friends waved their arms and joined the cheers. They smiled and then laughed, sharing even from their distance the joy and relief that Lars, his family, and their entire realm were feeling now that the light had been restored.

The fulfillment of Lars's mission pushed them to stride all the more quickly toward Carr's encampment. Surely the restoration of Periluna would be followed by the liberation of Parthogen. And Hamelin couldn't help hoping that maybe his quest too would soon find success.

Chapter 37

The Reunion outside Parthogen

H AMELIN, ERAINA, AND CHARISSA CONTINUED SOUTH-west toward the area where Eraina knew the king's forces would be encamped. She used her scarf often, but all three of them could see wolves sniffing and lurking about. Since they were not attacking, they were obviously scouts for Landon.

"This probably means that news of our arrival will reach Parthogen before us," said Eraina.

"Do you expect an attack?" asked Hamelin.

"I doubt it," said Eraina. "My guess is that Landon has heard all about your strength and our recovery of Charissa, as well as Tumultor's defeat by that army of locusts, so he's going to be cautious. And now that the jewel is back in place, Tumultor will know, or soon learn, that we survived the jump. So these scouts are here to confirm it's us, but I suspect Landon won't want to attack us head on, at least not yet. He'll mostly be just watching us for now."

Hamelin was amazed at how much Eraina seemed to know about military tactics, and right then it dawned on him that while he had grown up in an orphan's home, reading adventure books, doing chores, and playing baseball, she and her sisters were raised in a king's palace, no doubt living in luxury but also studying things like battles, war, and the use of weapons. And he also realized there was a lot he didn't know about these kingdoms and their conflicts. They walked on, alert to the prowling wolves and wild dogs.

By late afternoon, they found themselves some two miles from Parthogen's city walls. They soon entered a lightly wooded area that lay mostly southeast of the central gates of the city. Eraina continued using her scarf, and each time she did, Charissa and Hamelin would pause and wait for her report. This time, just inside the woods, she seemed to be looking longer than usual.

"What is it?" said Charissa.

Then Eraina's face broke into a big smile. "It's our father's colors! Let's wait right here." Not much longer after that, a small company of men appeared, led by Carr's most trusted leader and chief commander, Fearbane.

"We've come to escort you to your father, my ladies," Fearbane said after dismounting and bowing on one knee before the girls. His eyes lingered on Charissa, before he looked at Hamelin. "And of course your brave young friend," he added as he nodded a greeting. Now with armed support, the three friends were well protected as they approached the encampment.

Carr's camp lay just inside the woods southeast of Parthogen and was bordered on the north by a wide, flowing stream. The distance of about a mile between the camp and the city consisted mostly of grassy plains. Though the city was not on a hill, there was a slight elevation leading to the city walls. Landon obviously knew the location of Carr's camp, but he didn't need to risk a pitched battle outside the gates, since the city's elevation gave him a defensive advantage.

Carr made no efforts to hide his position, since his attempts to recover his capital city and lost kingdom were widely known and gaining strength. Men of all ages had come from the four corners of the kingdom to aid in its recovery. Landon's forces controlled Parthogen, the capital city, and his canine monsters were able to extend its boundaries for a half-mile radius outside the city gates. But outlying regions were rallying to Carr, and everyone knew it was now just a matter of time before a great battle would take place.

As they entered the king's camp, Eraina, Charissa, and Hamelin found tents and other lodgings of longbowmen, archers, and knights in well-ordered positions. There were also areas set aside for horses, military drills, and archery ranges, and there were caravans of baggage, equipment, and other supplies. These forces had been gathering for months, and now Carr, with Sophia always at his side, had come out of hiding to take command of his armies.

As soon as the girls came close to their father's tent, the old king came running to meet them. He laughed loudly with joy to see Eraina and was so overcome with emotion at the sight of Charissa that he could hardly stand. Sophia, the youngest of the daughters at fourteen, joined them too. She seemed tired and drawn, but her happiness at seeing her sisters matched theirs at returning home.

The entire encampment was overjoyed to see Charissa, who had been gone for almost four years. Most had assumed—and privately whispered—that they would never see her again. The king called for a celebration that night, but before all that, Charissa, Eraina, and Hamelin were to receive careful attention from the king's stewards. Their bruises and bites were given special oils and herbal ointments.

The sisters' return was the center of conversation, and everyone speculated that with the prophecy of the four thrones now being fulfilled, the time for the big battle was certainly near. And sure enough, Carr announced that the festivities that night would be followed by a council of war. Word of the planned council spread rapidly, and now it was only a question of how soon the great day of battle would come. Perhaps even tomorrow.

After seeing the king's doctors, but with no time yet for rest, Eraina and Charissa introduced Hamelin to Sophia and their father and began telling the king—as the servants hurriedly prepared a great supper to celebrate the reunion—of all their exploits. They told of Lars and his shoes, Hamelin and his gloves, Eraina's scarf, all their adventures since first meeting in the Forest of Fears, and of course the wedding and the great jewel of Periluna. King Carr embraced Hamelin and thanked him for caring for and protecting his daughters.

"I am forever in your debt," he said. "But forgive me, you are tired and must rest. Tonight, you will tell us more about all your exploits as we feast together!"

Hamelin was glad to rest. The king's servants took him to a tent that was furnished with a bed and had bowls for washing and even a sleeping gown. His things—except for his gloves and his pocketknife—were taken away to be washed.

But before they rested, Charissa, Eraina, and Sophia stole away to talk privately.

"How is our father?" asked Charissa.

"Not well, my sisters," replied Sophia. "Sometimes he is clear headed. Sometimes not. He seems full of doubts."

"But he looks so much stronger now," responded Eraina.

"Yes," answered Sophia. "He is better at the moment, most likely spurred by the excitement of your return. But for the last several days especially, he has had troubled sleep. In the night, he weeps bitterly for his three absent daughters."

"Three? But it was only the two of us absent, Sister," said Eraina. "So, you mean he called all our names?"

"Yes, he has called them all, but he especially cried for his three absent daughters."

"He calls my name and Charissa's and yours?"

"Yes. He has called my name too."

"But you've been here all the time, haven't you, Sophie?" asked Charissa.

"Yes, of course."

"So he's cried for all three of us, is that what you mean?" asked Eraina.

"I said it as I meant to say it," said Sophia.

Eraina let out a huffy sigh, not hiding her growing impatience. "Please! We've just returned, Sophie! I don't understand what you're saying, and I don't want to argue over words."

"Nor do I," answered Sophia quietly.

The conversation ended poorly, but before long they had all freshened up and the feast began. And soon their good cheer resumed and lasted throughout the entire meal. The retelling of all their adventures took them well through supper and on into the night. They laughed and hugged, and the girls and Carr occasionally cried with joy over seeing one another again.

After supper had passed—with only the king, his closest advisors, Hamelin, and the princesses still at the table—Fearbane approached and asked, "Your Majesty, what of tomorrow?"

Carr moved uneasily in his chair. He looked first to his daughters and then to Hamelin and finally spoke, "Yes, though it is growing late, there are still important matters to discuss."

Carr stood and stared into the distance. He began a deliberate and lengthy speech, which grew in intensity. "My daughters and friends, Fearbane and I have come to the conclusion that we must strike soon to regain the city." He looked all around as he spoke. He repeated in detail the tragedies of the previous four years: the death of the queen, the invasion of Landon and his wolves, and the capture of Charissa. Carr spoke at length, and it was evident that his listeners were restless, and he was growing tired. Finally, he concluded.

"We have suffered much, my people and kingdom. But now things have turned! My daughters have returned—Eraina has saved my beautiful Charissa." He looked at Hamelin and smiled. "Of course, with the brave assistance of the mighty Hamelin, whose feats of strength were whispered among my people even before your arrival."

Hamelin blushed.

"And now, with my three daughters alongside me, the four of us may take our thrones. The words of the prophecy are being fulfilled! All of you know the prophecy, don't you?"

Sophia said softly, "Father, we know the prophecy well. You have told us many times. But what does it mean when it says—?"

"What does it *mean*, my daughter?" Carr said. "Here, let me read it again for all of us and especially for our new young friend."

The king signaled for *The Enchiridion of the Sages* to be brought to him, and he opened it and read aloud, "'Pay heed to the words of wisdom, for ferocious beasts will come to take the land, but when the living heirs of the king are reunited and the four thrones filled, the evil . . .'" But Carr paused in his reading, his eyes staring into space. "Then . . . then . . ."

"It's okay, Father. You don't need to read it all. The *words* we know. But . . ." It looked like Sophia wanted to say more, but she paused.

The king's eyes fluttered. "Yes," he said, as he regained his focus and fixed his eyes softly on Sophia. "Yes . . . Sophie is right. It is clear . . . clear that . . ."

Carr's voice began to fade. He then abruptly sighed and sat down. Everyone was quiet. Hamelin scanned the faces of the three princesses, who quickly glanced at one another before looking back at their father.

Then Carr looked at Fearbane, and his trusted commander nodded to him. Once again, but in a slow and deliberate voice, the king spoke. "Now that all of you are here, and with these other signs in our favor, Fearbane and I believe that we must strike. Daughters and friend Hamelin, what do you say?"

Eraina spoke first. She looked the others directly in the eyes and said, "We must not delay. These last days have given us great success, and though every turn in our mission has not gone well, the end has been good. Now near the end of our quest, our friend Lars has already restored the jewel to his father's kingdom, which signals victory for us as well.

I believe it's up to us to restore our father to his throne. And we will join him in reigning, whenever he chooses."

The king glanced toward Charissa, and she spoke.

"Father, my greatest joy is simply being back here with you and my sisters. My vanity led me astray, and because of that, I've caused all of you great pain and sorrow. I am reluctant to speak, but this I promise—I will submit to the will of my father."

The king looked at Hamelin, but Hamelin didn't know what to say. He cleared his throat, stood, and said, "Sir, I have come to help and to serve. I am looking for my parents, but I know that my hopes are tied to Lars and to you and your daughters. I also know . . ." Hamelin stammered. "Your praise is wonderful and all, but I have not always acted brave. Years ago, I failed . . ." He paused and looked at Charissa.

He saw her soft, glistening eyes and remembered her words about his "fortunate failure," how it helped her in the end and made him fight harder. He began again, more confidently. "Well, we can learn from our mistakes, as a friend taught me." Charissa smiled at him. "I am here now, and I stand in your service."

"Well said," responded the king with delight in his voice. "These words of agreement, from all of you, have encouraged me!" Hamelin wasn't sure he and Charissa had agreed as strongly as Eraina, but he kept quiet.

He noticed that the king had not addressed Sophia for her approval, and she looked down silently. "Sir, may we also hear what Sophia thinks?" he said.

Sophia smiled and blinked a thank you to Hamelin. Her father nodded at her to speak.

"I do not claim to have answers," she began, "but I do have questions. Has the full price of this undertaking been considered? It is possible that we could lose not only the battle but our father's kingdom and our father as well. And what about the lives of all those in this camp with us and their wives and children? I do *not* fear a battle undertaken at the right time, when we know the cost and will accept the consequences. But I must ask again, have we truly understood the prophecy?"

Eraina spoke quickly and forcefully. "Sophie! After all we've been through! How can you possibly raise these questions now? We're all back together again, just as the prophecy foretold! Four of us on our respective thrones. We cannot wait!"

"Yes," Sophia responded, "you and Charissa and our father—and no doubt Hamelin too—have suffered a great deal. And it is true that our forces led by Fearbane are brave. But what do we three daughters have to do with this battle, we who, according to all, are supposed to join our father to fill the four thrones?"

Through a barely contained anger, Eraina said, "I have experiences of dangers faced, canyons crossed, howling dogs, and the bitterness of cold and dangerous weather. Not to mention being tossed up trees and thrown over walls! And, I might add, I have this *scarf*." She held out the scarf for all to see. "It sees at great distances, things both true and eerie, things of this world and maybe even the spirit world that surrounds us."

Everyone was silent. Then Charissa spoke. "My dear Sophie, your question is fair. I can only claim to have begun to learn from the sad experiences of one who trusted too much in herself, who suffered because of it and caused others enormous pain. But I do remember much of my former training for battle." She glanced at Fearbane. "So, again, I offer myself to serve whenever I am called upon, according to our father's wishes."

"And you, brave warrior?" asked Sophia, looking at Hamelin.

Hamelin didn't expect the question. "I . . . I've been through some tough spots. Honestly, I'm really not sure what to do, but I trust my friends, and . . ." Then remembering that Eraina had mentioned her scarf, Hamelin looked down at his gloved hands. "And these—I have these gloves of strength, given to me by the Great Eagle."

"Well, those are . . . very *large* gloves." The word *large* seemed to hang in the air. "And you, Father? What do you say about your daughters—all of them?"

Though surprised to be asked, Carr answered quickly, with almost a tone of rebuke. "Sophia, you three are the treasures of my life, my daughters, whom I would not risk if I didn't know with certainty what the prophecy says."

All eyes were on Sophia, since it was clear that she had something else to say. "I love you all, and I admire greatly your deeds of courage and strength. And, Charissa, my dear big sister, I am overjoyed that at last you are home—and that you, Eraina, and your courageous friend Hamelin have brought her back to us. But I do not agree. I trust the prophecy—but not our *reading* of it. We want it too much to hear it right."

"But it says plainly that when all the living heirs come together to rule, and the four thrones are filled, the beasts—which are obviously Landon's wolves—will be defeated," Eraina said.

"Yes," replied Sophia softly, "perhaps. But it does not say they *fight*. It says they are *reunited*. And, besides, are you sure that we are the heirs of the prophecy? And what of the four thrones? What does—?"

"We three, plus our father, make *four*! It is plain to see," said Eraina.

Everyone was quiet. Eraina then spoke again. "Are you afraid, Sophie?" she said.

The question bit the air and hung in the silence that followed. Sophia looked at Eraina and blinked once softly before answering. "Yes, my sister whose name means 'peace,' I fear all acts of foolishness and their consequences." There was a long pause, before Sophia spoke again. "I will sleep on it."

With that, she stood to leave but turned once more, looked at her sisters, and said, "I'm glad you are back."

There was a long and awkward silence after Sophia stepped away from the table and went to her tent. Finally, the king spoke, "Well, tomorrow we fight. As Sophia has said, all the sisters need only come together; they need not all fight. So at daybreak, we march."

The king then quickly stood up, stepped away from the table, and kissed his two remaining daughters lightly on the cheek. Then he nodded to Hamelin, who stood and bowed. The king left, followed by Fearbane and the other advisors.

Hamelin could tell the king had decided. Tomorrow, a battle would begin, and he had no idea what he would be expected to do.

Chapter 38

The Signal
Is Given

TWO HOURS BEFORE SUNUP, THE ENTIRE CAMP BEGAN THE final preparations for battle. The men dressed for combat; their horses were fed, watered, and outfitted; and all the weapons were checked—bows, arrows, spears, maces, mallets, and nets. The plans for attacking the city were reviewed and shared once again by Commander Fearbane.

As the sun began to show the top of its head over the eastern horizon, Fearbane commented to the king, "Sire, when the sun is risen, it will be full in their faces. I believe we should then begin our march, and I am confident of success."

"Agreed," Carr replied. But his face showed uncertainty.

The rows of longbowmen took their positions first, followed by the archers, then the lesser trained but nonetheless brave foot soldiers with their hand weapons, then the knights in full armor with squires and palfreys nearby. With banners flying and family colors displayed everywhere, Charissa, Eraina, and Hamelin were seated on their horses. Hamelin had ridden a horse before, but never one this big or spirited.

He looked nervously at Eraina and Charissa, who obviously were trained to ride. All of them were anxiously waiting for the king to give the signal to Fearbane, who would in turn pass it on to the next level of officers.

Eraina looked around anxiously for Sophia. Charissa noticed her looks of distress and said softly, "I don't believe she will come, Eraina."

"I'm afraid you're right. I don't care whether she comes for the battle, but I do want to ask her forgiveness. I was so wrong last night in what I said and in the mean way I said it. Sophie has experienced terrible hardships as well, enduring the long nights here with our father. She has seen him grow weaker, probably every day, but she stays by his side, protecting him from those who constantly push and demand . . . and now I've added to her burdens." Then Eraina looked about as the soldiers gathered into their formations. "And besides, what good are we here at the back of the battle lines?"

Hamelin replied, "Eraina, have you used the scarf to look around?"

"I've looked already at Landon's forces!" she said with an edge in her voice. "The central gate is a portcullis, and it is closed. His longbowmen are standing on the city walls and are three deep at the towers and two deep in the turrets. Then, through the walls, I see their archers, swordsmen, and knights, all massing in the bailey, ready to do battle."

"I meant—"

"And accompanying every group are those vicious dogs and wolves, snarling and foaming at the mouth."

"Yeah. You already told us all that," said Hamelin, "But have you looked around elsewhere? Is Tumultor on his way? And . . . what about the eagle? Have you seen him?"

In embarrassment, Eraina closed her eyes and let out a short breath. "Sorry," she said. She then pulled the scarf around her head again and peered deeply back to the north and northeast.

"No sign of Tumultor," she said. She then looked through and beyond the Forest of Fears, all the way to the mountain range, at the base of which stood Sue Ammi's house. "No sign of the eagle yet . . ."

Her eyes climbed upward, to a spot near the top of the mountain. There, in a hollowed out place in the rocky mountainside, she found the eagle's nest—and on it sat the great bird. Eraina looked directly at his face, just as he suddenly turned in her direction. She felt sure their eyes met. "Oh!" she said suddenly.

"Can you see him?" asked Hamelin. "Do you see the Great Eagle?"

"Yes, I do!"

"What's he doing?"

"He's *looking* at us, I'm almost certain," said Eraina with new energy in her voice.

"Is he moving? Is he coming our way?" asked Hamelin.

"No, but I *know* he's looking at me! But . . ." Her voice trailed off as she continued. "He's not moving . . . at least not yet."

And then, though he couldn't have explained it to the others, Hamelin heard a song or something in his mind. He could almost feel it. *What is that?* It was jogging a memory, something that reminded him of an earlier time, a different place. Was it the music from the cave that he, Bryan, and Layla had heard? He tried to remember but didn't have enough time to think.

The sun was now just above the eastern horizon. Landon's defenders would be looking directly into it as the forces of Carr formed up to march toward the city. Fearbane came riding up to the king and said, "My lord, the men are ready. All are arrayed in battle formation. They wait only upon your word. May I give the command?"

The king gave an affirmative nod. Fearbane, with a solemn acknowledgment in return, immediately turned his horse about and, looking at his officers who were awaiting the order from him, raised his hand to give the signal.

At that moment, there was a loud shout of *"Hold up, there!"* and a stir from the midst of the officers to their left. Suddenly a horse galloped furiously toward the king. The rider was dressed in the family's royal colors—it was Sophia!

When Carr saw her, his spirits soared. He immediately raised his left hand toward Fearbane to signal him to pause for a moment. The king's left hand remained in the air, as did Fearbane's right, waiting for Sophia to settle and for the reconfirmation of the order.

"I said I would sleep on it," Sophia said as soon as she drew up alongside her sisters. "I couldn't leave my sisters alone. I still won't fight, at least not now. But I must be with you. *Especially* now."

When Eraina first saw Sophia approaching, her hopes too had surged. So, once again, she had unfurled the scarf from her neck to her head and looked hard toward the eagle. But this time, instead of looking at Eraina from that great distance, the bird stood poised on his legs just outside the nest and then took flight.

"Oh!" she yelled out as her hopes for the eagle's help soared. All eyes turned from Sophia to Eraina.

"What is it, Sister?" said Charissa.

Eraina kept looking toward the north but then realized something was wrong. The eagle flew straight up, landed at the very top of the mountain, and then, no longer looking at her and the field of battle, turned his back and looked to the north.

Eraina glanced at Charissa, then Hamelin. She looked down and shrugged. "Oh, it's nothing."

All eyes turned again to the king, who breathed in deeply and looked again at Fearbane.

"Father," said Sophia, "will you wait just one moment more?"

"Yes, my daughter," he replied with a sigh but with his left hand still raised.

Sophia then looked toward the group of mounted officers from which she had emerged and gave a signal with her head to one of them. From the midst of that group, another horse trotted forth. It was very old but dressed in the armor befitting a knight's horse, with banners depicting the family arms flowing from its sides. No one rode it. The horse came toward them and stopped.

"What's this?" asked her father. "Is this . . . is this *Alathea's* horse?"

"The prophecy, as you understand it," said Sophia, "says that the *living* heirs must be reunited, and I thought it at least best to have your fourth daughter's horse stand with us . . . just in case."

"Just in case? Just in case . . . Why I . . . How dare you! You know your sister Alathea is long dead," Carr sputtered.

At this point, Hamelin was confused—he had never before heard of a fourth daughter.

"Is she? Do you know that for sure, my father?" Sophia said.

Eraina, trying to refocus her thoughts from the eagle and the mountain, saw the riderless horse and recognized it. And she heard Sophia's last question. "Sophia! What do you *mean*? You're hurting *Father*! Alathea is *long* since dead! *All* of us know that."

"Do we?" asked Sophia.

"Of course! For years we've been told that—"

"Oh, well, yes, of course," replied Sophia. "In our short lives we've been told many things, however well intentioned, that later turned out to be otherwise. I seem to recall hearing in recent days the fear that surely *Charissa* was dead. And maybe even *you*." She then turned to her father. All sat silent, waiting for Carr to reply.

Finally, Charissa spoke. "Father," she asked, "Alathea *is* dead, isn't she?"

Carr couldn't look at them. At last, he spoke, but with no certainty in his voice. "Of course Alathea is . . ." But he couldn't finish the sentence. Then, as if to change the question, he burst out, "I've mourned for her all these years!"

"Oh, yes," said Sophia. "I can attest to that. You have often cried out for her, especially in recent days. But is it possible you could only say in your dreams what your heart still hoped for—and perhaps still believes: that your *three* absent daughters—Charissa, Eraina, *and* Alathea—would return?" Sophia glanced at Eraina.

Eraina's eyes widened as she listened to Sophia. She quickly turned toward Carr. "Father!" she said urgently. "You must tell us. Is this an old, ageless grief, or is there an uncertainty in your mind? Do you have a lingering hope that our sister Alathea lives?"

The king sat on his horse in silence. His face showed anger as he looked impatiently at Sophia and the others.

Then with his body beginning to shake and his lips pressing hard against clenched teeth, a low groan emerged from the old king. It grew to a soft wail. Finally he spoke, "Yes . . . yes . . . I have prayed a thousand times that my dear child might still be *alive*." And now the king, with his left hand still raised but slumping at the elbow, cried softly, "Oh, Alathea, Alathea, my sweet daughter . . . my *Layla*."

At the name Layla, Hamelin's whole body tensed, and a bolt of fear shot through him.

Sophia continued, "So then, Father—"

"Please, my wise sister," said Eraina, "if there is any chance that what you say is true, let me now make amends with you for what I said last night. Let me be the one to ask our father this last question."

Then she looked at Carr and asked firmly, "Father, is there truly a possibility that our sister Alathea lives?"

Carr was silent.

"And Father, dear Father," said Charissa as she leaned over and touched Carr's forearm, "if you do not know of her death, and if you still pray that she lives, can you truly send us out on this day? You yourself have said things are turning. Is it still possible that Layla could return, as I have? Certainly we will go at your bidding, if you give the command. But if we are acting in presumption and against the ancient texts you so greatly trust . . ."

The old man's arm slowly dropped. He could scarcely hold himself on his horse. His hands gripped the horn of his saddle, and his forehead fell forward. He sobbed once, held his breath, and squeezed his eyes shut.

"Sire," yelled the commander, "may I confirm the order to the men?"

The great king raised his head and said, "No, my friend. I say now, relent. Stand down, good Fearbane."

"But, Sire—"

"Sir Fearbane," began Charissa, "you are the noblest warrior in all my father's kingdom. And all of us will join you in the march—upon *his* signal. But I have pledged myself to do my *father's* will. And now he says, 'Relent. Stand down.'" She held the commander's gaze and then added firmly, "Give my father's command now, or I will ride among the men and order it myself."

"As you—and your father—say," said the commander. His eyes dropped, but then he turned back to his officers and yelled, "Stand down! Draw the men back! Return to the camp!"

Hamelin was amazed at Charissa's strength. And the king's words—what did he say? Had Hamelin really heard what he thought he heard? *Layla*?

The great king, slowly helped off his horse, slid to the ground and was on his knees. He wept.

"My daughters," he said between sobs, "I am sorry. I have wanted this for you, to see you finally rule in my place, but I fear I have wanted it also too much for myself. These last years have been full of grief, and I have not seen things rightly."

Sophia also dismounted and kneeled on the ground next to her father. "Oh, Father," she said as she placed her arms around his shoulders, "your heart has been good. You wept for *all* of us."

Eraina quickly swung down from her saddle. As she ran toward her father, the king said, "Yes, yes, I dream of all of you every night, and in these last years, I mourned after Charissa was taken and cried for two lost daughters. Then when

Eraina left, I cried for three lost daughters. But now, two of you are back. But Layla, oh, my Layla . . . are you alive?"

Charissa also dismounted, and the three daughters surrounded their father on the ground, kneeling at his side. Their tears were mixed with sorrow and love—for their father and for Layla, their sister who, more than twenty years ago, had mysteriously disappeared. Now they all once again dared to hope she was still alive.

Chapter 39

Hamelin's Dilemma

T HE SOLDIERS WERE DISAPPOINTED TO BE ORDERED BACK. They were physically and mentally ready for battle. But within forty-five minutes of their return to camp, storm clouds quickly formed, and the skies opened up and poured. For three solid hours, the rains fell in torrents, turning the grassy plain between their camp and the city walls into a muddy pitch.

By noontime, the older soldiers maintained—and the younger soldiers came to understand—that the king, in his great wisdom, had actually saved them from a disastrous defeat by calling off the attack. The rains would have worked to their disadvantage, the old warriors explained. Their arrows would have been shortened in their flight, and their feet and those of the horses made treacherously unstable. The slightly elevated position of the city, under those changed conditions, with the sun behind the clouds, would have favored Landon's forces immeasurably.

Early that afternoon, the rains ended. A rainbow appeared, stretching across the entire breadth of Carr's camp. It gave, in retrospect, some cheer to the warriors who once again would have to wait.

Eraina, when she had the opportunity to visit with Hamelin, told him what she had seen with the scarf—that the eagle had left his nest but had turned his back on them. She then explained to Hamelin all about their other sister. Her name was Alathea, but the family had called her Layla, the name given to her by Charissa, who was only two years older than she.

Layla had vanished when she was four years old. Some said her nurse fell asleep, but the nurse claimed that one moment Layla was playing in the great area behind the castle and the next she was gone. Rumors abounded that the dark warriors of Chimera had snatched her. Her father, the king, had looked for the four-year-old girl, but after more than two years of searching, he had finally given up.

"So how old would Layla be?" Hamelin asked.

"Let's see, Charissa's ten years older than I am, so she's twenty-six. That would make Layla about twenty-four."

Hamelin was stunned to hear them use the name *Layla*. He knew that even though it was not a common name, it was not impossible that two people could have it. But it was jarring to hear the name of his dear friend used on this side. And what was it Layla and Bryan said about having a strange experience once with an eagle? He needed more time to think.

He certainly didn't want to get the family's hopes up regarding the Layla he knew—who, he was pretty sure, was also twenty-four. Besides, his own mission was still not done. SueSue had said he could find his family and learn his name, but he still had no clear idea how to do that. His only lead was the name Ren'dal, and Tumultor had confirmed that Ren'dal could still be found in Ventradees. So Hamelin made up his mind: since the plans to attack Landon had been indefinitely postponed, he would head to Ventradees to find Ren'dal.

He realized, however, that he couldn't just leave without speaking to King Carr and his three daughters, especially Eraina and Charissa. He knew the girls would be with their father, so that afternoon, he went to the king's tent. The guard immediately recognized him and allowed him to enter unannounced.

But just as he stepped inside, he heard Eraina's voice: "Father, please, you must not grieve so. We will search for Layla."

"But *where*? I looked for her all across these lands. And it has been twenty years now. Perhaps Chimera himself took her."

"We won't stop searching," said Charissa. "I was lost too, but now I'm back, thanks to Hamelin."

"Yes!" cried the old king. "Where is the boy? Perhaps he could find my Layla!"

Hamelin quietly stepped back outside the tent.

No, I've already found Charissa and the jewel. Now I want to find my parents.

Eraina, however, looked up and saw him just as he left. She followed him outside and found him looking at the ground, deep in thought.

"Hamelin," she said, "how much did you hear?"

"I heard your father saying that he wants me to look for your lost sister."

"Please—you don't have to do that. You've already helped us so much, and you have your own quest."

After several moments of silence, Hamelin said, "But yours is really not finished yet. We found Charissa, but your father's kingdom is not restored. And now we know you have another sister to find."

"But SueSue didn't send you for her."

"But SueSue said I wouldn't find my family until I had helped Lars and you. Besides . . ."

"Besides what, Hamelin?"

"I . . . might know something about Layla."

"About Layla? What?"

"I'm not sure, Eraina. It's all so strange, but . . . there are some things I would have to check on first."

"*What*? You must *tell* me!"

"Look, I don't want to get anyone's hopes up just yet."

"Hamelin, right now, hope is all we have. Please . . ."

"All right. Well, there's a girl back in my world who is twenty-four years old and has the name Layla. She was orphaned and at one time was helped by . . . an unusual creature."

"Hamelin!" Eraina said. But then she looked around to make sure they were alone and whispered, "You've got to go bring her here!"

"Eraina, I couldn't ask her to do that. She's my friend, and it's very dangerous over here."

"But if she's our *sister* . . ."

"But I don't know that. It could just be a coincidence. And besides . . . I don't think I can go back right now. My own quest isn't done yet, and SueSue told me not to 'turn aside' from helping you and Lars."

"But you would be helping me out by going back! You'd be looking for our sister!"

"But we don't really know if the Layla I know is your sister. There are so many strange questions. I mean, how did she get over to my side?"

"I don't know. Maybe with help from the unusual creature you mentioned—an eagle helped you, and a lion helped Charissa. Who knows? But like you said, it's all strange!"

"I know. But that's the problem. You can't just make these things happen. It's not that easy to get between here and there. I could get back to the pond from this side, but you can't just jump in and swim to the Atrium. It's . . . harder than you can imagine. Besides, I've never done it without the eagle."

"But," asked Eraina, "couldn't you get to the Atrium another way? Charissa did."

"Well . . . I'm sure it's possible. But Charissa was led there by a lion. And the eagle flew Charissa and me out of it through an opening high up on the eastern wall. But even if I climbed up the right hill and somehow got back inside the Atrium, I'd probably never find my way back through that cave. It's pitch black in there without the eagle and the light he puts off. And there's no way to pick the right path without him. He's the guide.

"Besides, even if I got back to my world and to Layla, I don't even know if I could get Layla back here. You can't just *decide* when you want to come here. The eagle said I was 'summoned' the first time. And after I failed to get through, I tried to come back on my own. But I couldn't. I think you can only come when you are called, and even then it takes a lot of help."

"I see," said Eraina thoughtfully.

"If somehow I got back there, I might wait forever and never get back here—which would mean I couldn't help you . . . or . . . find my parents."

"It sounds like you need to wait for the eagle," said a soft voice behind them. They turned. It was Sophia.

"Sophie!" said Eraina in a loud whisper. "Please don't tell Father—"

"I'm sorry," she said. "I wasn't trying to eavesdrop. I shouldn't have spoken at all."

"No, it's okay," replied Hamelin. "Please stay. But you're right. I've got to have the eagle's help."

"Maybe," Eraina said, "it's like before, when we were able to save Charissa and get the jewel at the same time. Maybe by bringing Layla here, you will find your parents."

"Maybe so. But the only clue I have—and I got this from SueSue—is that defeating Ren'dal is connected to finding my parents. Until now, no one ever mentioned Layla."

Hamelin again became silent. Eraina knew she had said enough for the moment and Hamelin would have to decide what to do. She nodded at Sophia, and the two sisters quietly stepped away.

For Hamelin, it was like a fight between two voices. One argued that he had to go to Ventradees to confront Ren'dal and find out about his parents. The other voice in his head—it also sometimes sounded like Sue Ammi—was reminding him that he would be tempted "to turn aside from helping Eraina and Lars, but . . . you cannot defeat Ren'dal until . . ." Until *when*?

He *had* helped them both! Surely it was okay now to look for his parents!

But the battle within suddenly ended. Hamelin didn't have to decide. He just knew. He knew that he hadn't finished helping his friends.

But where would he go? Wherever it was, he would have to speak to the king and also say a proper good-bye to his friends. No more running away or leaving any of his closest friends without an explanation. He went back to the king's tent.

"Sir . . . I mean, Your Majesty," he began, "I think it's time for me to leave."

"Where will you go, my son?" asked Carr.

"Sir, I don't even know myself. Maybe I should go to Periluna. Lars promised he would help me."

"I'll go with you," Eraina said quickly.

"No, I think you should stay. Your father and sisters need you here. But I promise to let you know if I learn about your sister Alathea." And then Hamelin spoke again to the king. "Please, Your Majesty. I don't understand all these things, but I do want to help. May I go?"

"Of course, my son," replied the king. "You have cared for my daughters and thus been kind to me in ways that I shall never be able to repay. We are in your debt. Go with our blessing and with our hopes. We hope that you can help us now in our search to find Layla, if she lives."

Hamelin nodded and left. Sophia told him good-bye and stayed with the king. Charissa and Eraina accompanied him outside. It was all happening so suddenly. They had just gotten home, and now Hamelin, their young friend, was leaving. Charissa first and then Eraina broke into tears. Charissa kissed him on the cheek, and Eraina hugged him hard. He told them both good-bye and turned before they could see his face. "I gotta go" was all he could say.

Hamelin began to walk back along the path they had taken to reach the king's camp from Periluna. Eraina watched but couldn't bear to see him walking away alone. She sighed and ran after him.

"Hamelin, I know you are strong, but at least let me walk with you a bit. I can use my scarf to make sure there are no enemies along the way."

"Sure," said Hamelin, glad to have some company, even for a short while.

At first Eraina looked toward Periluna, but she almost instinctively swept her eyes from there more directly north, toward the mountain where the eagle had turned his back on them. She saw that the skies in that direction were now bearing the full brunt of the storm that had earlier passed over Parthogen.

Her gaze lingered near the top of the mountain, and just as she looked, lightning suddenly cracked sharply over the peak, directly above the place where the eagle had stood. Eraina kept looking long and hard.

"What is it?" Hamelin finally asked.

At first she spoke in a whisper. "I think I see the Great Eagle . . . coming up from the other side of the mountain! Yes!" she said excitedly. "I'm certain he's flying this way. His eyes are right on us! Wait here!" Eraina ran back to the tent yelling, "Father! Charissa! Sophia! Come quickly! Hurry!"

Before long, Hamelin also could see the eagle, who was approaching with a speed greater than he had ever seen. Charissa came, helping her father, who was walking as fast as he could. Eraina ran ahead and got back to Hamelin first, but Sophia was just behind her, carrying a wooden object with the size and look of an ordinary jewelry box. She quickly handed it to him. "This may help you, if you study it carefully." Hamelin had no time to ask her what it was or what she meant.

The eagle—now very near—gave no signs of slowing down. The great bird let out a long, high screech, and Hamelin realized that he wasn't going to stop. However, he knew what to do. He turned his back to the direction of the eagle's approach and waved to the king and the three princesses.

"Eraina," Hamelin shouted, "go ahead and tell your father and sisters what I told you about Alathea!"

Eraina nodded, and seconds later Hamelin heard a powerful rushing wind. He started to run as he also lifted his arms, and with a thud that at first jarred him, he felt the legs of the eagle squeeze his sides and simultaneously pull him into the bird's feathery chest.

"Yoweee!" Hamelin hollered as he was suddenly airborne. He quickly twisted his shoulders and head and glanced back and below to see King Carr, Charissa, Eraina, and Sophia waving wildly, the girls jumping up and down.

"Good-bye, Hamelin! We love you!" they yelled. "Come back as soon as you can!" Their voices faded, but he watched them jump and wave until they were too far away to see. The wind in his face quickly blew away his tears.

He flew face forward under the wings of the great bird, not knowing where he was going but trusting the powerful creature who held him.

Chapter 40

Johnnie and Simon: Their Secret Revealed

THE YEARS HAD GONE BY, AND REN'DAL'S SMOLDERING anger had increased as each one passed. Simon and Johnnie had conceived no more children since the birth of the girl he had ordered Katris to get rid of.

Johnnie had wept for weeks after they seized her newborn. Simon had grieved in his own way, though not in front of her. And their grief had additional, and strange, results. Though she and Simon clung closely to each other as husband and wife, Johnnie no longer conceived. It was as if she willed her body to refuse Ren'dal's sinister plans.

They had been in Ventradees about five years when their daughter was born, and now the following years had added another six or so, making it more than eleven years since they were captured.

Long years of waiting were not new to Chimera and his sons, but late one night Ren'dal's patience ran out. He was drinking in his private quarters when word came to him that the great jewel of Periluna, which his plotting had helped his brother Tumultor acquire, had been recovered by Elwood's son. To make matters worse, Tumultor's would-be new bride, the daughter of Carr, had been stolen away at the wedding ceremony by Elwood's son with the help of another daughter of Carr. And there was a new adversary—some young boy who had great strength. Obviously Landon couldn't control his domains. But worst of all, somehow that boy with strength had used a magic sword to pierce the Great Rock, which caused the magic waters to stop. Their carefully devised schemes were falling apart.

These reversals of their efforts to expand Nefas would no doubt be humiliating to Chimera and thus produced fear in Ren'dal. To see their plans break down by such ineptitude on the part of his brothers, Landon and Tumultor, enraged Ren'dal. And in his drunken state, he couldn't stop thinking of his own failure—to provide Chimera with a male child from both sides of the Atrium. He knew Chimera would soon demand an accounting from him.

With these late-night fears playing on him, he insisted that Katris be awakened to report to him about Johnnie. He was not surprised to learn that she still had not conceived, but the drink took away what few controls he had on his fury. His mercurial temper reached a boiling point.

"Eleven, no, almost twelve years now is *enough*!" he screamed. "Bring them both to me!"

Simon and Johnnie were dragged from their bed and pushed roughly into Ren'dal's private quarters.

"Why do you still have no male child? You were brought here for that reason! We've made it easy for you—instead of making you work like all the *other* dogs here! You've been given private quarters and better food. You've had Katris assigned to you." Ren'dal's balance appeared unsteady as he turned toward Simon. "And *you*! You've had a lighter work-load than the others, the *real* men! But *still* no child!"

Simon and Johnnie stood before him, fearful but no longer quite the quailing young couple they were years earlier when they were first dragged before him.

"We *did* have a child!" Simon said.

"Silence, you fool! That miserable *girl* baby was not what we wanted. We must have a *boy* child!"

"You can't decide what kind of baby we're going to have!" he yelled back.

"I can decide whatever I *want*!" shouted Ren'dal. But then he grew quiet, staring at Simon—who glared back—for long moments before he began again. "Oh, you are very brave, young husband. Have you forgotten the lesson I taught you the first time you were in this room?" he sneered. "I remember how you left this room, whimpering and groaning after only *one* lash. Maybe that's the problem! You're just too weak, not *man enough* to have a son!"

Unlike years before, Simon wasn't held back by chains or guards. Enraged, he broke toward Ren'dal, but the son of Chimera, even drunk, anticipated the onrushing Simon. Hopping quickly on his right foot, he extended his left in a straight-legged kick that hit Simon in the abdomen and doubled him over. Then with his left hand, Ren'dal grabbed Simon by the back of the neck and lifted him at arm's length facing him, until his toes barely touched the floor.

"Don't think I couldn't break your neck with one flick of my wrist," he snarled. Then he threw him to the floor onto his back, and the guards immediately rushed over, kicking the helpless Simon while he lay there, before wrenching him back up on his feet.

"Yes. The problem is, you're just too *weak*! *That's* the whole problem! We've been too *easy* on you! Maybe if I made you work like all the other slaves here, you would be stronger and tougher. Maybe then you'd be man enough to sire a male child!" Ren'dal then glanced to his right and nodded, and from the shadows behind, the hulking figure of Snardolf emerged, holding the Scorpions' Whip. He allowed the whip to lightly touch the floor while he slowly moved it back and forth in a small arc with his right hand.

"Yes, Snardolf, come here. That's what this impertinent husband needs, more toughening up."

"No," screamed Johnnie, "please, not that!"

"Oh, listen while the young wife begs for her husband! No, I have made up my mind. We've done this all the wrong way. He needs more toughening! Snardolf, it's been a long time since I've applied more than one lash. Take him back to your area—I don't want to hear his screams—and see what *four* strokes will do. It'll either kill him, or he'll come back begging to be given another chance to father a son!"

"No, no," screamed Johnnie, "*please!*"

"Don't beg for him," bellowed Ren'dal as the guards grabbed Simon and began to lead him away with Snardolf following. "He's no man! If the four strokes kill him, don't worry. We'll go back to the other side and find you another husband, someone who can give you a *son!*"

As Johnnie wailed, Katris approached Ren'dal and spoke urgently but quietly enough that Johnnie couldn't hear. "Master, you must be careful!"

"Don't tell me what to do, old woman!"

Katris stepped even closer and spoke more firmly. "Master, I have served you for many years, and I know what your father wants to do. And I know well his ways. If you kill this man now, in a drunken rage, your father's anger will know no limits! You cannot simply get her another husband from the other side! You know as well as I"—and here she whispered—"that the *Ancient One* does not *permit* that. Remember! We got this one because he came *voluntarily*, and that was because he already loved her!"

Ren'dal shook his head as if to clear it. He wiped his mouth with the back of his hand. Then after a further pause, he jerked his head toward Snardolf, who, with the guards, had delayed in leaving the room with Simon. "Snardolf! Be sure you don't kill him! Only *three* lashes. But he must be punished for attacking me—as well as toughened!"

"Yes, Ren'dal," Snardolf replied slowly and heavily.

"No, *please*," begged Johnnie. Then, desperate to stop Ren'dal, she lost her will to protect the secret she and Simon had kept hidden between them for almost twelve years.

"Please, do not whip him! He *has* given me a son!"

"Oh, we know that! But he killed him! And now—"

"No! That's not true!" Johnnie screamed.

"*No! Don't*—!" yelled Simon, realizing what Johnnie was about to do. But it was too late.

"We *have* a son!" she blurted out.

Ren'dal stopped. His head jerked to the side. He could hardly believe what he had heard. "What?" he asked. "You have a son? No! All the two of you could produce was a—"

"Johnnie, no!" yelled Simon.

"No," Johnnie screamed, "our son on the other side—just before you caught us—we hid him!"

"What! That's *impossible*! How could you still have a son and I not know about it? Litchie always knows—"

Johnnie collapsed on the floor, head in hands. "It's *true*," she sobbed.

"Get me *Litchie*!" Ren'dal screamed to his attendants standing nearby, his fists clenched and his eyes blood red.

Then, to Johnnie, he snarled in indignation, "How is it possible that your son is alive and my spy does not know?"

Ren'dal turned to Katris and yelled, "He has been well rewarded to report to me all the things that go on near the entry to the other side!"

But all Johnnie could do was cry. "Please," she begged, "don't lash my husband!"

And now Katris approached Ren'dal again. "Master," she whispered, "perhaps you *should* let the husband alone this time. Harming him may cause her to despair, and then she will be no good to you. Besides, now you have learned what you needed to know. There is already a male child. He must be nearly twelve years old by now, and you can use his mother and father to find him and lure him here. The boy will have to agree to come, so you'll need them— looking strong and healthy."

"Hmmm," said Ren'dal as he pondered the whispered advice. "Perhaps," he said as his eyes narrowed.

Katris saw she was making ground, so she pressed her point. "Master, you've just regained almost twelve years in your plan! But until you get the boy for sure, you'll *need* his parents! *Both* of them. In the meantime, give the woman a reason to think there is hope. Besides, if you whip him now, he'll have to recover. It'll just delay using them to find the boy."

Ren'dal breathed loudly from his nose, then suddenly said, "Wait," to Snardolf and the guards who were still holding Simon. "I have changed my mind." Then he looked back at Johnnie and sneered.

"Well, my dear Magda. So you *have* a son. Very good. *Very* good! That is the only thing that has saved your husband's skin for now. I'll give you both another chance . . . but if I do, I'll have to have your help. Do you understand?"

"Yes," Johnnie mumbled.

Then as Johnnie and Simon were led away, Ren'dal spoke again to Katris. "My good woman, come with me. Tell me more of how to play the emotions of the woman on behalf of her husband."

"Yes, my lord," she responded. "And how to play both of them on behalf of their son."

"So," he said, to himself mostly, "they have a son. Perfect. The wait has been worth it. At nearly twelve years of age, the boy is almost old enough to do exactly as my father, Chimera, wishes. Oh, good news and joyous day! The child was born, and soon the son will be given to us! The coming of Nefas is near!"

Ren'dal then looked around at one of his attendants still in the room and clapped his hands once. "What are you standing there for? Go! Find the priests who know how to summon the trackers! And tell the trackers to *bring me Litchie—now!*"

Chapter 41

An Unexpected Destination

I T WAS MIDAFTERNOON, AND THE EAGLE WAS IN A HURRY. After snatching Hamelin from the ground, he gained altitude quickly. Hamelin expected the great bird to bank at any moment and head back to Periluna, or to SueSue's house, or maybe to Osmethan. He thought—if the eagle did what he always did and surprised him—that they might fly even farther north to Ren'dal's realm. But none of those places proved to be in the eagle's sights as he continued to fly south by southeast.

Hamelin then guessed where they might be going. Soon they would be in the vicinity of the pond. He was right, but wrong. The eagle made no effort to descend. If anything, he climbed a bit higher, flying at a speed Hamelin hadn't experienced before. Soon they were just above a plateau, and from above, Hamelin could see that it led toward a rounded dome.

At first he had no memory of this natural structure, and so he assumed they would fly directly over it. But as they approached the rounded area, the great bird began to descend. Then his descent leveled out, and just as Hamelin thought they would crash into the side of it, the eagle veered left and came to a soft landing that ended with both of them standing on a small outcropping of rock partway up the side of the dome.

Hamelin then saw a hole in the rock that was about six feet wide, and he knew where he was. It was the hole in the eastern wall of the Atrium of the Worlds. He had, of course, seen this hole before, but the last time, he and Charissa had been too busy hanging from the eagle to notice the formations around them as they flew away.

The great bird then took Hamelin through the opening and descended to the floor in a hard glide, and they both stood there, looking again at the glistening walls, now reflecting the fading light of the day. For a while, there would be no more flying.

Hamelin wondered if there were other passages in and out of the Atrium that he didn't know about. Would the eagle lead him through a new pathway to Ren'dal's kingdom? Or to somewhere else? But the bird led him on a dead run past the pond and out the Atrium door next to the smooth patio surface, then through the smaller adjoining corridor and the larger natural cathedral. They passed other caverns that Hamelin faintly recognized by the light of the eagle as they ran furiously through the long shaftlike stretch that had exhausted him so severely before, the Tunnel of Times.

Then, with almost no warning, they were back at the footbridge. This time, however, Hamelin gave it little thought, crossing it as if he wore Lars's shoes. His hands still held the box from Sophia, so he never even used the hand ropes. But then immediately on the other side of the bridge, the eagle, who was in the lead, stopped.

The path in front of them was narrow and shallow. The eagle circled behind Hamelin and once again lifted him. They plummeted down into the chasm of blackness.

This time Hamelin faced forward and could see—from the light that shone from the majestic bird—many of the features that they had passed before with such lightning speed. Once again he felt and smelled the burning heat that came from somewhere below him, from the bottom of that blackness. Again, shortly after that, he felt a rush of cold air.

Then came again the short period of slower speed, followed by the sudden, straight-up soaring of the great bird. Finally, again, there was the abrupt landing. This time, however, Hamelin was ready for it. Facing forward, as soon as his feet hit the ground, he rolled head and shoulders first in a perfect somersault, holding the box in one hand and using the other to push himself up to a standing position.

He saw a patch of light in front of him and recognized the spot. He was just around the corner from the opening of the cave. But now he could see that there was more to this chamber than he had noticed before. At the other end of it, back to his right, he could see what looked like another path that ended under a smooth, arched crack in the rock. The crack formed what could be a door-like opening leading—where?

"Does that go somewhere?" he asked.

"Yes," replied the eagle. "But this is the end of today's journey."

Hamelin immediately knew that the eagle was going to leave. He remembered what Sue Ammi had done when she bowed before the great bird, and he knew he had even more reason to do so himself. He was about to bend one of his knees and touch it to the floor of the cave. But before he could kneel, the great bird, as if reading his mind, bowed his head toward Hamelin and said, "Thank you, O Man. You struck the bear on my behalf and, with arguments beyond my wisdom, compelled us to return to the waters of death and life. There, with the Lady Charissa, and in her place, you fought the monsters of that watery grave."

Hamelin was struck silent by what the great bird said. What did he mean, addressing him with "O Man"? After a moment's pause, he said, "I hope I will see you again soon."

"Yes," replied the eagle. "When we are both summoned, we will meet, for Ren'dal will not sit back for long. His father, Chimera, is enraged at Tumultor's loss of Charissa and the jewel, not to mention the staunching of the water. But Chimera's plans are bigger than just recovering the jewel or kidnapping a daughter of Carr."

"What will I do?"

"You will be tested."

"What about Layla?" Hamelin asked quickly. "Is my friend Layla the missing sister from Parthogen?"

"It is best that you learn that yourself," replied the eagle. He turned to leave.

"What about these gloves?" Hamelin held up his hands. "Should you take them back?"

"No," replied the eagle. "They are yours, but you must use them only for the purposes for which they were given." And then he arched his head, hearing something in the distance. "I hear the padding of feet, and I must go."

The eagle disappeared back into the darkness of the cave. He was gone.

Hamelin turned back toward the opening and walked toward the light. He stepped out of the cave and could tell that it was just past sundown. Sliding with his feet and using one hand to grab shrubs and small trees for balance and the other to hold the box, he scrambled down the hill. He came to the road, turned south, and began to run. He could have walked. But he felt like running, as hard as he could.

As he ran, he stayed on the road. He began to wonder how long he had been gone. In some ways, it seemed like years, but as he thought back and counted the nights, he decided that it was nine nights and ten days. What day was it now?

He ran hard as long as he could, then slowed to a jog and finally to a brisk walk. Within thirty minutes, the house was in view, but with the sun fully down, the darkness of winter had settled in quickly. The air was brisk. He rushed through the gate and up the porch of the Upton County Children's Home. As he glanced through the windows, he could see colored lights and decorations inside. He silently opened the door, walked through the foyer, and slowly, quietly peered around the door to the dining hall.

At the far end of the room stood a giant Christmas tree, lighted and decorated as beautifully as Hamelin had ever seen. There were presents piled high around the base of it. Then he realized. It was Christmas Eve.

Everyone was there, the children, the Kaleys, and Mrs. Parker. It was quiet, but Hamelin could hear a voice—it was Paul! With a little help from Mrs. Kaley, he was reading aloud the Christmas story from the Bible.

"'Mary treasured up all these things, pondering them in her heart,'" Paul read.

And then Hamelin could also see, standing next to the Kaleys, two familiar figures. Bryan and Layla stood at the back of the children, heads down, looking sad.

Suddenly, as if feeling that someone was looking at her, Layla glanced across the dining hall. She saw him.

"*Hamelin!*" she screamed, and she ran toward him as fast as she could, bumping into chairs and maneuvering around the tables. Bryan and the Kaleys followed. The children, seated on the floor, were up immediately, and before he realized it, Layla had jumped at him, hugging him. He just stood there, in the middle of the dining room, with the entire Upton County Children's Home gathered around him, yelling his name, the younger children grabbing his legs, others patting him on the back, and Layla, the Kaleys, and Bryan hugging him.

"Where have you been?" some of the children asked, but Hamelin just smiled and laughed, and more than ever before in all his life, he felt the love of a family all around him.

———————

That night, after things were quiet, with the last stocking hung and the children all sent to bed, Hamelin, the Kaleys, Bryan, and Layla sat in the small living room.

They all sat there for a moment looking at each other, and Mrs. Kaley began to cry. Then it was Layla's turn again to cry. And the two men, one middle-aged and one in his twenties, lowered their heads so that others wouldn't see their faces.

"I'm sorry," said Hamelin. "I had to go. It was the right time, but I know I didn't leave here the right way." He then looked directly at the Kaleys. "I'm sorry. I should have done more than just write you a note. I know you . . . love me, and you're the closest people to parents I've ever had. And I'm sorry I worried you for so long."

They nodded and smiled, and Mrs. Kaley took his hands in both of hers and just looked at him. Her eyes still glistened, but her face was soft and full of peace.

"And," Hamelin said, looking at Bryan and Layla, "even though you knew I was going, I know you worried about me too. After all I've been through, I know what it feels like to worry about someone else."

They were all silent for a moment.

Then Mrs. Kaley said, "Hamelin, Bryan and Layla told us a little bit about what you were going through, but they've left most of the story for you to tell, and we want to hear it. But there are also some things we need to tell you. Things we probably should have told you before . . ." She closed her eyes and looked down.

Mr. Kaley put his arm around her and finally spoke up. "Hamelin," he said, "we have a lot to tell you, and we want Bryan and Layla to hear it too. But it's long and complicated, so we don't want to start the story tonight, if that's okay."

Hamelin nodded.

"The same with us," said Bryan. "We've got things to tell you too, but it'll take a while. When you were gone, we went back to Alpine and went through our aunt's things. We found a box of old letters—several of them from our mother. We've read them and learned a lot about our family, about Layla, and more about our parents' deaths."

Hamelin sat in silence. Then he looked up, first at Bryan and then at Layla. "And I want to hear about the eagle you met. I want to know if yours was like the Great Eagle. I've seen him again, and I expect to see him some more, maybe soon, but next time . . . I don't know . . . there's a lot more I have to do."

The Kaleys were quiet, but Mr. Kaley's eyes widened at Hamelin's mention of eagles. Hamelin looked at the Kaleys. "Bryan and Layla know some of my story, but whenever you say, I'll tell it to you from the beginning."

Layla was very still and quiet. Finally, she spoke. "It's so strange. All of us and our stories seem connected somehow. I wish we had more answers."

Hamelin remembered the wooden box that Sophia had given him and brought it out.

"What's that?" asked Bryan.

"It was given to me by somebody on the other side of the cave," Hamelin said. He lifted the lid, and inside was a very old book. He carefully removed it. Everyone crowded around him as he opened the book to see the writing on the title page. It said, in very ornate script, *The Enchiridion of the Sages*.

"What's it about?" asked Layla.

"Where I've been they all use this old book. I was told it might answer some questions."

"What kinds of questions?" said Bryan.

"Lots," said Hamelin. "Questions about families, kingdoms, and a missing girl."

Hamelin looked at Bryan and then at the Kaleys before setting his eyes on Layla and looking at her for long seconds. *Does she look like the three sisters? Is she the missing princess?* Then he said, "Who knows? Maybe it has some answers for all of us."

Acknowledgments

AS WITH BOOK ONE, I WANT TO THANK OUR CHILDREN, their spouses, and other family members for allowing me to borrow their names for the series. The names and places that are not fictional are, as with all other names and places, fictionalized, but it is also true to say that I received a lot of inspiration from using names and places familiar to me.

I also take a certain joy in mentioning in these stories the places known to me while growing up in Abilene, Texas. I have been significantly shaped by the strong, quiet individuals who inhabit that part of the world, and it is inevitable that their strengths and personalities would influence me in the creation of characters for this series.

Once again, as with book one, I must acknowledge my huge debt of gratitude to Judy Ferguson, my senior administrative assistant. Her work at every level of the series, from ferreting out comma blunders and word repetitions to advising with respect to plot consistency and character development, has been irreplaceable. It gives me great pleasure to dedicate this volume to her.

And then I have other friends and colleagues I want to mention. Sharon Saunders, Karen Francies, Ed Borges, and Sandy Mooney—whether they realize it or not—have helped me in many ways, and I want to acknowledge my gratitude to them. And a special thank-you to Margaret Patterson for the map of the Land of Gloaming that appears in this volume.

Jerry and Jeremiah Johnston have helped Sue and me extensively in matters related to marketing, promotion, interviews, and distribution. We are grateful for their experienced advice and constant encouragement.

I again want to think our partners at Scribe Inc., a truly outstanding company in all matters related to the production of books. Danny Constantino is a professional master of the copyediting process. I'm grateful to him for his expertise—and also for his cheerful, patient, and thoughtful counsel overall. Thanks also to Tim Durning, Jeff DeBlasio, and Jamie Harrison for their guidance and creativity in page design and cover creation. Another key member of the Scribe team is Steve Ushioda. He has been particularly helpful in bringing these volumes to printed completion. Finally, I am very grateful to David Rech, the principal of Scribe, for his friendship and guidance.

I also want to thank the Trustees of Houston Baptist University, past and present, who have allowed me opportunities to work on this project from time to time. As board members, they are amazing examples of wisdom and good faith. And they are also my friends.

Since the publication of book one, I've been reminded again of how grateful I am for many friends who have over quite a few years cheered this work. I'm thinking now of Hayne and Virginia Griffin, who years ago read an early draft while we were on vacation together and discussed it with me. And a special word of thanks to Jim Parker, a life-long friend. Jim is an extremely knowledgeable reader and critic of fantasy literature. He has read both volumes and been extremely generous in his support. Then there's Skip McBride, David Hatton, Gary Thomas, Jim Carroll, and Gus Blackshear, who, with me, belong to a men's group that meets (somewhat) regularly. They have been supporting me for years. Skip especially, not too delicately, has been pushing me to "hurry up and finish!" Sam and Annette Bailey of Mountain Home, Arkansas, are new friends, but it seems like Sue and I have known them for years. Their support has been deeply felt and appreciated. Recent months have also reminded me of the depth of love and appreciation I have for so many colleagues at HBU who have not only read the first volume but shared it with others. We have an amazing number of C. S. Lewis (and other Inklings) experts—among them Lou Markos, who read and generously reviewed the first volume—at the university. They have inspired me to continue. I hope this new volume meets with their approval as well, not to mention that of their children and grandchildren.

Most of all, I thank Sue, my wife of forty-seven years at this writing, who has never failed to support, encourage, and advise me in all things, including this project. There must have been a thousand times when I could have been more help to her in her extremely busy life, but she regularly enabled me to make extra time to write. And she never let me quit, even when I seriously considered the possibility. But in addition to encouragement, Sue is also my partner (and I hers) in the writing, editing, and production of these volumes. She has read them from the earliest drafts to the latest, and she is an extremely knowledgeable editor, critic, and now publisher. Thank you, Sue, love of my life.

Look for the third book in the Hamelin Stoop series.

nOW THAT HAMELIN HAS RETURNED TO THE CHILDREN'S HOME, what is happening in the Land of Gloaming? With Lars back in Periluna, will Hamelin ever see him again? Can Parthogen be rescued from Landon, the wolfish son of Chimera? What about King Carr's fourth daughter, Princess Alathea? Could she be Hamelin's friend Layla on this side of the Atrium?

Perhaps the biggest question of all—what about Hamelin's passion, his quest to find his parents and learn his name? Can that be done only in the Land of Gloaming? And what part will the Great Eagle play?

And what about the mysterious *Enchiridion of the Sages*— what secrets does it hold for Hamelin, his friends, and the Land of Gloaming?

- If you enjoyed *Hamelin Stoop: The Lost Princess and the Jewel of Periluna*, share it with your friends, small group, or book club.
- Mention Hamelin Stoop in a Facebook post, Twitter update, or blog post using the hashtag #HamelinStoop.
- Review the Hamelin Stoop books at Amazon.com.
- Books can be purchased at Amazon, Twelve Gates Publishing, or www.hamelinstoop.com. Or ask for them at your favorite bookstore.

About the Author

Robert B. Sloan is married to his college sweetheart, Sue. With seven married children and twenty young grandchildren, they especially enjoy large family gatherings with good food and lively conversation around the table. Favorite family activities include table and parlor games, writing and reading stories, coloring, and, of course, storytelling. The newest holiday activity includes original dramas, written and produced by the grandchildren.

CPSIA information can be obtained
at www.ICGtesting.com
Printed in the USA
LVHW032148230419
615328LV00001B/46/P